A DYSFUNCTIONAL *Family*

Meryl McCurry

Copyright © 2021 Meryl McCurry Publishing

All rights reserved. No part of this publication may be reproduced, distributed, or transmitted in any form or by any means, including photocopying, recording, or other electronic or mechanical methods, without the prior written permission of the publisher, except in the case of brief quotations embodied in critical reviews and certain other noncommercial uses permitted by copyright law. For permission requests, write to the publisher, addressed "Attention: Book Rights and Permission," at the address below.

Published in the United States of America

ISBN: 978-1-7358010-9-4 (SC)

Meryl McCurry Publishing
222 West 6th Street
Suite 400, San Pedro, CA, 90731
www.stellarliterary.com

Ordering Information and Rights Permission:
Quantity sales. Special discounts might be available on quantity purchases by corporations, associations, and others. For details, contact the publisher at the address above.

For Book Rights Adaptation and other Rights Permission. Call us at toll-free 1-888-945-8513 or send us an email at admin@stellarliterary.com.

Contents

1 5
2 15
3 23
4 31
5 42
6 48
7 54
8 60
9 68
10 74
11 79
12 86
13 93
14 101
15 106
16 112
17 118
18 127
19 136
20 142
21 148
22 155

23	160
24	171
25	177
26	183
27	188
28	206
29	219
30	225
31	231
32	236
33	243
34	253
35	259
36	267
37	273
38	283
39	291
40	300
41	312
42	320

1

After an extensively strenuous and exhausting day at work, Dylan sluggishly came in through the doors of his rundown apartment building. As he locked the door behind him, he dropped the recent mail on the nearest dresser and turned the lights on so he could see where he was going. Dylan then gradually strolled into the kitchen going into the fridge and grabbed himself a bottle of beer along with a pound of red meat. From the looks of the situation, Dylan seemed like your average everyday human going about their everyday life. However, Dylan wasn't a human being. The weird aspect of it was in fact that Dylan was an odd-looking creature, something out of an actual (hand-drawn) cartoon. Dylan was displayed as something of a reptile creature with two noticeable fangs, sharp claws for hands and feet, and long rabbit-like ears that usually flop down behind his shoulders. He had a long reptilian tail which normally dragged on the floor the majority of the time but occasionally would put to use as an additional set of claws. His color was a dark blue hue, while the underside of his stomach, inner claws and ears were light blue. He also had an apparent purple stripe that ran from the tip of his forehead to the back of his tail. His height was 6 ft and weighed around 170 lbs.

Creatures like Dylan aren't uncommon, mythical creatures that possess special powers even though they regularly stick out like a sore thumb in this world. They mingle in society like everyday normal human beings where they're regularly seen as conventional everyday individuals. Due to their cartoon-like features, they were faced with prejudice by some humans regarding some small differences they don't share with society. Their values and moralities are on a much higher level, leaving humans to either envy or hate them in the process leading to bias.

Dylan slowly enters his bathroom carrying the pound of meat in his claws. Fully opening the door Dylan's eyes focus on the individual who was already waiting for him in the bathroom. Lo' and behold sitting right in the tub was a fully-grown great white shark—mind you, an actual great white, baring a colossal cavity with several rows of bone-saw-sharp teeth. It is not a cartoon caricature. Barely even fitting in the cramped tub, the shark might have seemed uncomfortable in this small environment, but he was used to resting in this enclosure. The shark's coloration was that of a normal great white shark but his color was a more intense black and white, closely related to the same texture of a killer whale. There was a laptop sectioned on top of the closed toilet lid enabling the shark to watch various videos for entertainment. He noticed Dylan enter the bathroom and gave him his full attention.

"Well it's about time you got home," the shark groaned.

"What are you complaining about Jerry," Dylan argued, "this has always been my schedule for seven years. I thought you'd be used to it by now."

"The only thing I would get used to is finally getting out of this damn tub! When are you going to get that promotion?!"

"I don't know Jerry," Dylan sadly sighed. "We've been praying and working hard towards that for a long time. I'm finally at the end of my rope for how long it's taking. But the one thing I'm not is a quitter. Eventually, someday my hard work will pay off."

"So you keep telling me." As the shark props his body up he finally notices the meat in Dylan's claw and practically begs for it. "Hand over that beautiful juicy meat before I'll take your claw off with it by force."

"This is the daily routine," Dylan groans as he drops the meat in Jerry's mouth. "Half of our finances always go to buying those pounds of meat for you."

"And you've both have a done a terrific job," Jerry says while chewing the meat.

"Cause you know what will happen whenever my hunger gets the best of me."

"You're just lucky you're not a man-eating killer. The worse damage you do is by making a mess in our kitchen to satisfy your hunger needs. Last time it took us hours to clean up everything."

"Well I have you and your wife to thank that I'm not a man-eating killer," Jerry pointed out. "This environment isn't best suited for me but I wouldn't have any other family but you two."

"Thanks, Jerry," Dylan reflected emotionally. "I guess Katie and I have always had our hearts set on marine creatures than anything else. But don't worry buddy, sooner or later we're going to say good-bye to this stressful lifestyle and find a much better home. And you'll finally get to swim in that big swimming pool we promised you."

"And I'll still be holding you up on that promise until it happens."

"Well you had your meal and I'm bushed," Dylan says heading out the door. "See ya tomorrow Jerry."

"And another thing, why don't you and Katie keep it down when you're in the bedroom," Jerry claimed. "Last time you two made love you were so loud I couldn't hear my program."

Dylan blushed embarrassingly from Jerry's statement then groaned at him. "Whatever and goodnight," he said closing the bathroom door behind him.

As he walked back near the kitchen to reclaim his beer bottle he noted before he was able to fully relax other pets also needed feeding. Near the living room wall was a medium-sized fish tank. And inside of it were seven baby alligators. They were somewhat recent new additions to the family since they were still pretty small in size. All gators were the average color of a regular alligator, aside from just one who was an albino color. Unlike Jerry's poor living environment, the gators had a decent setting inside their aquarium with plenty of space and tools for them to run around and play in. However, Dylan knew they wouldn't stay this way forever. It was already hectic enough having a fully grown great white shark living in a small apartment building, but to add seven grown alligators to the mix would just be asking for nothing but trouble. Dylan is hoping and praying to get that promotion at his job to get his family out of this miserable cramped environment.

After feeding the gators, Dylan was finally able to relax as he sat in his comfortable recliner chair and turned on the television. He gradually drank his cold beer letting the sensation calm his nerves as he turned his head to the left. Sectioned on the wall was a poster protected behind a glass frame. On the poster was a picture of him and his wife Katie. Katie looked like a reptilian creature also but had more fur elements just like mammals. Her coloration was light pink while her underside and inner paws were light yellow. She had a somewhat slim feature with noticeable plump breasts where her areola was covered by her pink skin stripe which acted like a bra.

She had long, red silky hair, lop-ears but was much shorter than Dylan's and an enormous big bushy squirrel-like tail. She was just a few inches shorter than Dylan. The poster was back then in their teenage years when they were part of a heavy rock band. That was around the time the two became inseparable and it was a special moment for them. He closely studied himself and his wife which didn't even look like what they do now. They wore greaser attires, dark sunglasses and were playing heavy metal guitars while Katie's hair was displayed in a punk spiky haircut. Despite how they might have looked on the outside, it never changed who they were on the inside. Dylan and his wife have always stayed the loving couple they were then till now. After smiling at the poster, he turns his attention back on the TV and slowly browses through the channels to see if there was anything good to watch. After searching for a good minute or two Dylan gives up and just turns off the TV. He strolls over to his dresser and decides to retrieve the mail he put down when he first came in. He groans in frustration at each envelope noticing nothing but bills, bills, bills. Then something catches his eye. Underneath all the envelopes was a Playboy magazine, or in Dylan's case, it was a Playcritter magazine. He smiled with deep satisfaction as he held the magazine in front of him and dropped the other mail.

"This just made my day," he grinned immediately flipping through pages looking for the right picture. After searching for a while he stopped and found the right one for himself. "Aww perfect, you're the right one."

Dylan found the picture of a very seductive creature that almost looked like a cross between a squirrel and a skunk. She had about the same breasts and big bushy tail feature that Dylan was very interested in. Taking a pair of scissors out from the dresser he ripped the picture out of the magazine then cut the face off the female creature. Going through the dresser he found his photo album with plenty of pictures of him and his wife. After finding the right one he took the photo of his wife's head and placed it over the picture replacing it with Katie's. He smiled in satisfaction looking at it with admiration then kissed it.

Dylan finally headed to his bedroom where he found his wife soundly sleeping. He carefully made sure not to wake her as he scurried under the sheets right beside her. However, she wasn't fully asleep and instantly woke up when she noticed Dylan come in.

"Late night shift again," she said quietly.

"Sorry I didn't mean to wake you," he said.

"You didn't. I was only partly asleep. Those damn neighbors had their music pounding the walls again nonstop for hours. I was about to go next door and start something."

"Well, I'm glad you didn't. I don't want you getting into a conflict with these people," Dylan said worriedly. "They're unpredictable and dangerous."

"So am I!" Katie claimed nearly springing up.

"Yeah—I know," Dylan said trying to calm Katie putting his arm around her waist. "Just relax baby. You have that overtime expo at your job tomorrow."

"I know," Katie said relaxing her head back down on the pillow. "I just wish a change will finally happen for us. I hate this place and the people don't do it any justice either. I'm tired of living here."

"You're not alone on that," Dylan said bringing Katie in a full embrace.

Before Katie could fully savor the touch of her husband she noticed the paper from his claws. "What's this?" she asked taking it from him.

"Oh—just another picture I can add to my fantasy collection," Dylan said kind of embarrassed.

Turning on the light that was placed on the dresser right next to their bed, Katie was able to go get a good look at it.

"What is it with you and these weird fetishes of you cutting out Playcritter magazines and sticking my head on them?" she asked pretty weirded out.

"Call it a bad habit," Dylan admitted. "I've been doing it ever since I had a crush on you in high school."

"Well, we're married now and have been for nine years. So you can cut out these bad habits because it's just too weird for me," Katie said crumbling up the paper and tossing it aside. "It just makes me think you don't appreciate my body since you're always finding pictures of other creature's body features."

"Don't be ridiculous baby. I worship your body like a goddess and always adore it," he said caressing her. "By comparison, your body permanently outdoes the other creature's body features. It's just a continuous wayward habit that stuck with me since high school."

"If you say so weirdo," she said rolling her eyes to the ceiling.

"I don't know, I think it's pretty romantic to admire the creature I love so much," Dylan cradling her up against him.

"Yes, you are quite the romantic type," she giggled while her big bushy tail cradled Dylan into a full embrace.

It's something about Katie's tail that gets Dylan fully aroused. He savored her tail like a rich person fully embracing the feel and smell of an expensive fur coat.

"Are you trying to start something," he said looking at her seductively.

"I don't know," she smiled back at him, "are you?"

At that moment, Dylan placed himself directly on top of Katie and got to work.

"Now it's our turn to cause ruckus for the neighbors," Dylan smiled.

The intercourse between the two is no different than what humans do but they sometimes had an unusual way of doing things. For most, because all these creatures normally stroll around naked without any private parts being exposed their nudity is covered by their fur or skin, is as if watching clean, unexposed cartoon characters. However, when they make love to each other their private parts emerge out of their layer skin like a flower that blossoms. For females, the same, and when making love or breastfeeding their young, nipples would surface from their breasts under their skin.

Before taking the next big step he gently lays on top of her kissing her on the lips while caressing her head from behind. Katie slowly embraced her arms over his shoulders clutching him tightly not wanting him to let go. She could feel the pressure of his upper body on her stomach with his body temperature rising to correlate with this intimate moment. Eagerly grasping her he ultimately rushed himself inside of her. Katie moaned breathlessly with keenness once her husband made contact with her. Coaxing her at every heated moment he effortlessly thrusts himself back and forth inside of her savoring every pleasurable wave. The marvel from within both of them was at its peak. Something aroused inside of Dylan that triggered a spark he always felt with Katie. No other creature could ever make him feel as wondrous as she has. He couldn't let go of her. He continued grasping her as his body temperature begins rising causing both to sweat quicker than usual. His tail automatically works like a reflex were it ducks down and equally enters inside of her. Speeding up to the superb buildup, Katie and Dylan could no longer keep their moaning to a soft tone. It was becoming nearly impossible for Katie as she felt the physical response of orgasms exploding at an immense rate. Dylan could feel their intercourse at its summit, sparking an overwhelming sensation as he held on to her tightly. It spread like a wonder that scattered throughout their souls. Feeling the tension escalating at an inevitable pace, he held on as long as he could before ultimately releasing the overwhelming buildup. In that instant, both were gifted with a vigorous sensation beyond their wildest dreams. Letting out a pleasant moan Dylan gave one last pleasurable thrust before finally ending their sexual intercourse. Every time the two came together, they strengthened their bond even more profoundly than the last. Katie calmly tried catching her breath as Dylan did the same looking down at her with passion.

"It's no wonder I love you so much," he murmured. "I always knew you were destined to be mine."

He promptly began kissing and licking her to whereas Katie had to pull her head away. "Dylan calm down. I need to catch my breath and regain my strength before we continue again."

Finally removing himself from her, Dylan carefully removed his tail out from underneath her and laid on his back fully catching his breath.

"You know another weird habit of yours is you and that tail," Katie mentioned. "Whenever we go at it, why are you always sticking it in me?"

"Uh—I guess I just want to give you the whole experience," Dylan blushed. "Besides I can't help it. You drive me crazy in bed."

"And it's a wonder I love you so much too," Katie smiled caressing him across the chest. "If only I can stick my tail into you too."

"You can't fit that big bushy thing into me," Dylan laughed amusingly. "It'll never fit."

"Yeah well we'll just wet my tail a bit and you'll be surprised what I'm capable of. By the way, did you feed Jerry when you came in?"

"Sure did. And the gators as well."

"Thanks, sweetie. I just hope we'll be able to move out of here before the alligators start getting big. It's bad enough dealing with Jerry's big butt every day."

"Things will eventually work out for the better, I promise you, baby."

"And I trust you as I always have. Despite our situation, at least we have each other."

"Thank God for that," Dylan smiled licking her on the nose.

"Yes thank God—and goodnight," Katie said turning over on her side as she got comfortable into a sleeping position fully embracing her pillow.

"Good night Katie—I love you," said Dylan.

"I love you too," Katie said.

2

Early the next morning Katie drove down to her job which was a beauty spa. It was a job Katie didn't mind having until she and Dylan were able to be relieved of their current situation for a better occupation. She's been working there almost as long as Dylan has been working at his job. She was a manicurist which everyone in the salon appreciated, mainly because she would always compliment customers and friends on their beauty and never her own. She stepped out of her vehicle parking in the employee zone and headed straight for the door. As she walked inside customers were getting manicures, pedicures, and hairdos while others were getting bikini waxed, beauty treatments, and massages as a routine.

"Hey girls," Katie said gaining the attention of some of her friends and regular customers.

"Hey Katie," some of them called out to her as she passed by.

She trailed to the back room where she met her friend Shelley Morrison. Shelley was possibly her only close human friend who has stuck by her side since she first started working at the spa. Shelley appeared in her mid-twenties with attractive blue eyes, blonde shared with brown silky hair, and an etiquette personality.

"Hey Shelley," Katie said getting out her equipment.

"Hey Katie," Shelley replied who was preoccupied with blowing drying her hair.

"So how did your date with Devin go?" Katie asked.

"That no-good asshole!" Shelley snapped. "I found out he was cheating on me!"

"Oh crap," Katie said taking a seat next to her friend and placed her arm around her shoulder. "I'm sorry Shelley. I know you had your hopes high that it would work between you two."

"Save it, Katie," Shelley scoffed. "I'm just glad I found out now before realizing the type of man I would've been stuck with before it was too late."

"Well, you know what they say, there's plenty of other fish in the sea," Katie said trying to brighten her spirits.

"Maybe I shouldn't be looking for a man."

"What do you mean by that Shelley?"

"I mean look at you Katie," Shelley said bringing her hands out to her. "Creatures like you know how to hold on to what they've got. You guys don't harbor infidelity or cheating in your bones whatsoever. Plus creatures like you always raise their children and never abandon them. I would kill to have a male creature like yours that's highly dedicated to their spouse."

Katie blushed a bit hating whenever this subject is brought up. It appeared this was the main reason why some humans hate creatures like them. From the humans' perspective, the creatures are flawless regarding fidelity and never abandoning their kind. As a result, human beings perceived the creatures as depicting grandeur, holier-than-thou overviews. However, that was never the case. Creatures like Katie just wished humans would learn by example from them instead of hating them as a result.

"We're not perfect Shelley," Katie said embarrassingly rubbing the back of her neck. "Even Dylan and I still have arguments from time to time like any romantic couple."

"Yeah but your guy's relationships last forever," Shelley sympathized. "What's your guy's secret?"

"We don't have a secret Shelley. It's just simple to do the right thing to the person you're supposed to love. I also think humans are easily drawn to temptation. There's plenty of tempting distractions, especially with social media and cell phones. I believe it's one of the main reasons why relationships are so screwed up these days. Love is also blind in a lot of areas. Some people don't wish to see it even when it's standing right there in front of them. On the other hand, there are also cases where people go through drama from bad upbringings and they bring that toxic background into their relationships. There are just so many different topics."

"Do you really think I could find a creature instead of a human?"

"Uh—don't even go there, Shelley. That's going towards bestiality which is wrong on so many levels." Katie said quite unnerved.

"It's happened before—hasn't it?"

"Hell no," Katie made clear. "Creatures like me only solely stick to our kind. It's in our genes. We never mess around with humans. They're not our type. No offense."

"None taken," Shelley groaned. "That's why you guys are so perfect."

"Please don't say that Shelley. We're not perfect. Listen if it'll make you feel better how about we put you up on a dating website and find you somebody decent?"

"Ugh, I don't know if I'm up for that," Shelley said finishing up with her hair.

"Well, I'll stick by your side until you find the right guy for you."

"Why would you do that Katie?"

"Cause you're my best friend Shelley," she said placing her arm around her friend. "Best friends help each other out do they not?"

Finally bringing a smile to her friend's face, Shelley equally wrapped her arm around Katie's saying, "You're right. So you ready for the expo?"

"Not really," Katie scoffed looking through a booklet she brought out from her purse. "Dylan and I are just working on trying to find a new place sooner or later. We can't stand the apartment we're living in any longer."

"Is Jerry causing more trouble again?"

"It's not just him but what do you expect from keeping a great white shark in a small crapped apartment," Katie scoffed rolling her eyes.

"That's the other odd thing with you creatures," Shelley said shaking her head. "Your taste in pets is more on the—wild side."

"I don't know why. Perhaps it's in our genes as well. Some like keeping Arctic predators, wild cats, you name it. For me and Dylan it just so happens that we like any type of water animals or fish."

"Good thing you guys can handle predators too. You're able to communicate with them in a way we humans will never understand."

"It's true we can communicate with them which is probably why we can get away with having them as pets unlike humans but we can't physically communicate with every single animal. It only works on some like for instance, Dylan and I are only able to vocally communicate with Jerry but not with our new alligators."

"Still you're able to control them."

"I wouldn't call it controlling Shelley. I would say that perhaps we have a deeper connection with predators that some humans will never understand. It's like a spiritual bond or something."

"If you say so. Well like it or not we might as well get ready for the expo."

"I guess so," Katie groaned setting her booklet down.

At the same time, while Katie was at her job, Dylan was also at his. He worked as an assistant to an investment banker. It was one of the toughest jobs for Dylan to get into. He achieved a diploma required for the position but lacked the experience. Lincoln Edward Industries was one of the most highly competitive companies in the business and unfortunately, he was stuck in the same position for years relentlessly trying to gain his boss's approval. Today he sat at the big vertical office table with a few of his colleagues. He stuck out being the only creature while everybody else was human. He always wore a professional business suit and presented himself respectfully to everybody. Everyone in the company was well aware of Dylan's hard work and dedication but they didn't let it divert them from doing what they had to do. His only close friend in the company was Brandon Wells. A young gentleman in his late twenties, he was the only associate Dylan could always count on, someone to talk to or depend on as a loyal friend. Everyone in the room directed their attention to their manager who sat up front in the most exaggerated chair. He was known as Edward Charles the III. He took up the family name of the company after his father and his father after that. He was a hard businessman to please but a reasonable man nonetheless. Today he discussed with everyone how they had to design new marketing strategies to get their company noticed by famous investors. Usually, Dylan's job was to just sit and listen then to improvise on whatever his coworkers handed him.

"Another glorious day in the office, right Dylan," Brandon couldn't help but mock as he nudged him with his elbow.

"Oh—yeah, I'm just waiting on that promotion," he commented to him.

"Whatever you do, don't go reminding Mr. Charles about it," he warned him. "You know he'll never give it to you if you don't let up about it. The one thing Charles is a hard nut to crack."

"I know," Dylan sighed. "I was just hoping by now he would've noticed me."

"With someone like Charles and a company like this," Brandon couldn't help but chuckle. "Keep dreaming on buddy."

"Alright guys that'll do for our meeting for the day," Edward said rising from his seat while collecting his paperwork and briefcase. "If there are any further questions, come to me in my office."

As Edward left the room Dylan was hoping he would notice him or even acknowledge him but his efforts were dashed as he watched his boss leave the conference room.

"Let it go, buddy," Brandon said placing his arm on his friend's shoulder. "You try hard enough as it is."

The tense creature took a moment to relax as his head slumped down for a good moment. "I don't know what me and Katie are going to do if nothing changes around here Brandon. I really need that promotion."

"Sounds like you and Katie are pretty stressed out. Tell you what, how about you come by my place this weekend and we'll have a barbeque just like old times."

Smiling a bit from his friend's offer Dylan replied, "Thanks, Brandon. I'll see if Katie is up for it. That is if we don't have any plans."

The two friends left the main office along with the other associates as everyone headed to their cubicles. As Dylan headed to his workstation he immediately noticed a woman standing in the doorway of their office. At first, he thought he didn't recognize her but then he suddenly knew who it was.

"Chloe? I mean Miss Waters."

"Dylan," she smiled seductively. "I'm surprised you remembered me."

"How could I forget. Uh—what are you doing here?" he said scratching his head confusingly.

"I haven't heard back from you and Katie since the case was settled," the young attractive blonde woman made clear.

"Well, nothing else has happened since then. I don't know what else you want from us. I mean we appreciate everything you've done for us and we paid you fairly so what else is it?"

"A casual talk. How about you and I talk it over at dinner tonight?"

Taking a big gulp Dylan didn't like how she suggested that. "Uh—I think I should tell Katie if she'll be up for joining us?"

"No, no, no leave her out of this," she insisted walking up to him. "It's just you and me."

"I don't like where you're possibly going with this," Dylan said.

"It's just a casual talk. That's all. I mean a little dinner shouldn't be too much to ask for after everything I've done for you and your wife."

"Okay, okay," Dylan said giving in. "But I swear Chloe if it's nothing more than just casual talk then…"

"I assure you it'll be just fine," she reassured him taking his claw in her hands.

Not liking the vibes he was getting from her, Dylan snatched his claw away and said, "Okay. I really should get back to work. I'll call you when I get off."

"I'll be waiting," she smiled watching him take his seat. "We'll meet at The BBQ and Burger Steak-Out."

"That place," Dylan tensed up knowing it was the main place where he and Katie usually go on dates.

3

As evening drew in Katie's expo was finally over and after a long drawn out day she and Shelley were both exhausted. It took longer than they intended. She decided to drive Shelley back to her place but at the last minute, they decided to treat themselves.

"I think we deserve a great meal," Katie said driving on the driver's seat. "Have you ever eaten at The BBQ and Burger Steak-Out? It's a great place Dylan and I usually go on occasions."

"Only if they have shrimp salad, then I'm in," Shelley claimed.

"Girl they serve the best dish there, you'll see," Katie said quite excited and anxious to get there.

Inside the very restaurant of The BBQ and Burger Steak-Out, Dylan was uncomfortably sitting in a booth right across from Chloe. Not having time to change, Dylan still wore his business suit from work and constantly tugged at his collar trying to loosen the grip due to nervousness. All they had at the moment was a carbonated beverage at their table before the waiter was to come and take their order. As Chloe watched Dylan straightening his collar she purposely dropped her napkin on the floor near his feet.

"Oops."

"I got it," he said ducking down reaching for it.

With Dylan momentarily distracted the shifty woman saw her chance as she took something mysterious from her purse and poured it in Dylan's drink. Once he brought his head back up she quickly read through the menu then asked, "Would you like something strong to drink?"

"Huh? Oh no, I never drink under the influence when leaving a restaurant, even if I'm not driving."

"Such the gentlemen you are," she smiled. "Well, you can drink your soda pop until we order our food."

"Alright Miss Waters…"

"Please, call me Chloe."

"Chloe. This already looks unprofessional. What's this about?" Dylan said getting to the point.

"First of all Dylan, what you and your wife went through that day is something no one should experience. I could understand if you've been feeling distant from your wife since it's happened."

"What the hell are you talking about?" Dylan said greatly offended.

"When couples lose a child, the grief is overwhelming. Couples often drift apart so it's understandable if you've been feeling that way."

"Chloe, you don't understand anything," he said looking angrily at her. "Yes, what happened to Katie and I was heart-wrenching but no matter how bad things get I would never leave her. Creatures like us aren't one to abandon each other no matter how terrible a situation gets."

"Dylan, you're only living in a fantasy thinking by sticking with your spouse will make everything better," she said placing her hand on his claw.

"What are you talking about?"

"Dylan from the first time I met you, I saw something in you, unlike anyone I've ever met. I tried denying my feelings for the longest but—I really like you."

Dylan stood frozen for a moment unable to reply to Chloe's statement putting him in a state of shock. "C-Chloe, you're human and I'm a creature."

"People can break the rules once in a while."

"Haven't you forgotten that I'm married?"

"So, she doesn't have to know that."

"Oh really," said a voice that took the two totally off guard.

Standing right in front of their booth was Katie herself with Shelley standing a few feet behind her.

"K-Katie?" Dylan nervously stuttered.

"What are you doing here?" Chloe said.

"The real question is what are you doing here with my husband?" Katie angrily demanded.

"We were just having a casual dinner," she claimed.

"Save it you tramp, I heard enough by the time I got here."

"Tramp!" Chloe said defensively standing up. "You know Katie, you and Dylan owe me for winning that case for you. The defendant would've got off if it hadn't been for me. Not to mention I knew the money struggle you two were going through so I only allowed you guys to pay half price. After the generosity, I've shown you two, and this is how you repay me."

"Don't you dare turn this back on me," Katie growled. "While you won that case, I lost something more. So don't you dare tell me how I owe you anything. As far as I'm concerned I don't owe you a damn thing."

Knowing she crossed the line, Chloe wisely backed off without nothing else to say. Katie then looked at Dylan and said, "Let's go."

Obeying his wife, Dylan immediately got up from his seat and left the restaurant with Katie and Shelley. Chloe was left alone with her own thoughts. Although deep down she knew Katie was right, the only thing that was clouding her judgment was the fact she wasn't able to get Dylan the way she wanted. Discouraged that her scheme didn't go according to plan, she looked over at Dylan's untouched drink and mumbled, "Son of a bitch."

Outside the restaurant, Katie apologized to her friend saying, "I'm so sorry Shelley. I wasn't expecting anything like that to happen but..."

"Say no more," Shelley brushed off. "I'd lose my appetite too if I caught someone who talked to me that way. I'm sure you two would most likely want to be alone after that mess so I'll just go home."

"Sorry Shelley, I promise I'll make it up to you," Katie said sadly.

Later on, the two dropped Shelley off at her place then drove home in awkward silence. Dylan sat on the passenger's side looking over at his wife as she wore a depressed expression which reminded him of something they've been desperately trying to get over. He truly regretted that he ever let Chloe talk into having dinner with him. Finally breaking the silence, Dylan quietly said, "Katie. I'm so sorry I even talked with her. I never knew she was that type of person."

"Save it, Dylan," she replied without looking at him as she kept her eyes on the road. "I know your fidelity is something I'll never question. It's the fact that she mentioned..." Katie stumbled in her words unable to finish her sentence.

"I know," Dylan said calmly trying to comfort her.

Once they drove home, they entered their apartment room hearing the sound of Jerry splashing in the tub and shouting, "Feed me!"

"Keep your skin on!" Dylan shouted back not wanting to deal with him right now. He sadly watched his wife head over to the couch in the living room and sat alone in silence. He serenely sat down right next to her and said, "Is there anything I can get you?"

"No," Katie sniveled ducking her head down while her hair gracefully followed suit.

Unable to see his wife in this state, he fully embraced Katie keeping her in a tight but gentle squeeze. She then gradually let out all of her emotions as she wept uncontrollably in her husband's arms.

"It's okay," he softly told her. "Better to let the emotions out than to keep them bottled in. I'm so sorry Katie. For everything."

After gaining better control of herself, Katie stopped crying then removed herself from him. "It's not your fault Dylan. The only one to blame was that asshole behind the wheel that day. But we can't change the past. The only thing we could do is move on."

"Yeah, at least I have you," he said taking her by the paw.

Finally cracking a smile she affectionately responded, "And I have you too."

The two became enthralled by each other's charms wanting to plant a kiss on each other's lips until they heard, "Feed me now!"

"Ugh, damn shark," Dylan groaned getting up from the couch to tend to him.

Early the next morning, Katie woke up before Dylan deciding to make him breakfast. She was off for the next few days and decided she wanted to keep herself busy around the apartment not dwelling on the past, unlike last night thanks to Chloe who miserably brought it up again. A few minutes later Dylan came into the room after smelling bacon, sausage, and eggs.

"Mmmmmm, that smells delicious," he said coming up from behind her hugging her. "Feeling better?"

"Much better. A good night's sleep did the trick," she said giving him a quick kiss. "Get 'em while they're still hot."

"Thanks, baby," he said taking a seat at the dinner table. "Did you feed Jerry and the gators?"

"Yep, I'll take care of them while you're at work today. I'll be off for the next couple of days so I'll take care of things around here. So I forgot to ask, did you hear anything about your promotion?"

"Still nothing yet baby," Dylan sadly said poking at his food with his fork. "I'm sorry, I'll try harder."

"Dylan all you do is try harder. Please don't overdo anything. Everything will be alright okay. Just as you always tell me, have a little faith."

"You're right," he happily smiles as he begins eating his food. "I will keep trying but I won't overdo anything. Oh, by the way, I almost forgot, Brandon, asks if you and I would like to come over for a barbeque this weekend at his place."

"Good ole Brandon," Katie acknowledges. "It has been a while since we've been at his place. Sure tell him why not."

"Alright, then it's settled. I'll tell him today at work."

"Now hurry up and finish your food so you can get ready to go."

"Yes ma'am," Dylan said eating the last of his scrambled eggs.

A few minutes later Dylan was dressed in a new fresh business suit while carrying a briefcase in one of his claws. "Bye baby, I'll see you later this evening," he said kissing her on the cheek.

"Okay, I love you," Katie said waving to him.

"I love you too," Dylan says finally leaving out the door.

Once Dylan was gone, Katie decided to start her cleaning by vacuuming. While working she wore a red bandana over her hair and listened to music with headphones on to lighten the mood. From their small cramped apartment, there wasn't that much to look at or cleaning for that matter, other than a few adjustments such as vacuuming their living room floor and bedroom or dusting the furniture. The only thing that stuck out was the living room itself which took up most of the complex and their small kitchen area that was on the right-hand side. They only had two bathrooms; the first one which was always occupied by Jerry was sectioned across from the living room and the second one was within their bedroom. She studied their poor apartment from the crumbling wallpapers, decaying window seals, and depleted kitchen counter. The apartment including this neighborhood has certainly seen better days over the years but those days are long gone. Now it was a place which has been gradually taken over by thugs and drug dealers deeming it as dangerous, but affordable which is why Katie and Dylan were putting up with it for now. Plus if their landlord would just keep up with the alterations and updates on sustaining this building from falling apart, there wouldn't be complaints about the deprived living conditions. Only one thing she and Dylan were grateful for was that the landlord allowed them to keep pets in the building considering they have Jerry of all things, but from the conditions of their environment, it almost shouldn't come as a surprise what the landlord wouldn't allow coming in this place. Furthermore, there are far worse things their neighbors bring in this building they don't even want to know about it. Still, she and Dylan anticipated the day where they would no longer have to deal with this lifestyle.

After five minutes of vacuuming, Katie could've sworn she heard something over the loud noise and turned off the electrical apparatus along with the music from her cell phone. Snatching off her headphones, her suspicions were correct when she suddenly heard loud banging at the door.

"Oh what now," Katie groaned knowing it must be something drastic by the sound of the loud banging. Opening the front door,

Katie was met with a drugged-out disheveled woman somewhere in her mid-twenties dressed in dirty rags. Her short black hair was wildly out of place while the complete bags under her eyes represented a lack of sleep. If that wasn't enough to her ordeal, she was extremely skinny with multiple spots on her body representing the countless drugs she's taken throughout her life and she constantly fidgeted either still high or eager for her next fix. In her arms were two crying babies no more than a few months old. Katie already knew who the individual was stating, "Amber?"

4

Amber anxiously held the two crying infants in her arms unable to stop shaking while she tried sounding coherent. "Katie, I'm so glad you're home. I—I came by your place yesterday but you weren't here."

"If you're looking for more money then forget it Amber," Katie told off. "Every time Dylan and I help you out, you always spend the money we give you on more drugs. No more."

"P-please," Amber begged. "My babies, I—I got nowhere to take them. My friend kicked me out and…"

"Where's the father?" Katie asked but then in the back of her mind said, "Like I should even ask."

"He's gone," she admitted. "L-listen K-Katie, you're the only person—I mean friend I c-could trust. C-can you please just watch them for today?"

"Oh no! No, no, no," Katie angrily refused. "First it's money with you people and now you're kids. I'm no babysitter. Get your act together and take care of your own kids! You're not dumping them on me!"

"I promise it won't take long," Amber desperately pleaded forcing herself in Katie's apartment. "I just need to t-take c-care of something then I promise I'll b-be back for them tomorrow. Please, Katie."

"No, no, no," Katie kept insisting but before she knew it, Amber forced both of the babies into her arms.

"Please Katie, just help me out this last time and I promise I'll m-make it up to you," Amber said pulling out a few baby supplies. All she pulled out was two diapers, one blanket, and a broken toy.

Katie knew it was helpless beyond this point and just angrily glared at Amber. The drug addict woman awkwardly hugged Katie saying, "Thank you so much. I promise I'll be back for them."

After taking one last look at her babies, Amber took off leaving a bewildered Katie alone with two crying children. She looked down at the kids in her arms then groaned, "Ugh, how did I get myself into this mess."

An angry Katie brought the babies over to the kitchen sink realizing it wasn't only their diapers that needed changing but by the looks of them, they were in deplorable conditions. They haven't been given a bath in days and were terribly emaciated. Katie of course felt bad for the infants knowing it wasn't their fault but was furious of the fact Amber would dump this crap on her and to leave the children in this appalling state.

"Aw shit!" she cried out. "Why do these damn humans get away with spawning children when they don't even have the mental brainpower to take care of themselves. Birth control and condoms are around for a reason but these dumb people just ignore it. What I should do is call child protective services on that bitch. This is clearly child abuse what I'm looking at." Katie then breathed a big sigh then sadly said, "Unfortunately this is the ghetto and one of the deadliest projects. Even child protective services don't give a damn about people down here. They rarely come even when we call them. Looks like I'm in this alone."

Katie got to work first changing the little ones to find out they were a boy and a girl. She first gave them a proper bath, changed them into clean diapers then warmed up some fresh milk to feed them. Luckily she had some bottles stashed around due to a time she and Dylan thought they were going to become parents. The babies' constant screaming the whole time wore on Katie's nerves nearly making her lose her mind but she rationally put up with it. From their conditions it nearly took two hours just trying to clean them up properly, then Katie brought them over to the couch to feed them. They greedily accepted the milk as if they hadn't eaten in a long time. Naturally, they would only prefer their mother's milk, but by how hungry they were any food will suffice.

"Thank God," Katie breathed a sigh of relief. "I know this isn't your guy's fault. You poor babies are brought into this messed up world because of your dumb parents. You didn't ask for any of this. I know I shouldn't be feeding you this artificial milk but any milk is better than no milk at all."

"Hey Katie, what was all that ruckus I heard for the past hour!" Jerry shouted from the bathroom.

"Ugh," Katie groaned deciding to get up with the babies and meet Jerry in the bathroom rather than to shout and upset the little ones.

She opened the door to reveal to Jerry the unexpected new arrivals.

"Babies? What are you doing with human babies?" Jerry said in shock.

"Amber dumped them on me. She promised she'll be back for them tomorrow so until then try to lower your volume around here."

"What are you talking about? They can't hear me, only you and Dylan can."

"I know that but I'm not going to be shouting back and forth to you so no yelling."

"Well, you know what to do if you don't want me shouting. Feed me," he demanded.

"I just fed you three hours ago."

"Yeah and now I'm hungry again."

"Can you at least wait until the babies are taken care of? They're the ones that haven't eaten in a long time."

"Whatever, just don't keep me waiting for too long or you know what will happen."

"Ungrateful!" Katie couldn't help but shout as she closed the bathroom door with her tail.

Katie returned to the couch continuing to feed the babies until they were fully satisfied. However, their fast pace of drinking only caused the unnatural milk to come back to haunt them. From their emaciated condition combined with their fragile little bodies, it was apparent the babies weren't used to enduring this much milk all at once. Furthermore, this type of milk didn't go well with their physical structure. They felt the growing pain of the artificial milk compelling its way back up their esophagus, as the infants screamed their heads off then proceeded to vomit directly on Katie's chest. The flabbergasted creature froze in shock to witness the sickening green-white vomit dripping down her clean fur while some of it made its way between her breasts.

"DAMN IT!" she heatedly shrieked. Realistically knowing the only individual at fault was Amber, Katie rationally tried calming herself while dealing with the toddlers who were still crying from the aftermath. "I'm going to make sure that Amber pays for this," she grumbled bringing the babies over to her and Dylan's bathroom. She took a moment cleaning herself and the infants up then returned to the living room sitting on the couch while rocking the babies in her arms. Allowing their stomachs to settle before feeding them again, Katie had to put up with their ear-shattering screams which no doubt nearly made her go berserker. There was no way she was going to attempt to feed them that artificial milk again so she had to give them something else.

"Oh you poor kids," Katie sympathized. "What am I going to feed you?"

An idea suddenly popped in her head. For female creatures like her, they possess galactorrhea, enabling them to produce milk even if they have never been pregnant. She cringed a bit never having breastfed a child before. It will be equally uncanny if she attempted to feed human babies of all things. They rightfully weren't hers and she didn't know how they'll react to tasting a different type of milk to steer them off of what they were used to drinking from their mother. Katie gazed down at the distressed infants in poor health desperate for their pain to end for some type of liberation.

"I shouldn't but I..." she uncomfortably tugged at her fur not believing what she was about to do then anxiously looked back and forth hoping she wasn't being watched although she obviously wasn't, "uh, maybe just a little."

Katie gradually brought the crying infants near her breasts and moved her fur aside allowing them to suckle her milk. Normally babies would only accept their mother's milk but in a case such as this, these infants happily accepted this new rich protein. Creature's milk in comparison to humans was not only delicious; it equally has healthy nutrition to it. Katie was self-aware that creatures of her kind don't normally share their milk with humans, but felt it was necessary under these circumstances.

"At least you guys like it. This will be just our little secret okay."

Whether or not Amber has generally breastfed her babies, Katie's new milk was just the medicine they desperately needed to cure their anguish. The tranquil creature relaxed against the couch watching the children at peace for a while until the baby boy and girl were fully satisfied much to Katie's relief. She admirably watched them as their chubby fingers clutched onto her plumped breasts not wanting the delicious taste to end. She couldn't believe how convenient this moment was to have the right type of milk available for them as she chastises herself for feeding them the artificial milk first. A trigger of emotions penetrated her soul truly cementing this moment for Katie as she admired the children at peace. Almost waiting a half an hour later, the babies were out cold like a light. From the stressful morning they've had and now with content tummies have finally drained their energy into a deep slumber. Now exhausted herself, Katie gently placed the two babies on the couch wrapping them in the blanket Amber had given her. She walked over to the kitchen and grabbed a pound of meat for Jerry. Bringing it to him in the bathroom she said, "And that's all you're getting until dinner."

"Aw you're no fun," Jerry said eating the meat once she brought it to his mouth. "So have the babies finally calmed down?"

"For now," Katie said. "I need to run to the store and get the kids proper milk, not the one I had to feed them from the fridge. It didn't agree with their stomachs. And I don't feel comfortable giving them my milk when that's supposed to be Amber's job. I also have to get them more diapers. That dumb Amber only gave me two like that would make any difference."

"Like you can afford to take care of babies now. I thought you said that you and Dylan were on a tight budget."

"We are but it'll only be a few supplies for the babies. Besides they're going back to their mother tomorrow so I'm getting stuff that Amber will also need for them. Will you watch them until I get back?"

"Hey I ain't no babysitter," Jerry angrily claimed.

"All you have to do is watch them. I don't expect you to take care of them."

"Ugh I hate leaving this tub," Jerry complained.

"You only do it when you're desperate, now get up off your lazy butt and help me with this!" Katie angrily yelled losing her temper.

"Alright, alright, don't blow a gut," Jerry said flopping down from the tub.

Whenever Jerry gets around from leaving the bathroom, he usually flops around like an overweight seal using his pectoral fins to drag his heavy body. He wandered over to the couch where the babies were still slumbering.

"Aw, cute. Can I eat them?" Jerry teased.

"You wish," Katie groaned grabbing her car keys and purse. She equally took off her red bandana before heading out. "I'll try not to be gone long. And don't you dare think about going through the kitchen looking for your next meal. Wait until dinner."

"Yeah, yeah, I got it," he said not wanting to get into another argument with her.

Once Katie left the apartment Jerry directed his attention towards the sleeping children. He chuckled a bit saying, "Ironic, isn't it. If I wasn't living with Dylan and Katie then I would instinctively eat you two. They've tamed that side of me however and I just don't have it in me to do that anymore. So it looks like you babies were very fortunate to come across Dylan and Katie. As much as they'll try denying it, they will never turn away a person in need of help. And by the way you guys look, you definitely need help."

The babies were still in a deep sleep the whole time fully unaware of the great white shark just inches away hovering over them. As the evening stars settled in, Jerry reluctantly watched the babies which he found as a real tedious experience. Thinking he was about to lose his mind, he suddenly heard something coming from the window. It was on the fire escape outside. Surely enough there was a dark silhouetted figure covered completely in black peering on the side of the window. Jerry hid behind the couch before the intruder could spot him. To his surprise, it was a burglar. Not uncommon around these parts but the burglar just doesn't realize who's residence he's breaking into. Jerry at first grunted annoyingly then he chuckled saying, "This night just got interesting. Dylan and Katie did say humans were off-limits unless one comes as an apparent threat to the family." The intruder first looked inside the house only noticing the two babies sleeping on the couch. Without wasting a moment he broke the glass window, with his carelessness evident. The prowler easily walked his way into the room bringing out a pistol for protection. He suspected this was going to be an easy robbery as he placed the gun back in his pocket. "Like taking candy from a baby," he chuckled sinisterly to himself directing his attention towards the infants on the couch.

"You took the words right out of my mouth," Jerry said as he jumped out from behind the couch and clamped his jaws around the leg of the robber.

Taken totally off guard from the unexpected attack, the prowler released a bloodcurdlingly scream clearly waking the babies up. He frantically brought his gun out trying to fire at Jerry but couldn't get a good aim while his body was frantically being thrashed around uncontrollably. Noticing the stupidity of the robber ineptly firing his weapon, he couldn't risk the babies getting hurt in the process so thinking fast he released his jaws from the robber's leg and instead clamped onto his arm. Dropping the gun now, the only logical thing the robber could do was scream in pain. With just one more bite Jerry would've taken his whole arm off but in a desperate attempt to escape with his life, the robber viciously ripped his arm away from the sharp teeth of the predator. Large quantities of blood seeped from the flailing robber as he clumsily escaped with his life exiting through the window in which he came. Jerry stuck his head outside the window watching the foolish robber stumble about the fire escape nearly breaking his neck as he ran away from the area.

"Come back here!" Jerry cried out. "That was just an appetizer tasting that blood. I wanted your whole arm!"

From all the heavy commotion the babies were now screaming frantically. Jerry brought his attention back to them sighing, "Oh great. I'm unable to hold you guys so I don't know how I'm going to rock you."

As he gazed down at the babies' wrappings he gets an idea. Making sure they were properly secured in it, he steadily lifts the top part of the blanket with his mouth lifting both of them off the couch. He then begins the process of rocking them back and forth. They continue crying for a good few minutes until the gentle swinging actually does the trick and calmly puts them back to sleep. Once Jerry finally hears them slumbering again, he gently places them back on the couch.

"Thank God," he sighs annoyingly as he flops away from the couch and desperately tries to lick up the tasty blood left by the robber on the floor.

After a few more minutes Katie finally returned with a bag of groceries in her paws. Her eyes widened in shock witnessing the broken window and speared blood which Jerry was still trying to clean up. As much as she wanted to shout, she didn't want to disturb the babies so she angrily stomped towards the preoccupied shark saying, "What the devil happened here?"

"Some damn robber came in here so I took care of him," Jerry simply explained while still licking the floor.

"Damn it," Katie groaned as she fell back against the nearest kitchen chair. "That's the fifth robbery this year. I'm surprised someone is still stupid enough to steal from us knowing we have a shark."

"I don't mind. More food for me to eat."

"Jerry I appreciate you looking after us but Dylan and I can't take care of our finances if our property is always going to be constantly damaged. Now I'm going to have to go to the department store tomorrow and replace that broken window. And stop licking the floor. It isn't practical."

"I can't help it," Jerry claimed. "Just the taste of blood drives me crazy."

"Well here," Katie said grabbing more pounds of meat from the groceries she just bought. "For protecting the kids and taking care of that robber, think of this as a treat before dinner."

"Now you're speaking my language," Jerry happily said as he grabbed the meat with his mouth and flopped his way back to the bathroom.

Katie looked at the mess before her and groaned in aggravation. "Ugh, we really need to get out this nightmare."

She first checked on the babies satisfied they were still sleeping and decided to take this opportunity to clean up the place. She used a mop cleaning up the blood and placed a 3x5 flat wooden board temporarily against the window. After that, she put all the groceries away then flopped down on the couch from exhaustion. Just when she thought she was getting a break, the babies began to stir and cried indicating it was time to be fed again. Katie forced herself up once more gathering a top brand baby formula she picked up at the store and warmed it up. After pouring it in freshly clean bottles, she fed them both at the same time sitting back on the couch. Just greedy for any type of ration in their tummies, the babies accepted whatever was given to them. After another hour Dylan finally came home. He had a bouquet of roses in his left claw while holding his briefcase in the other.

"Honey I'm home!" he called out.

"SHHHH! I just got them to sleep," Katie scolded.

"Well, what is this?" Dylan said coming over to the couch with Katie while she rocked the babies in her arms.

"Amber dumped them on me this morning," she explained. "I told her no but she just forced them into my arms."

"Wow. They look so skinny," Dylan acknowledged taking a good look at them.

"I know. From the lifestyle that Amber is living how do you expect these poor kids to turn out."

"How long are you suppose to be watching them?"

"She said she would come back for them tomorrow so it's just one day."

"Okay, well I got these for you," he said handing her the roses.

"Oh you're such a sweetheart," she said taking the gift with her free paw and affectionately embraced Dylan with her big bushy tail.

"Are you trying to start something," he slightly chuckled.

"Who says I'm starting anything," she giggled at his remark.

"Uh—what happened to the window?" Dylan said taking notice of the wooden board covering it.

"Another uneventful day in this dump of a neighborhood," Katie groaned as she began to tell Dylan about everything.

5

Now with Dylan home, Katie was able to have extra help with taking care of the babies. He assisted in helping change their diapers when duty called and then clean them into proper clothing that Katie bought from the store.

"Good thing we have Jerry watching over this place like a watchdog otherwise we would've been burglarized multiple times or worse," Dylan stated cleaning up the baby boy's face with a wet rag.

"I agree," said Katie sectioning the diaper correctly on the baby girl. "I just wish we didn't have to put up with prowlers in this crappy neighborhood."

"I know, I'm truly sorry we live in one the crappiest and horrible neighborhoods around but it's all we can afford until we make it."

After cleaning up the boy, Dylan noticed a slight red mark behind the boy's ear and another one on his arm. After studying them a bit it possibly indicated child abuse. "Hey, this poor baby's been abused."

Katie brought the baby sister overlaying the infant on the counter right next to her baby brother to take a closer look. "That does look peculiar."

"Are you sure it's a good idea to return these babies to their mother. We already know the type of person Amber is. Ever since we've moved here she's always come around asking for money, food, and a place to stay whenever her family or friends kick her out. All she does is go back to doing drugs no matter how many times we convinced her to go to rehab to get clean. And now that she has kids in the mix, they're going to suffer under her abuse."

"The only thing I want to do is protect these kids, but you honestly know we can't keep them from their biological mother."

"Can we at least call child protective services on Amber and have them removed from the situation?"

"Dylan remember the last time we did that. We got a lot of death threats from the neighbors by always calling them. Besides, no one gives a damn about people or creatures down here like us. It's one of the many reasons why cops hardly come down here either whenever a robbery takes place. The only thing we can do is look out for ourselves."

"I still feel guilty leaving these innocent children with a drug addict who's already abusing them."

"Then we'll watch over them," Katie stated. "Whenever Amber has them, we'll always come by and check in on them to babysit and make sure they're taken care of. I even bought extra baby supplies for Amber to take so she can properly provide for them. We'll take it upon ourselves to watch over them and call CPS before any more abuse comes to them."

"That will add another workload to our schedule, but I'm willing to do it for the innocent babies," Dylan agreed.

"Then it's settled," Katie said taking the little girl in her arms while Dylan held the boy. They both walked them back over to the couch and gave them their last feeding for the night.

"You know Katie, you're already a natural," Dylan acknowledged as he watched his wife feed the little girl. "You would've made a great mom."

Katie blushed a bit saying, "Thanks dear. I guess this is the best substitute would could ask for. Of course, I ain't that good. The first milk I fed them caused the poor dears to vomit all over me."

Dylan briefly chuckled then instantly put on a serene feature commenting, "Well—there's a first time for everything."

"Uh—I'm afraid to admit that I had to feed them a little bit of my own milk before buying them the baby formula at the store," she revealed. "Just don't tell Amber."

"Hey, it's Amber's fault for leaving them in this state so my lips are sealed."

After the babies finished drinking all their milk, they were out like a light again. Since Dylan and Katie didn't have anything like a crib or a bassinet, the best thing they had for them right now was by pulling out the couch bed and tenderly placed them in the center of it. They properly bundled between the covers making sure they wouldn't roll out of bed. It's ironically the first time the babies ever had anything comfortable so they relaxed peacefully throughout the majority of the night. Dylan opened the door to the bathroom telling Jerry if he hears anything don't hesitate in attacking anybody who comes in. Dylan then tended to feed the alligators which he was pleased to see were still little, however, they were growing and he knew it will only be a matter of time before they'll grow out of the fish tank. He then walked into his bedroom with Katie joining her on the bed.

"What a day this turned out to be," Dylan said coming alongside her.

"I know," Katie exhaled. "I just hope Amber will get her act together and try to do right, especially by those kids."

"Don't worry. Now that we're going to be watching them from now on, we'll see to it that'll she'll get her act together."

"I guess so."

Now with his mind focused on something else more personal, Dylan wrapped his arm fully around Katie bringing her closer to him. "How about we get back to having a little fun and relieve you from this stressful day."

She giggles as he turns her over on her back so she's looking up at him. "And how are you going to make it all better?"

"Well let me show you," he happily said positioning himself directly on top of her.

At first, he started with a simple kiss first trailing from the top of her head down to her chest. He then clutched her hips towards him arranging himself in the right spot while spreading her legs open with his tail. Unable to delay the inevitable any longer he immediately plunged himself inside of her causing Katie to gasp from the first contact. Pumping her full of extreme passion Katie completely reacted by digging her claws into his back while also wrapping her legs around his body. Katie was Dylan's only genuine soul mate to link with and knew how well she liked it sweet and rough always pleasing her whenever they connected. Getting rougher by the minute, the two suddenly heard the babies crying.

"Damn it!" Dylan complained squinting his eyes in frustration.

"We're going to have to stop," Katie said between pants.

"But I'm not finished," he cried.

"Then hurry up and finish it!" she screamed at him.

Destroying the mood of what could've carried on as a pleasant enjoyment for countless hours throughout the night, Dylan begrudgingly brought up the speed. Sure it was always pleasurable but to be interrupted by kids now taking up residence in their home along with having to finish it so quickly brought a melancholy mood to the whole situation. Feeling the immense climax, Dylan reluctantly emptied all of his gratifications inside of Katie causing them both to shout in the end. After they finished Dylan released himself from her as both took a moment to catch their breaths. Katie then quickly got up from the bed to go and tend to the babies. Before Dylan could join her, he looked up at the ceiling above him rubbing his claws against his face.

"Ugh, I guess with kids around, sex won't be a daily routine anymore," he complained.

After regaining some of his strength, Dylan came into the living room finding Katie with both of the babies in her arms as she tried calming them down.

"What's wrong with them?" he asked.

"They're not hungry and they're diapers don't need changing so I don't know what it is?" she said gently bouncing them.

"How old are they?"

"I don't know but judging by their small size they only look to be about a few months old."

"Maybe they miss their mommy or we're dealing with colicky babies."

"Oh God no," Katie heavily breathed with disappointment.

"Here let me help you," Dylan said taking the baby girl this time.

"If we're dealing with colicky babies then none of us are gonna get enough sleep tonight," Katie upsettingly whimpered. "Why don't you let me deal with both of them? You at least have to get up for work tomorrow and you need all the sleep you can get."

"No Katie, we're in this together and I'm gonna help you on this," he insisted.

"Okay Dylan, you just better not fall asleep at work tomorrow," she warned him. "Drink plenty of coffee."

Dylan was right about the kids being colicky babies. To their horror, the babies kept up their ear-piercing cries for about four hours straight. The two exhausted creatures did their best by constantly walking them around the room while also bouncing them on occasions. Katie kept on telling Dylan to hit the sack but he refused to leave her alone as he stayed up suffering with her through the whole ordeal. Jerry even came out unable to tolerate the ongoing crying.

"For crying out loud, can you two shut those kids up!" he shouted.

"Shut up Jerry!" Katie yelled back. "We're doing the best that we can. This is our first time dealing with human babies. Just put up with it until tomorrow. Go back to your bathroom and turn up the volume on your laptop."

"It's already all the way up," he complained flopping back to the bathroom. "Geez, and I thought you guys making love was loud and annoying."

Katie was about to go after Jerry for his snarky statement but Dylan simply said, "Let it go, Katie. We're all going through a bad time here."

Too exhausted and tired to even argue, Katie sluggishly continued trying to calm the baby boy she was carrying. For what seemed like an eternity, the babies had finally stopped their crying and fell asleep from tiredness. Dylan and Katie both gently placed the babies back in their natural spot in the comforter. Too tired and fatigued to even do anything else, both creatures returned to their bedroom and collapsed on the bed immediately falling asleep in a quick flash.

6

Around 7:00 a.m. the next morning the babies began their next round of crying like clockwork. Dylan and Katie woke up with apparent bags under their eyelids representing the lack of sleep they both shared. This time Katie insisted getting up knowing Dylan only had a few minutes before getting ready for work.

"Oh no you don't," Katie said pushing her husband back down with her tail. "You stay in bed while I'll tend to them."

"If you're sure," he said groggily.

"Yes I'm sure," she insisted getting up leaving the bedroom.

Dylan took whatever little minutes he had left while Katie went to go and take care of the babies. She realized both of them needed diaper changing and got to work changing them on the couch bed. After disposing of the dirty diapers, she then got their bottles ready to feed them. However much to her surprise, they refused the bottles this time. Probably realizing they wanted more of her milk instead, Katie reluctantly gave in by breastfeeding them again which generally satisfied the babies. After all, her milk was far more appealing than the baby's formula by comparison. After ten minutes they finally finished and were content for now. Placing them back in the comforter, Katie went to the kitchen trying to hurry and make her husband breakfast. She made him the same thing as yesterday along with a hot cup of coffee.

"Dylan, it's time to get up now," she shouted to him.

After a few minutes later he finally emerges from the bedroom but was still groggy and extremely tired.

"I warned you. You should've gone to bed last night when you had the chance," she told him.

"I know, I know," he said sitting down at the kitchen table. "But I just didn't want to leave you alone to do all the work."

"Well thanks, sweetie," she said handing him his breakfast. "Always thoughtful and considerate. I'm also sorry about cutting our romantic time so short."

"Yeah, you owe me big time for that," he sneered.

"Well the babies are going back to Amber today so we'll have plenty of alone time tonight," she said.

"I'll certainly be looking forward to it," he smiled taking a drink of his coffee.

After finishing up his breakfast, Dylan was fully dressed and ready to head out the door with his briefcase. "Alright baby I'll see you again tonight," he said giving her a quick kiss before heading out.

"Bye Dylan," she said going to the refrigerator and grabbed a pound of red meat. She walked over to the bathroom finding Jerry asleep in the tub with the laptop gone to sleep as well.

"Hey, Jerry wake up. It's feeding time."

The great white shark woke up groggily the same as Dylan indicating he didn't get much sleep like the rest of them. "Five more minutes," he groaned drifting off back to sleep.

"Fine, your food is right here when you wake up," she said placing the meat on the bathroom sink.

Once Jerry was taken care of, she tended to the baby alligators. Much to her amazement, they were actually growing. Not big enough to where the tank was overcrowded but they weren't the same size anymore from when she and Dylan bought them.

"Oh boy, you guys are going to be an extra handful when you get big," she said dropping small amounts of food for them to eat. She then took a moment caressing some of them on their scaly heads. When they first bought them, they were naturally terrified and skittish but after a while, the charms of Dylan and Katie's creature connection began to rub off on them and they were now fully comfortable in their new environment.

Katie was pulled from her thoughts about the gators when the babies began round two of their crying. "Here we go again," she groaned strolling back over to the couch bed.

Morning turned to mid-afternoon and Katie found herself still taking care of the babies. Throughout most of the day, all they did was cry. She was lucky enough to catch an hour break but what she really found frustrating was that Amber never returned. She decided to give her the benefit of the doubt figuring she was probably getting herself together or running a last-minute errand but after another hour went by and then another and another, she began to lose to her mind.

"Damn where is that woman!" she angrily screamed.

Pacing the room back and forth now with both of the babies in her arms, she constantly kept glancing at the clock realizing it was now about to turn evening. She was beginning to dread the worse thinking Amber wasn't coming back. She decided to give her friend Shelley a call on her cell phone. Unable to put the babies down, she used her tail grabbing her cell phone and dialed the number to her friend. After three rings Shelley picked up.

"Hey Katie, what's up?" Shelley said at the other end of the line.

"Hi, Shelley. You won't believe what's happened?" Katie said using her tail holding up the cell phone to her ear.

"What's going on?"

"Remember that crack head Amber that Dylan and I told you about?"

"Yeah. She still causing trouble for you two?"

"You don't know the half of it. Now she's dumped two of her babies on us yesterday. We've been trying to take care of them and she was supposed to return today to retrieve them but she hasn't come back."

"Uh oh. Looks like you've been played. Knowing how generous and gullible you two are, no offense, she probably thought she could get away with dumping her babies on you and Dylan."

"She wouldn't do that!" Katie said losing her temper. "She's stupid but not that stupid! She wouldn't dare take advantage of me and Dylan like that."

"Do you need help watching them or something?"

"Thanks, Shelley but Dylan will be home in a little while and he'll help me with them so thanks for the offer but that's okay. I just wanted some advice on what I should do if she doesn't come back?"

"If you know her address you can confront her. But I'd be careful if I were you. I know your neighborhood isn't one of the safest places to be around."

"It's okay Shelley. Dylan and I know how to take care of ourselves. Knowing the drugged up junkie that she is, I'm going to give her one more day. If she doesn't come back tomorrow then I'm going to do just that and confront her."

"Alright, Katie. Good luck with that and with the kids."

"Oh by the way Shelley, Dylan invited me to his friend's barbeque this weekend. Would you like to join us? It'll certainly make up for the dinner I had to cancel on us the other night."

"Uh, sure. A family barbeque sounds like a good idea to get me. I'll be there."

"Okay Shelley, I'll pick you up at your place on Saturday. You take care and I'll see ya later. Bye."

"Goodbye Katie," Shelley said hanging up the phone.

Placing the phone on the kitchen counter with her tail, Katie continued pacing the room back and forth as the babies continued their nonstop crying again.

"Oh God, I'm going to strangle that Amber when I get my paws on her," she grunted.

A few minutes later Dylan finally returned home and was shocked to see Katie still with the babies. Her hair and fur was disheveled representing how stressed out she was. The way she looked actually turned Dylan on but he immediately snapped out of his fantasy element and focused on the task at hand.

"Um Katie baby, what are the babies still doing here," he said placing his car keys and briefcase on the nearest counter.

"Amber never came back," she said.

"What?"

"You heard me. She never came back!"

"Oh great," Dylan sighed with absolute frustration. "So what are we going to do now?"

"I'm giving her one more day. If she doesn't come back tomorrow I'm going to find her and confront that bitch."

"Okay, okay, just don't cause anything that'll start trouble," Dylan said helping loosen the load off of Katie by taking the baby girl.

"She already started trouble the minute she dumped these babies on us."

"I know. But tomorrow's Friday. It's my only off day along with the weekends so do you want me to take care of it instead?"

"No. I want to be the one to confront her since she's the one who dumped them on me," she claimed.

"If you insist," he said truly exhausted taking a wide yawn. "How long have they been up?"

"For the last four hours," she revealed. "Hopefully they'll start to feel tired in a little bit. I haven't got much work done today."

"That's understandable in dealing with a colicky baby. Two at that."

"I don't know what's the matter with human beings? All they like to do is have sex and pump out babies but don't have the guts to even take care of what they created. Sometimes I wish there was a law to sterilize certain people."

"I know how you feel but sometimes life just throws curve balls at you and you have no choice but to go along with it."

"Whatever," Katie groaned still trying to soothe the baby boy in her arms.

After another twenty minutes, the babies had finally calmed down and fell asleep. The two couples were hoping a chance to finally relax but were interrupted by Jerry who called out, "It's feeding time!"

7

After taking care of the babies as well as the animals, Dylan and Katie retreated to their bedroom flopping down on the bed.

"Oh God what a day," Katie exhaled.

"Yeah," Dylan groaned wrapping his arm around her stomach. "I'm praying every day that we'll get out of this mess."

"Me too," Katie said faintly with a yawn. "By the way, I talked to Shelley and invited her to Brandon's barbeque if that's alright?"

"Sure. The more the merrier. I'll try as hard as I can next week to ask my boss for that promotion. I don't want to pressure the matter but I will certainly remind him."

"Okay," Katie said more faintly than the last.

"So—now that we're alone, remember that promise you made me by making up our little romantic time cut so short yesterday?"

Without hearing a response, Dylan was discouraged to find Katie already fast asleep.

"Ugh," he frustratingly complained lying on his back. "Now you owe me double time woman. That is if we'll ever get free time with those two little ones on our hands."

Into wee hours of the night, the house was peaceful and quiet until the babies once more began their next rounds of screaming and crying. Because Katie had to deal with them all day, Dylan took it upon himself this time to take care of them. For about an hour he changed them and fed them until they stopped their crying and promptly fell back to sleep. Dylan returned to bed but unfortunately, he and Katie weren't going to get a good night's sleep. Throughout the rest of the night, the babies continued with their colicky agenda leaving no end where the two couldn't get a moment's peace. This time the two worked together trying to soothe both babies. It generally lasted until 3:30 a.m. until the babies were finally worn out. Dylan and Katie both were so drained they fell asleep on the couch bed with them. They slept opposite sides of each other while the two babies slept in between them right in the middle. The babies were too young to understand anything but it almost seemed like at this exact moment, they were finally at peace to know who their true parents really were.

In the morning before the sun could make its peak over the horizon, the babies woke Dylan and Katie up giving them a bad headache. Both were still drained and exhausted and weren't looking forward to another stressful day.

"Mornin'," Dylan said rubbing his red eyes.

"Mornin' yourself," Katie said groggily as she removed herself from the couch bed and headed over to the kitchen getting the babies' bottles ready. "Damn it. We're almost out of the baby's formula already. They drank it up quicker than I thought. I knew I should've bought more."

"You couldn't have known," he said joining her in the kitchen. "From how skinny and unhealthy they were, they were obviously hungry. Until we buy them more, you can still give them some of your own. Besides, you thought Amber would return so don't blame yourself. Speaking of which, are you still going to confront her today?"

"Of course I am! I've given her one more day but if she doesn't show up I'm going to find her and confront her on the matter."

"Certainly someone with her poor living conditions, the babies need all the proper care they can handle. How about I go out baby shopping for them today?"

"Are you sure you can afford that?"

"We are on a tight budget but the babies deserve the best care as possible. Besides the savings we've been saving up all this time for our new future house is something that we can sometimes dip into if an emergency arises."

"Alright, when do you want to go out shopping for them?"

"Probably later on this afternoon. We'll wait for Amber until then. If she doesn't return then you can go and confront her and I'll take them out shopping with me."

"Are you sure you can handle all that extra weight bringing them along?" she asked him.

"Hey, look at how we're doing so far," he halfheartedly teased.

"Okay tough guy. And also while you're out baby shopping, be sure and get Jerry some more food too. He's also running low."

"Sure thing baby. Oh, and by the way, you owe me double for falling asleep on me last night."

"Well we're just going to have come up with a special night to really spark the occasion," she said caressing her tail around his head.

"Girl do you want me to do you on the kitchen counter right here now," he claimed getting aroused.

"That would be interesting but I'm not going to traumatize the kids," she smirked.

"God I hate that tail of yours," he pouted. "It always fully arouses me."

"Wimp," she teased.

As the morning went on, Dylan and Katie both tended to the babies taking care of the basics like changing and feeding. They also dealt with their crying outburst but luckily it didn't last as long as it did yesterday. Once mid-afternoon finally came and there was still no sign of Amber, Katie was determined to find her one way or the other. Before heading out, she first breastfed the babies making sure they'll be settled for the second half of the day so Dylan won't have too much trouble dealing with them.

"Well I'm off to find that tramp," Katie said getting ready.

"Just be careful baby," Dylan warned her. "You know how rough this neighborhood is."

"Please Dylan don't talk to me like I'm a child. I told you I can take care of myself. We didn't survive in this neighborhood as long as we did for nothing."

"Alright but the minute anything happens, don't hesitate to call me."

"Yeah, yeah, I'll be fine," she said giving him a quick kiss before heading out. "I'll see ya later."

After Katie left, Dylan directed his attention towards the babies lying down on the couch bed. "So, are you two up for shopping?"

Knowing he would have his hands full, Dylan constructed the babies' blanket to act as a baby carrier around his chest. Once he got it sectioned into place he positioned both babies inside of it. They were firmly but gently placed from falling out safely secured around Dylan's chest. Before leaving he stopped by the bathroom to tell Jerry where he was going.

"What do you mean you're going out?" Jerry complained.

"It'll only be for an hour or two," said Dylan. "The babies and you need more rations so I must go out and take care of business."

"But I'm hungry now!" Jerry whined.

"Jerry you're not going to starve," Dylan scolded. "You can wait. Just please be on your best behavior and don't cause any trouble."

Once Dylan was all set and ready he left out the door with the babies leaving a desperate Jerry on his own. Jerry's main problem is unable to control his hunger on occasions. Since he no longer lives the predator life in the ocean like other sharks, part of his instincts would go into overdrive of wanting to be fed almost every three or four hours. He tried controlling his tremendous appetite but throughout all the years he lived with Dylan and Katie, it still wasn't an easy process to maintain. He miserably sat there in the tub while continuing to watch stuff on the laptop. The videos didn't help when different advertisements would pop up of food commercials.

"Aw don't do this to me," Jerry complained. "Go away stupid advertisements."

After another random advertisement popped up, Jerry had enough saying, "Screw this!" Unable to control his desires he gave into his temptation leaving the bathroom. He immediately wandered into the kitchen searching for anything edible. Opening the fridge with his large snout he came across all of Dylan and Katie's food. It might not have been meat but as long as it was something to munch on Jerry would dive right into it. "Come to daddy," he cried out making a mess everywhere. All of Dylan and Katie's leftovers and food items not yet opened where being devoured by Jerry in a split second. Heck, he even went for the beer and soda cans, munching away at them like they were nothing. After he devoured everything in the fridge, he went to the cabinets next finding stuff like bread, chips, cereal, and so on. He consumed whatever was in the cabinets as well just leaving mess after mess which would take hours to clean up. Feeling much better after pleasing his desires, he felt giddy flopping towards the alligator's fish tank.

"Hey guys, want to join the party?" he said trying to topple the tank over with his snout.

However, trying to topple something at this angle with his snout was awkward so he clumsily dropped the tank leaving it crashing to the floor. Luckily none of the alligators were harmed but the tank was damaged beyond repair.

"Oops," is all Jerry could say.

The baby alligators didn't waste a minute wandering everywhere throughout the apartment now that they were free.

"Oh well, can't make a big fuss about it now," Jerry said flopping over to the couch bed and decided to watch something from the TV in the living room. "Now this is the life," he said fully relaxed turning over on his side. However, the couch bed couldn't withstand the great white's bodyweight causing it to collapse underneath him.

8

Katie knew exactly where Amber lived and didn't have to travel far to locate her. She just traveled down the block then made it across the street to another apartment building that was very similar to her and Dylan's. From just the moment she began entering the area, there were already unpleasant indications of drug dealers, crack heads, a woman vomiting, five thugs arranging their pit bulls to battle against each other, and many more distasteful catastrophes. Katie kept her focus on heading inside the apartment building ignoring the repulsive sight of her neighborhood. Once inside she headed upstairs coming across more drug dealers who caught sight of her in an instant.

"Hey baby, what's a sexy thing like you doing wandering around in a place like this?" one of the men remarked who essentially sounded like a pimp.

Katie ignored him as she continued walking up the stairs but the drug dealer wasn't one to be ignored by anybody. He followed her already getting aggressive grabbing Katie by the tail.

"Hey sweet thang I'm talking to you," he said firmly. "It's not polite to ignore someone who's talking to you."

"And it's not polite to put your hands on someone you don't know," Katie said pushing him back with her tail.

"Hey looks like someone needs to teach you some manners," the man said getting quite aggressive as he moved up closer like he was about to sexually assault her.

"I'm warning you to back off," she informed him.

"What are you going to do about it?" he said seizing her by the arm.

However, Katie was ready for him as sharp claws emerged from her paws. Like a cat, she scratched him across the chest causing the man to fall backwards in pain.

"Awww! Crazy bitch!" he yelled holding on to his now bleeding chest.

"I'd keep walking if I were you scumbag. Now get out of here before I'll scratch something more precious and valuable to you you're not willing to risk losing."

Underestimating the female creature he's come across, the man wisely fled the scene. Now that she was alone, Katie continued on her way as she walked down the hallway after making it up the steps. The apartment already resembled theirs with numerous excessive graffiti speared everywhere, peeled off rundown wallpaper and cockroaches roaming the area. Coming across many doors she eventually found Amber's. Not hiding her frustration, she angrily knocked on the door. She heard screaming and shouting from the inside indicating that Amber wasn't alone. Katie knocked again only to be met with a different woman who opened the front door. From her apparent attitude, the woman was stressed and straight-up ghetto with a bad attitude.

"What the hell do you want?" the woman scoffed.

"I'm looking for Amber. Is she here?"

"What's it to you?"

"Listen lady, Amber dumped her children on me and I'm not leaving until I talk with her. Now, where is she?!" Katie demanded.

The rude woman was about to slam the door shut on Katie's face until the assertive female creature held it open and forced herself inside much to the woman's surprise.

"Hey!" the woman cried out but there was no stopping the determined female creature as she walked her way into their apartment.

The smell of marijuana, heroin, and many other unpleasing aromas already hit Katie's nose the minute she walked inside affecting her sinuses. Trying to block it out she aggressively searched around the apartment until she finally spotted Amber. Compared to the day she brought her kids to Katie, she was in worse shape now. She sat down in the far corner of the bathroom with her right arm spread across the open toilet completely drugged beyond her comprehension. There were needles everywhere basically indicating she recently just had her fix. She could even make out the pulsating purple veins, displaying themselves through Amber's white skin tone. Her red bloodshot eyes were half open and close, representing how she wasn't in her right state of mind. Katie was beyond furious to catch Amber like this who promised her she would return for her kids.

"Amber what the hell are you doing?!" Katie shouted at her.

Although drugged up, Amber still had enough common sense to notice Katie standing right in front of her. "Oh—K-Katie, w-what are you—doing here?"

"I came looking for you since you forgot about your kids," she growled at her.

"Oh yeah," she said as if she forgot she even had kids. "I-I promise I'll pick them up tomorrow. J-just give me one more day."

"Grrrrrr. Amber for crying out loud look at you! You're in no condition to look after children. You need to get your act together and stop this shit!"

"Don't yell at me," Amber complained like a spoiled child.

"Amber, I know you've had it rough growing up. All of us did which is why I see everyone the way they are around here but you gotta try hard to put that past behind you and think what is best for those kids. They didn't ask for this."

"And neither did I!"

"So now your kids gotta suffer because you suffered?"

"Yeah! Other people should feel the pain of what I've gone through."

"This horrendous cycle is just going to keep repeating itself with them suffering from what you suffered. They at least deserve a fighting chance. Do what's right for them!"

"Who are you to tell me what to do with my life! You're not my mother. This is my life and I choose to do what I want with it!" Amber retorted.

"Fine! Do whatever you want with your life. Dylan and I are through with trying to set you straight. I don't care if you so much as jumped out on the streets and got hit by a car. But your kids don't deserve your bullshit. They still deserve a fighting chance. Tomorrow you better come and retrieve your kids. Dylan and I only offer to help you for the kid's sake. Not you. We will make frequent visits to babysit and check up on them whether you like it or not. The next step we'll be calling the authorities and the CPS on you. If you're going to see it as an annoyance, you just better be grateful that we're willing to do the right thing for them. We tried with you but you're a lost cause."

Amber didn't say anything else. She just shamefully turned her head away unable to look at Katie in the eyes then passed out.

"Tomorrow. One more day to get yourself together. I'm not playing any more of these games with you Amber," Katie claimed then decided to finally leave feeling she's said what she needed to.

Leaving the bathroom she came across the woman who tried shutting her out and just gave her a dirty look walking right past her leaving the apartment.

Deep down Amber knew how right Katie was about trying to get her act together. There were numerous times she promised her and Dylan that she would do better, but her pride would take over always giving into her deepest temptations. The more she dug her grave, the harder it was to climb out of. She was stuck in the past with her demons and tired of trying.

While Katie was visiting Amber, Dylan was at the store during the same time. He walked down the grocery aisle checking the items on his list. The babies were somewhat enjoying this new experience never having been inside a store before. At first, Dylan didn't think anything of it but he suddenly got the impression he was being gawked and stared at by random people. What he failed to realize was that creatures of his kind had never taken in human babies before. Due to their status of never abandoning their own kind, they would only take care of their own children. It was unusual yet cute to witness a creature taking care of these babies as if they were his own. Some citizens couldn't help taking pictures of him from their cell phones. Once he came across the baby aisle he noticed a mother grabbing a handful of diapers.

"Uh excuse me?" he said gaining the woman's attention. "I'm sorry, I'm new at this but do you know what are the best diapers to get that'll last long."

"Oh that's so cute," the woman said first witnessing the babies on his chest. "Did you adopt them?"

"Oh no. My wife and I are just babysitting them for a friend as a favor."

"It'll still so adorable if you did adopt them. Anyway, I think these are the best diapers that'll last you a long time," she said handing him a certain brand.

"Okay, thanks," Dylan said first reading the instructions carefully and felt the woman was right. He then grabbed at least five diaper bags and continued down the aisle. He came across many other baby products which the children desperately needed. Knowing Amber didn't obtain half these items, he thought it was best for the kids to preserve these materials. He knew he and Katie were on a tight budget but the babies needed the proper care provided for them so Dylan reluctantly grabbed more material which he normally didn't intend on buying. He stuffed the cart with a few toys, pacifiers, more baby formula, baby monitors, clean sheets, baby powder, two child car seats, and even a bassinet.

"Oh crap," he said looking at his full cart when he finished. "Looks like some of our hard-earned savings are going into this. I generally don't like touching our savings but the babies here are an emergency so it's worth it."

After paying everything at the cash register, Dylan left the store with an armful of items. After storing everything in his trunk, he placed the new child car seats in the back of his car. It was difficult at first but once he got them set in place he safely secured the babies in their new car seats. He drove back home hoping he'll make it there in time before Jerry does anything stupid. With the babies once more safely secured in his blanket baby carrier, he holds a few of the items in his claws while he decides to come back for the rest. Right as he walks down the hallway to his apartment he spots Katie indicating they've just come back home at the same time.

"Hey Katie," he says.

"Hey Dylan, perfect timing," she says taking one of the bags from his claws. "You certainly bought a lot."

"I didn't plan on it but the babies really need half of this stuff," he said.

"Amber better be grateful for this. I've met her and she was ten times worse than she was the first day she left the babies with me."

"Well, hopefully tomorrow she'll be better."

"Fat chance," Katie said unlocking the door with her keys.

The minute she opened the door, one of the baby gators ran out. Katie was quick and grabbed him by the tail before he could scurry away. "Hey, how the heck did you get out?"

Once Dylan and Katie walked inside, their eyes extended in horror to witness the outrageous mess everywhere. The fish tank, the kitchen and everything in the living room was trashed. They found their culprit lying down on their now broken couch bed watching the TV. He tried turning his head to them already knowing how pissed they were with him.

"I know you guys are mad with me but look at it this way—things could be a whole lot worse."

Katie lost it as she bellowed in frustration and rushed at Jerry. She jumped on top of his huge body trying to move him. "You stupid shark!" she shrieked. "We should've dumped you in the ocean where you belong!"

"Hey calm down," Jerry said trying to roll over to get Katie off of him.

"Look at what you've done Jerry," Dylan said angrily looking at the broken fish tank. "Now the alligators don't have a home."

"Get back in the bathroom!" Katie desperately screamed pulling him by his fin and tried pushing him at the same time. "We've had it with you!"

"What do you mean?" Jerry said trying to move so Katie doesn't waste her energy pulling and pushing him.

"We're calling the wildlife aquarium and we're going to transport you back to the ocean," Katie claimed.

"What? No! I don't want to go!" he whined.

"We only ask you for one thing and that's to control your hunger. We can't afford to replace every single item you break and always buy groceries because of you eating up our food!"

"I promise I'll do better, just don't send me away," Jerry begged as he was shoved back into the bathroom.

"I'm too angry to discuss this with you right now. You just stay in there until we clean up the mess you made," Katie said as she slammed the bathroom door shut.

"Please, don't send me away! I like staying with you and Dylan. Please!" Jerry cried but he was ignored by a frustrated Dylan and Katie who now had a tremendous matter to attend to.

9

After Dylan placed the babies down on their bed inside their bedroom, he helped Katie to first retrieve all the baby alligators. They found them all in odd places such as the kitchen sink, the refrigerator, and even the toilet. The last one they found was the obvious albino gator and placed them all in a shoebox for now.

"Well I guess that's the last of them," Dylan said placing the box on the kitchen counter.

"Great, I'll get the broom and mop," Katie groaned with absolute frustration.

The couple worked together for the next two hours cleaning up the mess everywhere they could. The fish tank and couch bed were damaged beyond repair and had to be disposed of. Luckily Dylan bought a bassinet for the babies so there was no need for them to sleep on the couch bed anymore, however it was still a comfortable sofa Dylan and Katie had grew fond of and hated to part with it. As for the alligators, they both knew they had to find a temporary home for them until buying another fish tank.

"Good-bye precious couch," Dylan said after helping Katie move it outside their apartment building placing it on the curve of the sidewalk.

"That's the second one this month," Katie said rolling her eyes.

Heading back to their apartment Dylan brought the bassinet up to their bedroom placing it on the right-hand side of their bed and set the babies inside of it. The comforter they added to it did the trick on helping set the mood for the babies to quickly fall asleep. Pleased that the babies were satisfied and will probably be slumbering for a little while, they still wanted to take advantage of seeing what they could do for the alligators and especially Jerry.

"So what are we going to do about Jerry?" Dylan asked. "You're really not going to get rid of him are you?"

"Nah, I just said that in a fit of anger," Katie confessed. "He's family and I can't bear it if we ever got rid of him. But I don't know what we're going to do with him constantly causing this mess. We can't afford it."

"How about we make him think the more damage he causes, we'll threaten to get rid of him then maybe that'll cause him to straighten up his act," Dylan suggested.

"It's worth a try. Let's go and tell him."

When Dylan and Katie opened the door to the bathroom, it was hard to read Jerry's expressions with his blank shark-like appearance but knowing him well as they have for years, they could undoubtedly see hurt in his eyes. He sat there in the tub with his laptop off just waiting for their answer.

"Well Jerry, it's all settled," Katie announced. "We called the wildlife aquarium and they're coming to pick you up tomorrow."

"NO!" Jerry cried.

"Sorry, Jerry but we can't keep doing this with you. We figured you'd be much happier to be back in your natural habitat where you can eat all the food you want without restrictions from us," Dylan said.

"But I like you guys. I don't want to go. I promise I'll better control my appetite," he pleaded with them.

"How can we be sure Jerry? This is the tenth time you trashed the place because you couldn't be patient. Despite the tight budget we're under, we've always been fair with feeding you your daily routine of breakfast, lunch, and dinner and yet you still are greedy for more."

"Please don't get rid of me," he begged jumping out of the tub flopping over to them. "I promise I'll try to do better. Please call off the wildlife aquarium before it's too late. I don't want to go!"

Whether or not he would keep to his word, just the fact he was already guilty and remorseful for what he's done was enough to convince them.

"Alright Jerry, you're forgiven but just remember if you do it again I won't hesitate to call them and send your butt to the wild," Katie made clear.

"Oh thank you, thank you, thank you," Jerry happily cried lunging his huge body on top of Katie trying to hug her.

"Get off of me!" Katie screamed in frustration as the heavy shark removed himself from her. "Geez, I can't wait until we get you into a swimming pool."

"Well Jerry since you destroyed the alligator's home it looks like you're going to have to share your tub with them until we can find them another fish tank," Dylan said bringing them in the bathroom.

"Aw man," Jerry complained.

"You brought this on yourself so quit your complaining," Dylan said dumping the alligators inside the tub which was always filled with water. "We'll bring your dinner later."

Once Dylan and Katie left the bathroom, Jerry first stared at the seven baby gators who are now taking up residence in his comfort zone.

"Look you guys let's get something straight, just because you're in here with me doesn't mean we're friends. We're more like acquaintances, alright?"

The alligators typically ignored the shark as they happily swam in their new enclosure.

"Ugh, when I'm I going to learn to do what I'm told," Jerry sighed in defeat.

Since the couch was now gone, the only thing the couples had to sit on in the living room was the recliner. Dylan first took a seat on it while Katie lied down on his lap.

"Another hard working day, huh baby," Dylan said caressing her by the arm and hair.

"It's like things keep escalating from bad to worse for us," Katie groaned.

"Well you know what they say; things will only get worse before they get a whole lot better."

"I guess it's true but I'm praying our big break to come soon."

"Me too," Dylan said. Hoping to relieve some of the stress from his wife he began to gradually kiss her around the neck then gently massaged her breasts.

"Are you sure you want to do this now?" Katie giggled getting aroused.

"Better now than never," he smiled pulling her fully on top of him while suckling her breasts. "Are you sure I can't get some of your delicious milk too?"

"Sorry big man, but they're only reserved for the babies," she chuckled.

As Katie got in place ready to give Dylan a night he'd never forget they suddenly heard the babies' crying coming from the baby monitor.

"Not again," Dylan frustratingly cried out throwing his head back against the cushion.

"Sorry honey, duty calls again," she said removing herself from him heading to their bedroom.

After taking care of the babies which just needed diaper changing and feeding, the couples decided to order some pizza since Jerry devoured all of their food. Once the pizza arrived, the two ate their meal for the night sitting on the recliner while watching whatever was on TV.

"Hey Katie, after everything that has happened today, are you still up for going to Brandon's barbeque tomorrow?"

"Sure," she replied. "Just because we're having a bad time doesn't mean we still can't have fun over your friend's place. Not to mention it'll be great to be at your friend's house offering us food since Jerry ate up all of ours. Besides I promised Shelley I would bring her along and I already feel bad for having to cancel on her the other night."

Since Katie brought up that specific night, Dylan still felt guilty he went out with Chloe and felt this was something he should get off his chest.

"Um, Katie—I know you probably don't want to talk about this but—I'm still sorry about going out with Chloe. I didn't realize she had a thing for me."

"Forget about it Dylan. I never trusted Chloe but she was the best attorney recommended and we really had no choice at the time so that's why we went with her. She certainly has a sick mind for being attracted to you."

"You know the funny thing about it, she isn't the first. Other humans are sometimes attracted to creatures like us."

"Some humans are crazy," Katie stated. "They should just stick to their own kind like we do but half of them have mental problems which causes them to do crazy things. I don't hold it against those that can't help it but those who certainly know they're sick and don't do anything about it, I can't feel sympathy for them."

"Yeah like Amber. By the way, what did she say to you?"

"She basically told me not to judge her and she can do whatever she wants with her life. I made it clear to her though that from now on how we're going to be watching over her babies whether she likes it or not."

"Should we wait until she comes and picks them up tomorrow and then head to the barbeque?"

"I doubt we're going to drop off the babies at her place by the way she looked but we'll see if she'll come to her senses for the sake of her children and if not, we'll take other measures then head on over to Brandon's barbeque."

"Okay, sounds like a plan," Dylan said eating the last bite of his pizza.

10

Throughout most of the night, Dylan and Katie once more dealt with the kid's crying over and over again leaving very little sleep for them both. But they were thankful in just a couple of hours they would return them to their mother so they could get back to the way things were before they arrived. Don't get them wrong, it's not that they didn't love the kids but they weren't their responsibility. Around 7:27 a.m. the babies began their crying outburst ready for breakfast. Dylan and Katie both got up helping tend to fill the babies' little tummies in the kitchen.

"You know what's so funny Katie? We don't even know they're names?"

"You're right Dylan," she chuckled. "Amber never told me and I never got around to asking her. Oh well, when we return them today we'll find out."

"How about after the kids and pets finish eating, we'll get things together and head on over to Amber's place?" Dylan suggested. "Then we'll catch a quick breakfast on the road heading on over to Brandon's place."

"Sounds good," she agreed.

After the babies were fed, they were placed back inside their bassinet while Katie started to pack some things that Amber will need for her kids. Dylan wandered over to the fridge grabbing some meat for Jerry and alligators. When he opened the door to the bathroom, he was surprised to find Jerry and the gators getting along pretty well. All seven gators were on top of Jerry's head and body while they watched various shows from the laptop.

"Well it's good to see you guys are getting used to each other's company," Dylan stated.

"Oh yeah," Jerry said just noticing Dylan come in. "I thought I'd hate it but they're alright."

"Good cause its feeding time," he said lifting the meat over Jerry's mouth. "But you know since you ate up all the food last night, you're going to have to share this meat with them."

"Alright, alright, just give it," Jerry complained opening his mouth wide.

Dropping the meat inside Jerry's mouth, the shark only chewed half of it allowing the other half to be devoured by the baby gators.

Dylan returned to the kitchen with his wife saying, "Looks like Jerry and alligators are getting along quite well. Speaking of which, you know we never even gave the alligators names yet."

"That's true. Maybe when we get them their new fish tank, we'll start giving them names."

"Well I'll give Brandon a call and let him know when we'll be on our way," Dylan said bringing out his cell phone.

After everything was packed and ready aside from the bassinet which was too much to carry, the two couples carried each baby in their arms along with their diaper bags and left the apartment heading on over to Amber's place. Unlike last night, the area seemed quiet and deserted with hardly any citizens present. The only people around were small children playing hopscotch, jump rope, and patty cake on the streets. Watching them for a minute, it got Katie thinking just how it would feel to raise a human. So far it was stressful but at the same time, it filled a certain hole in Katie's heart that needed healing from a past occurrence. Finally entering inside the apartment building the two of them took the rundown elevator refusing to climb the stairs with all the extra weight they were already carrying. When they made their way to Amber's apartment Katie knocked on the door, not as aggressive as she did yesterday. After hearing nothing she decided to knock a little harder.

"They better be home," Katie said handing over the baby girl to Dylan. "Hey Amber! I know you're in there! Open up!"

After a while still nothing. Katie began feeling the same anger wash over her again and couldn't help banging loudly against the door. "Amber! Amber!"

"Geez lady, do you know what time it is? Are you trying to wake up the whole neighborhood!" said an irritable neighbor coming out of his apartment. "Amber isn't here."

"What do you mean Amber isn't here?" Katie demanded fully alarmed.

"She and some other woman packed their bags and left last night," the neighbor claimed. "If you ask me, good riddance. I could always smell their crap in my apartment."

Katie and Dylan first stared in shock at each other not knowing what to do.

"Are you sure she just went up and left?" Dylan asked.

"From the look on her face, I'm guessing she had enough of this neighborhood like the rest of us," the neighbor said going back inside his apartment.

Desperate to find out for herself, Katie rammed the door open only to find the room empty and deserted, aside from some garbage, a worn-out bed cushion, and a few cockroaches. The minute Amber left she had officially abandoned her babies leaving them with Katie and Dylan.

"AMBER!!" Katie angrily shouted to the ceiling.

Now leaving Amber's apartment a confused Dylan and Katie didn't know what to do as they headed to their vehicle. Dylan still held both babies in his arms as he turned toward his wife saying, "So what are we going to do now?"

"I don't know," Katie said pinching the bridge of her nose with her paws trying to concentrate. "That dirty bitch deliberately abandoned her children on us. I wonder if the fact I confronted her yesterday must have spooked her into leaving."

"I doubt that. That woman always had so many issues. She just couldn't face up to her demons and ran away."

"I guess we're going to keep the kids a bit longer than we intended," she said crossing her arms against her chest.

"Well, we can turn them in. I'm sure the system will put them in foster care where someone will most likely adopt them," Dylan suggested.

Her husband's words sank deep into her subconscious as she continued watching the little children still playing on the sidewalk just across from them. She wondered how lucky they were to have parents or even had the slightest chance of happiness due to not having parents at all. She then noticed one mother call for her child from her stoop. The child ran to his mother as she happily embraced him in her arms giving him plenty of love and affection then gradually carried him back into their apartment. That's the type of love she just wishes all children could receive.

"No," she told Dylan. "We're not sending them away only for them to be abandoned again. The system treats everybody the same way and the risk of them going through different foster homes can be a hellish experience. And if they did get adopted then they'll most likely be separated. They don't deserve that. Amber might have turned her back on them but we won't. For right now, we're keeping them."

Fully agreeing with his wife, Dylan simply nodded his head kissing her. "So I guess that means we're taking them to Brandon's barbeque with us."

"I guess we are."

11

Since the children's car seats were already placed in Dylan's car, they decided to take his vehicle heading to Brandon's place. They first stopped by Shelley's place picking her up. Unlike Dylan and Katie's neighborhood, she lived in a decent-sized region which the couples practically envied. She lived in a condo complex that was well-groomed and modest but way too expensive for Dylan and Katie to afford. The reason Shelley can afford it because she was left a reasonable size of money after her deceased mother passed. Instead of spending it all, she would only use it wisely by paying rent and utilities and food if her job couldn't sustain her.

After receiving a phone text from Katie letting her know they were here, she heads outside meeting them parked near the sidewalk. She didn't expect to see the babies with them and is surprised to meet them as she goes in the backseat to greet them.

"Oh you guys, they're so cute," Shelley says as she cuddles with their faces. "I didn't expect you to bring them along."

"Neither did we," said Katie. "Unfortunately their no-good mother has abandoned them."

"She's gone?" Shelley said surprised.

"Yep. She's just packed her bags and left town."

"So what are you two going to do with these little ones?"

"We're keeping them for now until we can figure out what to do," Katie claimed.

"Are you guys thinking about adopting them?" Shelley said.

Everyone in the car fell silent for a minute. Dylan and Katie certainly were possibly considering it but never has a creature such as their kind ever taken in human beings before. It's pretty much because the system deems them inadequate for several reasons. They know that these creatures aren't intentionally dangerous but some of them have characteristics such as claws, spikes, etc. while most love keeping predatory animals as pets which are considered too dangerous for innocent children to be around. Another is due to not knowing if a child will function properly in life by being raised around cartoon creatures. It's not illegal, but it's not necessarily socially acceptable either. No one has yet to attempt it, until now and so far Dylan and Katie have done a far better job taking care of them than their biological mother.

"That would be interesting Shelley but you know no creature has ever adopted a human being," Dylan stated.

"What's wrong with you guys being the first," she brought up. "I've known you guys for a long time and I think this is your chance to get the children you never obtained. Perhaps it's a sign from God."

"You think so Shelley," Katie said looking back at her from the rearview mirror.

"Hey if it doesn't work out, you know there's plenty of parents out there who are looking to adopt children but if not, it's your guys chance to get the family you never got. I think there's a reason why Amber gave them to you in the first place."

Dylan and Katie pondered on what Shelley just said. Who's to say they couldn't risk taking care of human beings. If the system is always adamant by just dumping kids into redundant homes, then why can't the creatures take a shot at doing a much superior and better job at turning them into model citizens which society desperately needs.

Either way, the subject is dropped for now once the friends made it to Brandon's place. Brandon lived a decent neighborhood like Shelley's but he lived a wealthy two-story house. He's worked a bit longer than Dylan as an investment banker and his finances have done him well. Dylan promised Brandon once he got that promotion his neighborhood would be the ideal place where he and Katie could thrive in. Shelley has never met Brandon before and she didn't quite know what to expect from Dylan's coworker. Brandon came at the front door opening it for his friends to enter.

"Come on in everybody," he said blissfully wearing an apron and holding a cold beer in one hand which indicated he was already barbequing outback. He just witnessed the two new babies and Shelley. He commented, "My you sure did bring more friends then I intended but that's fantastic. Come on right inside and make yourselves at home."

Being respectful to Shelley, he brought his hand out to her saying, "Nice to meet you, senorita."

He then gave her a quick kiss on the back of her hand making her blush deep red in the cheeks. "Uh, thanks," she smiled embarrassingly.

He led them outside in his backyard which had multiple chairs and a wide folding plywood table with plenty of food and drinks. Brandon worked at the grill cooking all types of meats that everyone found tremendously delectable. There were a few other friends present that Dylan knew of from his job and others he didn't know of which were probably Brandon's close friends and family members. Dylan and Katie set the babies down in their carriers to grab their plates of food at the table. Once everyone caught sight of the little ones, they couldn't help complimenting how cute they were and how lucky Dylan and Katie were to have them. The two just wholeheartedly accepted their complements and were glad they took Brandon up on his offer by coming here. Being around friends who care about you to get away from the stressful past couple of days was exactly what Dylan and Katie both needed. After a while, Dylan mingled with some of his friends while Katie tended to the babies by feeding them both. She then took notice of how Brandon was spending a lot of time with Shelley. He seemed really attracted to her and she was quite taken away by his charms. She was hoping this was the break that Shelley needed. She's been her best friend for a long time and in almost every single relationship, every guy ended up hurting her. But she somewhat knew Brandon just as much as Dylan and knowing the decent guy that he is, she knows he'll never do her that way. She keeps her paws crossed hoping those two will end up as a possible couple.

"So, do you always make it a habit kissing women on their hand the old fashion way?" Shelley questioned Brandon.

"Old habits die hard with me," he embarrassingly confessed. "So, you're good friends with Katie?"

"Oh yes, since the first moment she started working at the salon. Probably my only best friend."

"Dylan is the same with me. When he started working at Lincoln Edward Industries, we almost clicked immediately. I guess that's one thing we have in common; having two creatures as best friends."

"I guess it is," she slightly chuckled.

"So what do you do at your salon?"

"I do manicures, pedicures, and hairdos, that sort of stuff."

"You must be talented."

"Not really. I don't feel doing people's make-up is typically a talent."

"I feel what you do for a living is still a talent and at least you're content with your employment. Aren't you?"

"I don't know. I haven't given it much thought. Why you so interested?" she said getting to the point.

"I don't mean to pry as some sort of nuisance but—I guess I just want to learn more about you—if that's okay?"

Shelley had to admit, although she was at first skeptical, she enjoyed her conversations with Brandon. "Alright, ask me anything you want. I'm a big girl who's taken enough garbage from men and know what to expect from them."

"I hope you won't put me in that category of garbage men. Don't blame all of us for what the dirty ones have done to you."

"Okay, fair enough. I'll give you a chance."

As the day wore on, mid-afternoon turned to nightfall, and Dylan and Katie both knew they had to get the kids home and tend to their pets before another disaster takes place like last night.

"Well Brandon we really outta be going but thanks again for inviting us," Dylan said shaking his friend's hand.

"It's no problem buddy," his friend smiled back.

"Well come on Shelley, we'll drive you back home," said Katie carrying one of the babies in their carrier.

"Uh, if it's alright with you, may I drive Shelley back home instead?" Brandon offered.

Dylan and Katie both looked at Shelley if she was alright with it. She looked back at them with reassurance saying, "It's okay. I don't mind."

"Okay Shelley, you take care then," Katie said giving her a quick hug.

"Treat her right man," Dylan said to Brandon hoping his friend won't screw anything up.

"Don't worry buddy. I'm not the type of guy to mistreat a woman," he assured him. "Luckily I had two loving parents who raised me with enough compassion. Even if that wasn't the case, I could never harm a woman."

"That's good to hear," Dylan smiled in return.

After helping store some leftovers from the barbeque, Dylan, Katie, and the babies were well on their way back home.

"That was quite unexpected but I hope Shelley and Brandon will become more than just friends," Katie said.

"Me too," said Dylan. "I've always known Brandon as a decent guy and I think if he's serious about a relationship then Shelley's the perfect match for him."

"Yeah poor girl has been hurt so many times, she actually discussed with me that she wanted to be with a creature. I had to talk her out of that nonsense."

"Whoa. Good thing you changed her mind about that. Well, at least we'll have some food that'll last us until tomorrow. I'll go grocery shopping on Monday after work."

"I can go grocery shopping instead since you have to go back to work."

"Well now that we're taking care of two new additions to our family, I think it's best if you stay home with them."

"Alright but I only hope something will happen sooner or later before we end up in a bigger financial crisis as it is."

Once they made it back to their apartment, the two were afraid to find their place trashed again but when they opened the door they were pleased to find the place just as they left it. They found Jerry in the bathtub with the gators still enjoying themselves together.

"Well Jerry, nice job not trashing the place for once," Katie said.

"See, I told you I could do better," he said with pride. "Now feed me and the gators."

"Watch that mouth of your buster," Katie warned leaving the bathroom.

After taking care of the pets, Dylan and Katie placed the two babies back in their bassinet which for now was placed in the living room and put away all their leftovers in the kitchen. After another long day, the two relaxed on their bed together in each other's arms.

"Well maybe this day turned out stressful at first with Amber leaving but the rest of the day was pretty nice," Dylan commented.

"Yeah you're right," she sighs embracing him with her tail.

"There you go again," he said this time aggressively snatching her close to him.

"Are you sure we have time for this," she smirks. "The kids are in the other room."

"They'll be fine. They're sleeping right now. We have the baby monitor with us and Jerry is close by if anyone is stupid enough to come in here again. Right now it's our time," he said spreading her legs open lowering himself over her. "You owe me, double!"

"Okay, you win," she smiles unable to resist him.

12

Dylan and Katie slept peacefully after rather extreme lovemaking which lasted for about three hours into the night. They were just lucky enough the babies slept the entire time because now, their colicky systems were going off. Waking them up from the baby monitor, Katie was the first to get up and attend to them. Dylan shortly followed behind to help assist his wife. He grabbed the baby girl while Katie seized the baby boy. Their diapers didn't need changing and they weren't hungry so they both knew they would be up for a while dealing with their crying tantrums.

"Are you sure you can get used to this?" Dylan asked.

"Of course not but it's part of life dealing with things that are hectic," she told him. "Besides we wanted to be parents anyway and we knew the responsibilities we'd be facing."

"Would you really be up for adopting them?"

"Well—Shelley was possibly right when she said maybe it was a sign from God. We'll never have children of our own and maybe this is our second chance to take on a different path. I would like to see how these kids will turn out despite the fact their mom is a drug addict and a junkie."

"Well, we're going to have a long way to go if we're going to fight to get these kids to be ours. But I'm willing to support you every step of the way."

"That's why I love you so much. Truly devoted the way a husband is supposed to be," Katie smiled embracing him close with her tail.

"Alright missy, because I have my hands full you'll get off this round."

The tired couple dealt with the crying babies for about three to four hours straight until they finally calmed down. By then they were so exhausted they just collapsed on the recliner together unable to bring themselves back to their bedroom.

Before they knew it, it was already early morning around 6:47 a.m. and the babies were demanding to be fed. The two groggily woke up, still extremely sleepy, and too tired to be doing this so soon.

"Baby why don't you let me take care of it right now so you can continue catching up on your sleep," Dylan suggested. "Then you can take your next turn later on so I'll catch up on my sleep since I have work tomorrow."

"Are you sure honey?"

"Of course I'm sure. You go on back to sleep."

"Thanks, sweetie," Katie said giving him a quick kiss then headed straight to their bedroom.

Dylan grabbed the two crying infants out of their bassinet and brought them over to the kitchen counter. He realized their diapers also needed changing so he took care of that first then properly fed them both. While providing the restless infants their milk, he fed one using his claw while he used his tail to feed the other. As he nourished them, he decided to head to the bathroom to check on Jerry and alligators. Pretty much just like yesterday, the animals were fairly getting along with each other. Only this time the alligators were in different areas all over the bathroom.

"Hey guys, good morning," Dylan said.

"Mornin' Dylan," said Jerry who was too focused on whatever he was watching from the laptop. "I heard those babies ongoing screaming again last night. Are you sure you and Katie can put up with them?"

"It's still a continuing process but we're pretty much left with no choice since their mother had abandoned them."

"You guys are already on a tight budget as it is. You know by just taking care of us things weren't going to be easy. And now adding two babies in the mix is really going to put you guys in dept."

"No matter how rough things get I'm always one who's going to keep pushing forward, looking to the positive side."

"I wish I had your optimistic nature. So when are you going to feed us?"

"After the babies are taken care of. From now on you're going to have to wait because they come first."

"Great, I used to be first fed around here. Now I'm second place to a bunch of thumb sucking crying infants," Jerry pouted.

"I'm already sensing sibling rivalry," Dylan teased.

About two hours later Katie woke back up feeling she obtained enough rest. Eager to help her husband, she came back in the living room to catch him sitting in his recliner while watching the babies who were happily comfortable in their bassinet while sucking on their pacifiers.

"Hey Dylan," she said sitting down on his lap. "So how are they?"

"Other than just needing some feeding and changing, they're fine," he said embracing her close to him as she relaxed her body against his chest and stomach.

"It is silly that we still haven't named them yet," she chuckled.

"Well, you did forget to ask Amber."

"From the way she got rid of them, I don't even think she gave them names. We might as well so we don't have to keep referring to them as, "the babies."

"We always did say if we had a boy we would've named him Zachary and if it was a girl we would've named her Rena. Since we now have both a boy and a girl would you like to name them those?"

"I don't know. What do you think? Do you think it suits them?"

Taking a look at the babies in their bassinet just admiring their blissful appearance, Dylan simply smiled saying, "I think it suits them perfectly."

"Zachary Lloyd and Rena Lloyd, the first two human beings adopted by Mr. Dylan and Mrs. Katie Lloyd, the creatures," Katie happily quoted.

"I would certainly like a judge to say that in court and then put it down in writing."

"Remember when Chloe represented us for our case, that judge who was in charge helped us out. What was his name?"

"I believe it was Judge Malcolm."

"Yeah him. He was really a generous guy. We met up with him again after the case and somewhat became friends with him. Hopefully if we do try to adopt them, we should look to him as someone who can possibly help us. We can even try to represent ourselves. After dealing with Chloe, I don't trust looking up another lawyer."

"That's a long shot but adopting is going to have to come much later until I get that promotion. I hope and pray I get it. It seems that after all this time something would come up but it seems to be futile the way things are going."

"I know things are getting more stressful honey but the one thing you always tell me is that you never give up. As long as we have each other and keep trucking forward, our break will eventually come," she said caressing him by the cheeks. "Hang in there baby. As bad as things are, we've gone through worse than this."

Breathing a big sigh, Dylan wrapped Katie closer to him saying, "You're really my motivation. I don't know if I'd make it without you."

"The same goes to you baby," she said giving him a deep kiss on the lips.

Their kiss was momentarily interrupted by one of the baby alligators that somehow managed to escape from the bathroom and leaped at the junction where their noses met.

"Hey you," Katie said grabbing him by the tail. "You guys are already going to be a handful just like Jerry."

"That's what we get for having a soft spot for dangerous predators," Dylan remarked.

As the day continued, the babies were moderately on their best behavior for once, that is until evening came. They began their screaming tantrum yet again as the two tired creatures did their best to soothe them. Their only method was to constantly pace different parts of the room while rocking them at the same time. Katie told Dylan whether they calm down or not, it was her turn to take care of them so he could catch up on his sleep. He offered to at least stay up with her for one more hour before hitting the sack. As the two braced themselves for another long night, they suddenly heard a knock at their door. While holding the crying baby girl, Dylan answered it. Once the door was open, they came to witness a stressed-out man in his mid-fifties wearing nothing but raggedy overalls.

"Larry?" Dylan said surprised.

"Those damn baby's screaming and crying have been going on for the past few days now and they're driving me crazy!" he yelled.

"Sorry Larry," Katie said coming alongside her husband. "Something unexpected has happened and we're trying to take care of them."

"I've already been getting complaints from the neighbors about you two the most and I've had it. I want both of you out of here by next week."

"What?!" Katie shrieked.

"You can't do that Larry," Dylan maintained. "We've always paid our rent on time and don't nearly cause as much trouble, unlike the drug dealers who constantly roam the hallways."

"I don't care. I want you two out of my building by next week one way or the other," Larry ordered as he left.

Slamming the door shut full of frustration, Katie screamed, "That asshole! How dare he kick us out!"

"I never liked him. He'd much rather have drug dealers as tenants than loyal individuals who'll pay their rent honestly."

"What are we going to do now Dylan?"

"I don't know. Maybe we can ask Brandon or Shelley for help."

"We can but we can't burden them with Jerry and the alligators."

"You're right," Dylan said sadly as he continued trying to console the baby in his arms. "Maybe we can dip into our savings again to find another apartment?"

"No Dylan. That hard-earned money we've been saving up was for our dream house. Not be constantly used to live from one apartment to the next that are in worse condition than this. Besides, no other apartment around will allow us to keep our pets. We were fortunate to find this place that allowed us to keep them."

"Then I don't know what we're going to do. Things really aren't going our way."

"Ugh, please God help us," Katie cried.

"Shh, shh, shh," Dylan said comforting her. "Don't stress out. I know things keep escalating from bad to worse but we have to hang in there."

"I'm trying but it's getting harder and harder. In times of desperation, some people do drastic things and I can understand why."

"Yes but we're smarter than that. You would never go down that path to do something you'll later regret in life."

After breathing a big sigh and calming down a bit, Katie wrapped her left arm around Dylan while holding the baby boy in her right arm. "You're right Dylan. I wouldn't be able to live with myself if I did something radical. It's just not in me."

"We'll be okay," Dylan assured her. "We're strong and we're going to get through this together."

13

An hour later, Dylan was forced to go to bed while Katie took care of the babies and pets for the rest of the night. Luckily the babies' crying only lasted for about two hours so once they were finally asleep, Katie joined her husband in bed. As she pulled alongside him, she noticed a piece of paper sticking out of his claw. Pulling it out she groaned seeing yet another Playcritter magazine with a picture of her head replacing whoever used to be on it. She crumbled it threatening to hit him over the head with it but realized he needs his beauty sleep and decided not to wake him.

"You and your weird fetishes," she slightly chuckled as she gradually went to sleep herself.

Due to the unfortunate news of being evicted by their landlord, their night's sleep was disrupted with unease. Because of the babies and for the sake of pushing forward, they forced themselves to get as much sleep as possible. The only luck they got were the babies not waking them up in the middle of the night. However, it was broken early in the morning around 6:27 a.m. Dylan figured he might as well stay up and get ready for work so he'd be out the door as soon as possible. He took care of the babies first by feeding them and since their diapers didn't need any changing, he placed them back in their bassinet and quickly tried getting ready. By the time Katie got up, he was already dressed and ready after taking a quick shower from the bathroom in their bedroom. Katie found him in the kitchen grabbing a quick toast as he grabbed his suitcase on the counter.

"Oh Dylan baby, I'm so sorry I didn't have breakfast ready for you."

"It's okay. All we still have are the leftovers from Brandon's barbeque anyway so it's no big deal. I fed the babies so they should be fine but I have to run so I'll see ya later," he said giving her a quick kiss and quickly headed out the door.

"I love you too," she called out but he was already gone.

"Feed me!" Jerry called from the bathroom.

"Coming your majesty," Katie angrily scoffed.

Forty-five minutes later, Dylan made it to work on time as he headed to his cubicle. As he brought out his paperwork from his briefcase, Brandon popped his head in from the divider next door.

"Hey Dylan," he said quite cheery.

"Hi, Brandon. Katie and I want to thank you again for that family barbeque you invited us to. You have no idea how the leftovers you've given us really helped."

"It's no problem buddy. I want to thank you for introducing me to Shelley. She's a fantastic woman."

"How did it go with her?"

"Well I asked her out but she said she needs time to think about it because of the past men who mistreated her so I'm taking things slow and easy with her."

"Smart move."

"She really is wonderful. I don't understand the shitty men she's chosen and how they could treat someone as sweet as her like that."

"I'm glad you really like her but if she does give you a chance, don't take her for granted. Relationships are a sacred thing. I bless the Lord every day that I have someone like Katie in my life. I hope you'll do the same."

"Spoken like a true man," Brandon happily acknowledged. "So are things going alright with those two new additions to your family?"

"Actually, things had just gotten worse. Because of the babies, our landlord is kicking me and Katie out by next week," Dylan sadly revealed.

"What?!"

"Yeah, he said they've been causing a lot of noise and he's been getting complaints from the neighbors so he's kicking us out."

"Son of a bitch. It sounds like a complete asshole who's prejudice. Do you and Katie need a place to stay?"

"Yeah, but we can't burden you or Shelley."

"You wouldn't be burdening any of us," Brandon said quite offended. "I'm your good friend."

"I know Brandon and I appreciate it but you remember that Katie and I have those pets. We wouldn't feel right bringing them around other people's property other than our own. They may not attack you but they'll cause a lot of property damage if not fed properly."

"Well just to let you know, I'm always around if you need it."

"Thanks, Brandon."

The two of them were interrupted by their little conversation when Dylan's office telephone went off. He answered it saying, "Hello? Oh, yes sir. Yes, I'll be right there."

After hanging up Brandon anxiously asked, "Well who was it?"

"It's Mr. Charles," Dylan said worriedly. "He wants to see me right away."

"I hope it's nothing serious. Good luck man," Brandon said sitting back at his workstation.

As Dylan left his desk, butterflies ran rampant throughout his stomach. The firmness in Charles's voice could only indicate it was something serious. He mentally prayed for nothing negative to happen. So far he and Katie have been suffering strenuous delays and countless hardships one after the other. They couldn't keep going through this again and again. They desperately needed a break. Dylan steadily stepped into the elevator which took him to the top floor to Edward Charles's office.

"Please dear Lord," he quietly prayed trying to fight back the tears that threatened to make their way out of his eyes. "Please, please, please, please."

Taking a deep breath Dylan progressively knocked on the door after hearing a sturdy, "Come in."

Walking inside his manager's office, Charles was seated right next to a fancy telluride desk. There was an additional seat on the opposite side of the desk for visitors such as Dylan to take a seat in. After respectfully taking his seat, Dylan tried reading his boss's demeanor seeing if there were any signs of frustration but Charles was always a hard man to read with his thick brown eyes and stoic expression. At the time he was too busy typing information from his laptop that was nestled on his desk as if he almost forgot Dylan was even there. Only predicting the worse, all Dylan could do was shake uncontrollably. Finally, after what seemed like an eternity, Charles brought his attention to Dylan.

"Dylan."

"Y-yes sir," he nervously said trying to sound as professional as possible.

"How long have you been working here?"

"Uh—seven years."

"And in all those years you've always done your job without any complaints. I know you've been looking forward to that promotion but I had to wait and see if you would beg for it. I've gone through many employees who were greedy by always expecting it when they need it. Instead, you've been calm and patient about it. It's no secret that I'm a hard and firm man but I'm also a reasonable one. You may be a creature Dylan but you remind me a lot of myself when I was little. Hardworking and determined and that's exactly what you are. You've done good work for this company and you deserve your big break. As of today consider yourself promoted."

Feeling a rush of overwhelming excitement, Dylan almost broke down crying after hearing this news. "R-really sir?"

"Your pay will also be doubled and take another day off if ya like."

"Oh, Edward—I mean Mr. Charles, thank you so much!" Dylan cried out springing up from his seat shaking his supervisor's hand uncontrollably. "You don't know how much this means to me!"

Charles managed to notice a single tear that escaped from Dylan's eye and couldn't help to feel proud of what he's done for him. "It's okay Dylan. Just keep up the good work as you always have."

"I will. I will. Thank you again. Thank you so much!" he said now leaving the room. Once outside Charles's office, Dylan first laid his back against the door looking up towards the sky saying, "Thank you. Thank you. Thank you. Thank you!"

Once Dylan was free to go home after work, he raced home as quickly as he could while picking up a bouquet of flowers on the way there. He couldn't believe the big break he finally got and was overwhelmed with happiness thanking the Lord for this miracle. Now he and Katie can truly live the content life they desperately deserved. As he walked inside the building, he briefly came across his landlord's room. Larry just so happened to stick his head out at the time and called out, "Hey Dylan. Those damn kids have been crying again all day while you were out! I'm not waiting until next week. I want you and Katie out by tomorrow do you hear me!"

"That's fine by us Larry cause Katie and I are through with this shithole you call a building," Dylan scoffed.

"What did you say to me?" he demanded.

"You heard me, shithead," Dylan grinned. "You and all the other drug dealers can keep this dump. We wouldn't spend another minute in this hellhole if our lives depended on it. Now if you'll excuse me, my wife and I have some packing to do. So go on and crawl back to that little rat hole of yours Larry."

"Asshole!" Larry shouted.

"Yeah the same goes to you too," Dylan happily said heading upstairs to his apartment.

As anxious as he was to tell his wife the news, he joyfully knocked with a theme at the door. Once it opened he saw his wife with both of the babies in her arms feeding them at the same time.

"Hey beautiful," he said showing her the flowers.

"Well hello handsome," she said taking the flowers with her tail then gave them a sniff. "This was so sweet of you but we really got to watch what we spend from now on."

"Oh I think we can afford it," he smiled walking in closing the door. "By the way, I just ran into Larry and he says he's kicking us out tomorrow."

"WHAT?!" Katie yelled. "He can't do that! He said at least by next week."

"He's not giving us much of a choice."

"I'm going to have a word with that idiot," Katie ranted. "He can't get away with this!"

"Don't waste your energy on him cause I got something to tell you."

"Please no more bad news," Katie groaned. "That's all I can take right now."

Pulling out his laptop from his briefcase, he opened up the screen and set it down on the small desk in the living room.

"Come and see," he said sitting in his recliner.

Once the babies were finally settled down, Katie placed them back in their bassinet and sat with Dylan.

"I was looking up these houses today at work," he explained. "Brandon helped me since he lives in the same neighborhood and he's familiar with the area. We came across this great bargain where the realtor is allowing clients to stay within the residence as long as the papers are signed and eventually paid for. It's a two-story house with five bedrooms, three bathrooms, a large kitchen, and a living room and a big backyard with a large swimming pool. Almost exactly what we were looking for."

"It looks great but why are you showing me this?"

"I called the realtor today and made the arrangements with her. We can move in there tomorrow."

"Dylan we can't afford this. Even with our savings, we wouldn't be able to pay for it."

"We can now," he smiled at her lifting his eyebrow.

"You mean..." she stammered almost too perplexed to believe this miracle.

"Yeah, I got that promotion."

Screaming with excitement, Katie wrapped her arms around Dylan nearly knocking him over. She gave him plenty of kisses nonstop as he chuckled while trying to pull her off.

"Oh, baby I'm so proud of you! Is this really happening?"

"It sure is. We don't have to buy the house if you're not pleased with it but it's a place we can temporarily stay in just to get out of this dump."

"Oh, honey I just might fall in love with it regardless. You were right all along to keep pushing forward and that everything would be alright. You never gave up and I'm proud of you. God has finally answered our prayers."

"Yes he has. It might have taken a long time but it finally happened," he said kissing her around the neck.

"Hey, what's all the ruckus about?" Jerry said leaving the bathroom.

"Consider yourself lucky Jerry cause you're finally getting that swimming pool you always wanted," Dylan happily claimed.

"You finally got promoted!" Jerry said shocked himself.

"Yep and our lives are going to be a little less stressful."

"Yahoo! Good-bye rotten tub!" Jerry couldn't help but flop around causing a bit of commotion with his massive body weight. "When are we leaving?"

"Tomorrow, so we're packing everything tonight."

"Don't you have to go to work tomorrow?" Katie asked.

"My boss gave me some time off so we'll have all day tomorrow to get settled in our new home," Dylan said.

"I can't believe our luck. It couldn't have come at a better time," Katie smiled truly proud of her husband. She then looked back over to the babies and said, "And we'll finally give these kids the life they deserve too."

14

Throughout the whole night, Dylan and Katie packed everything they could into both of their vehicles. Because Jerry would already take up a lot of room in one car alone, Brandon offered to help by bringing his van to help transport some of their heavier furniture like the bed, recliner, TV, and so on. No one got any sleep that night but they didn't care. After all the stressful years of wanting to get away from this ghetto neighborhood, they were too excited to sleep and move on to a better region. By the time they finished packing everything, it was already the next day, around 7:53 a.m. Before heading inside their vehicles, the group met together.

"Thank you for coming over and helping us Brandon," Katie said for maybe the fifteenth time.

"You don't have to keep thanking me Katie," Brandon chuckled. "I'm just glad you guys are finally leaving this dump and are going to stay in my neighborhood. We'll practically be neighbors if you decide to go with the house you picked."

"We just might," Katie said. "It looked good from what Dylan has shown me."

"Well the little ones are already secured in the backseat," Dylan stated. "Are you guys ready to go?"

"More than anything," Katie happily said giving him a quick kiss. "Let's blow this dump."

Happy to leave this sad, doomed neighborhood behind them for good, everyone retreated inside their vehicles. Katie drove her vehicle with the babies in the backseat of her car, while Dylan drove with Jerry in his backseat. The alligators were secured in a temporary fishbowl sectioned upfront in the passenger's seat. Katie followed Dylan and Brandon to their new destination. It only took thirty minutes but they finally made it to their new residence. The neighborhood already felt soothing and much more relaxing. The air was intoxicating while the birds could be heard singing instead of loud, crude rap and ambulances roaming the streets twenty-four seven. Parking their vehicles in the driveway of the house, the real estate agent stood by the front door waiting for their arrival. She seemed like a modest woman around her late twenties with light curly brown hair as she wore black and sleek office attire that perfectly fit her personality. She seemed generous since she was considerate enough to allow Dylan and Katie to stay within the residence although they haven't quite finalized all the financial obligations.

"Mr. and Mrs. Lloyd I presume?" she said extending her hand out to them.

"Yes, I'm Dylan Lloyd and this is my wife Katie Lloyd," Dylan said shaking her hand as he motioned towards Katie.

"It's nice to meet you both. I'm Mrs. Cathy Milliken. When I got your phone call yesterday I was happy to hear someone finally was zoning in on the property. I'm sure you both will love it."

As Mrs. Milliken took them inside to grant them an official tour, Brandon thought it best to stay with the babies, deciding to keep them company. The interior of the place was a luxurious environment almost anyone would adore. The square footage in its entirety was impeccable, enough for two families. As she took them on a grand tour throughout the whole house the couple already came to the conclusion they loved it. By the time she took them to the backyard, they were sold. The garden stretched far as it did wide with perfectly lush green grass and even an additional landscape housing gorgeous plants, flowers, and a small outdoor water fountain decorated with elegant stone mermaids seemingly dancing around its foundation. Last but not least was the swimming pool. It had attractive landscaping that surrounded it and was big enough for Jerry and even the alligators when they reach their full potential size. After witnessing this, Dylan and Katie both said, "We'll take it!"

"Excellent!" Cathy said. "I knew you'd love it. Now I'll have you two sign a few papers then everything will be set. I just need to know at the soonest convenience when financial arrangements can be made. . ."

"This weekend!" Dylan happily proclaimed.

"Perfect," Cathy said leading them back inside so they can sign some of the papers.

After Dylan and Katie signed all the required documents, Cathy placed them back into her briefcase and wholeheartedly thanked them for their business. She then left saying her farewells until the next time they reconvened. Dylan and Katie finally went back to their vehicles knowing how stressful Jerry must be cramped in the backseat all this time.

"When can I come out for crying out loud!" he complained.

"Your wait is over," Dylan said opening the car door. "Go check out the pool."

Jerry excitedly flopped out of the vehicle as Katie opened the gate to the backyard, enticing him to discover the surprise that waited for him. The anxious shark desperately dragged his body to the pool like there was no tomorrow and the minute he touched the landscaping ledge he dropped inside of the water. Dylan and Katie both watched him with anticipation hoping he loved it. He was under the water for a while, leaving them a bit worried if they made the right choice but when he rose to the surface he shouted, "I LOVE IT!!" The happy Elasmobranchii fish presented himself as if he were a dolphin or killer whale contentedly rising from the water. The pair were satisfied to finally give Jerry the home they always wanted for him. Dylan then went to retrieve the baby alligators. He contently dropped them in the pool with Jerry and by the way they were swimming, he could tell they were pleased as well.

For the next three hours, Brandon helped his two friends transfer all of their furniture into the house until their vehicles were empty. Everyone was extremely tired and bushed, especially since none of them got any sleep. Once the babies started their screaming and crying, Dylan and Katie tended to them while offering Brandon some refreshments for his generosity, but he politely declined their offer since he just wanted to get home and rest. As he got in his van, they once more thanked him for his help and promised they would make it up to him. Once the babies were fed and taken care of, Dylan and Katie placed them in their bassinet, which was placed in the living room for now. They sat on the floor together right next to them too tired to move. They lied down on the soothing clean carpet truly satisfied and thankful for their hard work and where it led them to right now.

"I still can't believe this," Katie sighed. "It's almost like a dream, a dream come true."

"I know. We certainly have come a long way."

"There's still a lot more to go. But realistically, we wouldn't be here without you."

"And you too," he said looking at her while raising one side of his eyebrow.

"No, my job barely made ends meet. It was you and your hard work that got us here right now."

"Katie, you always played a big part in this. No matter how much you deny it, you did help. You helped with groceries, staying on top of different payments, and helping me pay bills. You especially helped played a big part in adding to our savings too. So don't you dare say it was just me. Without you, I never would've gotten that promotion because I only pushed forward for you. If I didn't have you in my life then I never would've had the confidence to keep going. We did this, together," he said intertwining his claw with her paw.

Staring deep into his attractive and appealing eyes, Katie smiled saying, "You're right Dylan. We did it together."

Without saying another word, the two laid together in each other's arms then fell asleep right next to the sleeping infants in their bassinet.

15

As the week went by, Dylan paid off the house to Cathy, officially making the property now theirs for the keeping. All of their hard-earned savings over the years and Dylan's now promotional payroll has made it a done deal. During the same week, the couple went major grocery shopping and shopped around the department store buying new furniture for their new big house. They chose one of the bedrooms solely for the kids and did their best designing it the way a kid would love it. Jerry and the alligators were content with staying in the backyard and rarely came in the house unless when necessary. After an uphill struggle and a week of hard work, their new family house was finally coming together. Now that they accomplished one of their major goals, their next goal was to adopt the babies. They knew it was going to be a challenging process but they were willing to go through with it. Katie tried as hard as she could to get in touch with the same judge who once helped them in the past refusing to see anybody else but him. Before they could locate him, the first thing they had to do was take the little infants to the hospital to be examined. It was something they logically should've done from the start when they first cared for them but considering their previous situation it was understandable. So today on this bright Saturday morning, the two walked down the busy hallways of the hospital with the babies securely in their grasps. After signing themselves in, Dylan and Katie sat in the waiting room patiently waiting for their names to be called. A woman sitting just two chairs from them who happened to have a baby of her own noticed the creatures with the human babies.

"Excuse me I don't mean to intrude but do those babies belong to you two?" she asked.

"Not biologically of course but yeah, I guess they do," Katie said.

"Amazing, I never heard of creatures adopting humans," she said surprised.

"I guess that would make us the first," Dylan said proudly.

After a while, their names were finally called and the two followed a nurse which led them to their room.

"Hi I'm Mrs. Johnson, it's nice to meet you Mr. Dylan and Mrs. Katie," the nurse respectfully announced. "And who might these two be."

"This is Zachary and Rena," Katie said. "I believe this will be their first checkup."

"You see their mother abandoned them so we're taking care of them now and we like to be sure that there's nothing physically wrong with them," Dylan explained.

"People always talk down on you creatures but your devotion to doing the right thing never ceases to amaze me. They're very lucky to have you. Alright, we'll do a proper examination and also give them a blood test just to be sure there's nothing physically wrong."

The two were worried for a moment knowing Amber was a drug addict which could've negatively affected the babies' health. Dylan and Katie had to sit and patiently wait as the nurse transported the infants into a different room.

"Oh Dylan, we probably should've taken them to the hospital the minute Amber dropped them on us," Katie said shaking. "They were already underweight and emaciated the first day we had them and now something could be wrong with them because who knows if Amber was doing drugs while she was pregnant with them."

"We did the best we could, Katie. We weren't expecting to take care of them, besides, we were going through our own problems. All we can do is pray for the best," Dylan said wrapping his arm around his wife's shaking body.

The two anxiously waited for a long time since the doctors and nurses were giving the babies a thorough examination. Mrs. Johnson finally came back into the room as Dylan and Katie rose from their seats.

"Are they alright? Is something wrong?" Katie nervously begged.

"Calm down Mrs. Lloyd. Your babies are fine. We just took their blood test and we're waiting for the results to come back so it's going to take a while," she told them. "You guys might want to grab something to eat or come back later if ya like."

"No, we're staying right here," Katie maintained. "Until those babies are safely returned to us, we're not going anywhere."

"Very good ma'am. I'll come back and give you two updates on how they're doing but in the meantime just relax," she said leaving them alone again.

"Okay, thank you," Dylan said a bit worried himself but tried to remain strong for his wife's sake.

"I don't like this Dylan. What if they find something and take them away from us for child abuse. They have the right to do so because they don't legally belong to us."

"Katie please calm down. Don't think that way. We didn't put all the hard work and effort for nothing only to have them taken away from us. Remember no matter how bad things get, we'll get through this together. We'll fight to keep them."

Katie continued pacing the room back and forth just anxious to hear some type of news. "I just need to hear something. I hate being kept in suspense."

"Alright, that's enough. Sit down missy," Dylan said pulling her by the tail and forced her to sit down right next to him. "What would you do without me?"

"Let's not find out," she said calming down a little bit.

For the next few minutes, Dylan grabbed them both snacks from the vending machine down the hallway and they casually watched TV which was mounted on the far upper corner in the room. Forty-five minutes later the nurse finally came back.

"Oh please don't sugarcoat anything," Katie anxiously cried. "I don't care how bad it is, just tell me!"

"Please calm down Mrs. Lloyd. I do have some good news and some bad news," she said looking through her notepad.

"Oh crap. Just give us the bad news first," Katie cringed.

"Their breathing was a bit low possibly due to lack of oxygen in their systems when they were born. However, the good news is because of the continuous baby formulas you've been feeding them daily, they are pretty good and healthy. What have you been specifically feeding them?"

"Mostly a top brand baby formula we occasionally pick up at the store," Dylan clarified.

"And the other half?" the nurse questioned.

Katie blushed heavily in the cheeks to reveal something she hoped wouldn't have to come out. "Uh—I kinda—breastfed them some of my own milk."

"Is that so," Mrs. Johnson said scribbling down notes. "That's quite a dedication if you went that extra mile. It's possible with your milk and the combination of the baby formulas you've been feeding them has exceedingly strengthed their health, otherwise, they would've been in bad conditions."

"Oh thank God," Katie sniveled falling up against Dylan who had to help her stand back up.

"Let me ask you when you said their mother abandoned them, was she a drug addict and were her babies malnourished?" the nurse asked them.

"I'm afraid so," Katie replied. "Will it affect their health?"

"If the infants were frequently premature, they would've developed malformed kidneys and seizures, but luckily that didn't occur with these two."

"Thank God for that. We also found slight red marks around Zachary suspecting there was possible abuse taking place," Dylan said.

"The malnourishment they suffered would've triggered future health problems, but because you two have been persistent with feeding them around the clock, there isn't any reason that Zachary and Rena will grow into healthy human beings. As for the red marks you mentioned, we didn't find any indication that Zachary's been abused, however, if there were any signs of abuse, we wouldn't know because he's healed up quite nicely."

"That's good to hear," Dylan said breathing a sigh of relief.

"They're also colicky babies," Katie pointed out. "How long will it last?"

"It's very common for most babies. It will most likely last for a few weeks or two to three months."

"Two to three months!" Katie cried out. "I guess we might as well say good-bye to a good night's rest for a while."

"Due to their early malnourish state, their crying could go on quite longer than usual but as long as you two remain persistent with their feedings, the sooner you'll be out of the woods in that department," Mrs. Johnson clarified. "I'll also recommend new baby formulas this hospital will provide that'll improve their health."

"Thank you so much," Katie said shaking her hand.

"Also, are you two their legal guardians?" she asked.

"Not yet but we will be. We're finding a judge that'll hopefully grant us full custody of them but before we do that, we thought it would be wise to have them checked out first," said Dylan.

"Yes, that's always the number one priority. The minute you guys get the approval from the judge, they must be brought back here immediately for another checkup. I'd also hate to tell you this but if the judge doesn't grant you two custody of them, child protected service will have to take them and keep 'em here until they're legally adopted by someone else."

"Yes—we understand," Katie said feeling hurt in her voice.

"But from the way you guys took care of them, I truly hope the judge will grant you guys custody of those two lucky kids."

"Thanks, we hope so too," Dylan said sadly.

16

The drive back home was in depressive silence. They were pleased that the babies were fine and healthy thanks to them, but the thing Mrs. Johnson said afterward just couldn't escape their minds. "I'd also hate to tell you this but if the judge doesn't grant you two custody of them, child protected services will have to take them and keep 'em here until they're legally adopted by someone else." Dylan and Katie have grown attached to the kids, despite how overwhelming they were. At first, when Amber first dumped the babies on them, they didn't know what to think but after bonding with them due to the fact they felt it was a blessing in disguise to finally care for children, they just couldn't bear to part with them. Katie extremely felt the bonding experience after sincerely linking with them through breastfeeding which is an experience only a true mother and child will share. While Dylan drove in the driver's seat, Katie sat in the passenger's seat each in their own thoughts. The babies slept peacefully in the back of their car seats without a fuss. Katie kept glancing back at them feeling her heartbreak at the thought of them being absent from her and Dylan's life. Dylan finally broke the silence saying, "Are you okay baby?"

"Huh? Oh yeah, I'm fine," she said unsure of herself. "It's just—it's just I don't wanna lose them."

"I know baby, me too. We're going to do everything in our power to keep them."

"I'm not going to rest until I find that judge. The minute I do, we're scheduling an appointment to meet him. Will you come even if you have to work?"

"Of course. My boss is more understanding now that I've been promoted. If it lands on a workday, I'll ask for some time off."

When the four of them made it home, Dylan and Katie were so pleased to walk into a driveway of an actual house instead of a broken-down apartment building. Once they settled the babies in their bassinet, Katie went online desperately trying to find Judge Malcolm by any means necessary. When she got his number she didn't waste a minute calling him. Considering how busy he was, it was natural for him not to pick up so Katie left as many messages as possible until he was able to return her calls. Keeping her cell phone close by, she joined her husband who was outside in the backyard with Jerry and the alligators.

"So are you guys still enjoying it?" Dylan asked.

"There's plenty of room in here," Jerry happily replied, "especially for the gators. Oh, one thing I miss was having a laptop to pass the time. Do you mind setting one up out here?"

"Sure thing," Dylan said going back inside the house to retrieve the portable computer.

"So you don't mind sharing the pool with the gators?" Katie asked. "Cause you know they'll get big sooner or later."

"I don't mind, besides they can't outgrow me. I'm the biggest predator in these parts."

After making sure Jerry and the alligators were fed, Dylan and Katie returned inside to watch over Zachary and Rena. Just like clockwork, they were ready for their next feeding. The two tried the new formulas which the hospital had given them and properly fed them. During their feeding, Katie's cell phone began vibrating.

"Oh shoot! Here Dylan, take Rena," she said handing the baby girl over to him so she can answer her phone. "Yes hello! Yes! Yes your honor. I'm sorry if I called you at a bad time but do you remember me and my husband Dylan? Oh of course you do. Yes well, the reason I called you is that my husband and I recently came across two human babies who were abandoned by their mother. We want to adopt them. No. Yes I'm serious. No. It has nothing to do with filling any void, it's just we feel it's a second chance for us— and the babies. Yes sir. Yes I understand. We were hoping you would take our case and grant us custody of them. Yes. I'm fully aware of the guideline status but we just want to do what's right. No, we want to represent ourselves. Yeah but I—oh no! We have no intension of wanting to work with Miss Waters ever again. She did help us last time but trust us your honor, we have a good reason why we don't want her to represent us again. That's one of the main reasons why we want to represent ourselves instead. We believe we have a good case to prove. I understand it's risky but that's why I called you because you're not only a great judge, but a trustworthy old friend. Yes. You will? Oh, thank you honor. When? Okay, we'll be right there. Thank you again and goodbye."

"From that conversation, I'm taking it he'll take our case?" Dylan said while comforting both babies in his arms.

"Thank God he will but he warned me because the status of our reputation being very strict, our chances are very slim so we shouldn't give our hopes up but he'll try with us anyway."

"That is some good news. I'm equally surprised he's willing to see us considering we're representing ourselves and don't need a lawyer."

"Well consider this blind luck because next time if we do go to court again, we're just going to have to find one. Anyway, he's expecting us to meet him down at the courthouse next Monday. Are you sure you'll come?"

"Of course I will. I wouldn't skip out on something like this even if it was the end of the world."

As the day continued, the two still had the babies in their arms while singing peacefully to them. Dylan rocked Zachary while Katie cuddled Rena. For the very first time since they had them, both babies reacted with happy squeals and laughs.

"Well would you look at that," Dylan said fully astonished. "They're finally coming out of their cranky shells."

"I think maybe they're recognizing us," Katie said. She then gave Rena a raspberry blow on the belly which made the baby cry out with blissful laughter. Rena playfully grabbed Katie by her hair with her chubby hands and tugged at it aggressively. Prying Rena's hands free, the baby girl kept her hand on Katie's paw holding it tightly. Looking deeply into each other's eyes, it truly connected how much Katie appreciated her, like her own daughter.

"That's right Rena, I'll soon be your mommy," she said hugging her closer to her face. "I'll always be your mommy no matter what."

"And I'll always be your guy's daddy," Dylan said to Zachary.

A few hours later, Dylan and Katie brought the babies to their bedroom which now had a crib when they did their furniture shopping. They gently placed them both inside while adding soft plush animal toys to keep them company. The one that stuck out from the rest was an alligator plush toy as Zachary pulled it close to him while drooling on it. The two creatures then began to proceed by singing them a soft lullaby. The soothing sound of the two individuals they've grown so accustomed to was harmonious to the baby's ears. The soft melody was like a calming force with a wave of pleasure that only parents possess as a gift providing for their children. Their song glided them to dreamland until they were finally in a deep sleep. Dylan and Katie happily watched them both over the crib for a good long while truly thankful for these small beings in their life. Finally leaving the room quietly, they retreated to their bedroom which was just next door down the hall not too far from them. They collapsed on their bed only thinking about what will occur on Monday.

"I'm so worried what will happen when we walk into that courtroom on Monday," Katie said.

"I know, me too," Dylan sighed. "We'll just keep praying and hoping for the best."

"But what if the judge can't do anything about it and that'll be the last we'll see of Zachary and Rena?"

"Katie," he groaned.

"But I just..."

"No butts," Dylan said bringing himself alongside her. He placed his claw ever so gently across her lips while his other caressed gently around her hips. "Let's put aside our worries for the rest of the night and spark up some excitement around here."

"I guess you took the words right out of my mouth," she smiled kissing him.

Their kiss is sweet and passionate at first until Dylan can't control his rising impulses. Giving to his deepest desires, he aggressively turned Katie onto her stomach. Katie intuitively raises her hip in the air as Dylan clutches her by the rear. He first moves her tail aside finding the entrance to her backside and then restrained her arms from moving. Already heated with utter passion, he instantly inserts himself inside of Katie causing her body to immediately tense up. Her tail embraces itself around him as he holds tight, thrusting in and out of her effortlessly. Letting go of one of her arms he grabs her hair, feeling her and his aggressive passion rise to the extreme. She felt the gripping sensation flow through her body truly making her and her husband in sync. Supreme pleasure flourished through both of them resulting in their spirits intertwining like a tight rope. When they go, he tries to make it last holding off for the grand finale so it'd be worth it in the end. He plunges hard and deep inside of her getting devastatingly embellished by an obsession that possessed his soul. Dylan's tail then instinctively goes inside of Katie, unable to contain himself. In that instant, her orgasms multiplied in numbers then reacted in the form of fireworks once they reached the pinnacle of their climax. Katie moans becomes louder unable to control her volume. Dylan felt the buildup and rushed harder by the minute giving her everything he's got. Finally, at his own climax, he cries out emptying his fluids fully inside of her. After giving a cry of her own, Dylan collapses on top of her, both extremely exhausted but feeling overwhelmed with sheer satisfaction.

"I love you, Katie," he inhaled and exhaled.

"I love you too," she said trying to catch her breath.

17

Now that it was Monday, the two were up bright and early ready for the big day. Dylan was able to call today off as he and Katie were both worried and anxious to see how the day would take place. They've been praying really hard for this small miracle to come through for them. They were already thankful to be in better surroundings but their family truly wouldn't be complete without little Zachary and Rena in it. While Dylan was getting ready in the bathroom, Katie took care of the babies by changing their diapers and feeding them.

"Well guys, today is the day," she said looking down upon them in their crib. "We're praying that this thing will allow us to adopt you guys. I don't want to feel empty and lonely again without children in my life. If we can just convince people and the judge, I know we can try to be a happy family. Not perfect by any means, more like a weird and eccentric family, but I'm sure we can still be happy nonetheless."

The babies happily responded to her statement by laughing and gurgling up bubbles in their mouths.

"I'll take that as a yes," she smiled.

While Katie was getting the kids ready, Dylan rushed outside in the backyard feeding Jerry and the alligators.

"Be good while we're gone," Dylan warned them. "And keep your fins and claws crossed that we'll be able to adopt Zachary and Rena."

"It's risky but I do wish you two the best," Jerry remarked. "You deserve it."

"Thanks," Dylan said rushing back inside the house.

He and Katie were dressed in their finest suits trying to present themselves properly for court. After packing a diaper bag for the babies and some paperwork, the two were ready and headed out the door. As they drove down to the courthouse, the two were taken by surprise to witness a crowd of people in front of the building which looked like the media. As soon as word got out, the media wanted to hear the story of creatures being the first to adopt humans.

"I wasn't expecting this," Dylan said, pulling up near the curb.

"Me neither," Katie said looking on in amazement but also in disgust at the thought dealing with these types of people. "How are we supposed to get inside with the babies if they're going to be blocking our way?"

Dylan swiftly replied, "The best thing we can do is push. You grab the kids and I'll protect you as you all squeeze through."

After Katie grabbed both babies in her arms, Dylan wrapped his left arm around her while using his right one to push the random media circus out of their way. A pandemonium of pictures was taken while countless people began chattering at the same time. They could barely make them out all at once but got a few coherent words out of some of them.

"Mr. and Mrs. Lloyd! What made you come to the conclusion of wanting to adopt humans?"

"What do you think the judge will say?"

"Are you going to treat these kids as if they're your own flesh and blood?"

"How do you think this event will affect other creatures from around the world?"

The loud noise and pictures began to frighten the babies as they began crying hysterically. Desperate to get his wife and kids away from this crowd, he forcefully pushed forward saying, "No comment! Please let us get inside!"

As soon as they got inside the building, the two breathed a sigh of relief while Katie tried to calm the babies.

"It's alright guys. Those arrogant people don't have respect for people's privacy. It's okay, there's nothing to be afraid of. Mama's here."

The calmness of Katie's voice did the trick instantly settling Zachary and Rena down.

"The nerve of those people," Katie growled.

"When this is over, maybe we should head around back to avoid them."

"Good idea."

Walking further into the building they showed a security guard their case as he led them to the courtroom. There they encountered their friends, Shelley and Brandon where they reluctantly handed the two infant children to them. It was hard for Katie to let go but she eventually did. A tight-lipped, awkward smile formed Shelley's face as tension was thick in the air. The two watched in anguish as the babies were taken into the courtroom by their trusted friends to prepare for the commencing trial. Feeling the absence of their parents, the kids began screaming their heads off which affected Katie and Dylan significantly.

"It's okay guys, we'll be back," Katie called out trying hard to convince herself.

"Well this is it," Dylan said putting his claw on her shoulder. "Are you ready to do this?"

"Yeah, let's do this," she said firmly puffing her chest out.

Inside the courtroom, there were a few citizens in the aisles such as Brandon and Shelley comforting the infants. There were also a few of their coworkers from both of their jobs who came too. And of course last but not least a few citizens from the media. Sitting down at their table, everyone patiently waited for the judge to arrive. Finally, a bailiff appeared by the stand announced, "All rise! Honorable Judge Malcolm presiding." Everyone rose as they watched Judge Malcolm enter the building. He appeared around his late fifties to early sixties with short, gray hair and wore stylish, prescription eyeglasses. Holding an envelope folder in his hands, he took his seat while everyone else did the same.

"I didn't expect this type of news to get this type of attention this morning but I guess it's not much of a surprise," he commented bringing out papers from his envelope folder. "Mr. and Mrs. Lloyd, it's nice to see you all again."

"You too your honor," Katie said respectfully.

"So as I recall, you two actually want to adopt human babies. You do understand this is the first case of this stature on record, so tell me why did you two come to the ultimate decision of wanting to do this?"

"Well your honor," Katie spoke, "I think considering how much we're law-abiding citizens like everyone else, we should be given a chance to take care of kids who desperately need all the love and attention they deserve. Zachary and Rena were deliberately abandoned by their mother who is a drug addict and didn't care about them in the slightest. They were malnourished and possibly abused when she gave them to us. The neighborhood we used to live in doesn't give a crap about anyone down there. There were numerous times we called the police and even child protective services but they hardly ever came to our streets. We decided we wanted to do what was in the best interest of the children giving them the life all kids deserve." Taking a deep breath for a moment, Katie tried finding her voice again knowing what she was going to say next will greatly affect her.

"Take your time," Malcolm said sensing the hurt in her.

"Y-your honor, you already know what happened to me and Dylan when you took our case awhile back. I'll never have children of my own. That was wrongfully taken away from me. I'm not trying to fill some empty hollowness to replace what I couldn't have, but rather experiencing the joy and love only a mother knows. No matter what species, I would wholeheartedly accept them into my home."

"I understand where you're coming from," Malcolm acknowledged. "My absolute condolences for you and Dylan's loss. However, there is the issue as to why everyone is pretty reluctant to allow creatures to adopt human beings. After all, your ways are—unusual."

"We understand," Dylan finally spoke. "Yes we keep dangerous pets, but under our guidance, they wouldn't harm a fly. We have this type of connection with them that pretty much tames them in a sense."

"Can you really assure me they won't hurt anybody?"

"Never in history have you heard of creatures owning dangerous predators that have actually attacked people unless provoked or assaulted for any other different reasons. No one has ever even tried having humans live with creatures owning these predators to prove they wouldn't hurt anyone."

"And what type of predators do you own?" he said writing notes on his paper.

"We have a great white shark and seven alligators," Dylan admitted.

The courtroom grew talkative with people mumbling all sorts of gossip which didn't look good on Dylan and Katie's part.

"Please hear us out," Dylan said. "For example, when we had errands to run, our shark watched over the kids and babysat them for us. He took care of them and protected them from intruders which was a common occurrence that Katie and I had to deal with. It's the same as people owning a dog but our ways are just more extreme."

Malcolm didn't say anything for a minute which pretty much frightened the two, so Dylan spoke up again while grabbing a few pieces of paper from their folder.

"Your honor, if we may," he said holding up the papers in his claws.

The bailiff took the papers from Dylan and handed them over to the judge.

"What you have there your honor are the documents of their report from the hospital. The nurse told us if it wasn't for Katie and I, they would've gone through major future health problems. After coming out of the hospital that day, the babies have been healthier than they were with their own mother. If you think the babies are better off with their biological mother, how is it when they were with her, they were left in deplorable conditions while when they were with us, they were in much better health than they've ever been. Their mother abused them while they never suffered a single scratch with us despite our appearance and dangerous pets. We lived in the same appalling neighborhood as their mother, but that didn't cause us to ever mistreat them. Yes she had a terrible upbringing and we don't hold that against her, but we didn't think it was right that her children should suffer the same fate and deserve a chance at a better life. It'll be just a repeated cycle if kids have to suffer the same abuse as their parents. We want to break that cycle."

Malcolm went through all the papers then stated, "You do make a good point. It amazes me how humans are so prejudice for the stupidest reasons. From what I see, you two are good souls only wanting what's best for these kids. And you're right. I've yet to hear a drastic report on creatures like you owning predators that haven't attacked people unless like you said, due to being provoked or assaulted by assholes. Excuse my language."

The courtroom slightly chuckles a bit as Dylan grabs Katie's paw bracing themselves for the final verdict.

"Your guy's records are clean and you're still rightfully employed. If you guys were able to do all this when their mother couldn't, I don't see why creatures shouldn't be given a chance to adopt human beings. However are you sure you're willing to meet all the requirements of what these children will need in life?"

"Yes your honor," Katie said nearly crying with tears of joy. "We'll do right by them every step of the way. We'll put them in the best schools, we'll save up for their college funds, we'll raise them with the best love and care. We just want to be given a chance."

Examining them very closely, Malcolm officially made up his mind. "I'm going to go forward with granting Mr. and Mrs. Lloyd custody of the two babies."

The courtroom roared with excitement as all of their friends clapped and cheered for them. Dylan and Katie both rose from their seats giving each other tight hugs.

"Alright settle down," the judge said pounding his mallet.

"Thank you so much, your honor," Katie cried.

"Yes! You don't know how happy you've made us," Dylan said equally crying.

"You guys aren't out of the woods just yet," he told them. "You'll be checked upon by social workers who'll keep us up to date on how you're doing."

"We understand," Katie said.

"If you guys can pull this off, then who knows? Maybe every creature will be given a chance to adopt human beings and give them a good home. But I'm giving you guys the chance you deserve as well as those innocent kids."

"You don't know how blessed we are for this big miracle," Katie murmured a bit.

Signing a document on his desk he asked, "So what are the baby's names?"

"Zachary and Rena," Dylan and Katie both announced in unison.

"Zachary Lloyd and Rena Lloyd," Malcolm read out loud then left his desk handing over the signed document to the bailiff which then delivered them to the outstretched arms of the new parents. "Congratulations."

The two creatures couldn't help but cry out in joy as they took the paper which solidified that they finally adopted the kids. When the judge left the courtroom, their friends greeted them with hugs and praise congratulating them as well.

"Well honey, it looks like we did it," Dylan said kissing his wife on the head.

"Yes we did," she said kissing him back.

Shelley handed them the children who were still slightly whining, but the minute they were embraced by the only two individuals they knew as their real parents, their crying instantly subsided. Katie cuddled Zachary against her chest while Dylan did the same with Rena.

"Now that's what I call a true family," Shelley acknowledged. She couldn't help but take a few snapshots of them with her cell phone cementing the moment.

"Way to go you two," Brandon said. "Now looks like you're a family of four."

"Make that twelve," Katie said. "Our pets are also members of our family."

"Sure whatever you say," Brandon chuckled.

As they made their way to the front of the building, the media was still waiting anxiously for them outside.

"You still want to go out back?" Dylan asked her.

Thinking hard for a moment, Katie said, "You know, they should know how this played out. That way if we get the word around perhaps other creatures like us will be given a chance to also adopt humans, just like Malcolm said. But we'll make it as brief as possible for the babies' sakes."

"Sure," Dylan said supporting his wife every step of the way.

Once outside the media didn't crowd them like before but still surrounded them anxiously waiting to hear what happened. Surprisingly the babies tolerated the media this time allowing for some good photos that'll certainly make history. Dylan and Katie answered the right questions as best as they could and if a question came off as insulting they would be sure to answer with appropriate clarification. However much to their amazement, it went by pretty smoothly. Before they knew it, they made the front papers and social media for the world to see. "FIRST CREATURES TO ADOPT HUMAN BABIES."

18

It seemed just like yesterday as Katie held the picture of the event in her hands showing it to Zachary and Rena. The two children happily relaxed on the living room couch together with their mother admiring the event.

"Mommy, is that me?" Rena asked.

"Yes that's me holding Zachary and daddy is holding you, honey," Katie told her.

"I look so fat," Zachary complained.

"Nonsense," Katie chuckled. "Believe it or not when we first got you two, you guys were really skinny."

"Skinnier than that table?" Zachary pointed to the furniture across from them.

"No, skinnier than that," said Katie.

"Nobody's skinnier than that," Rena protested.

"You'd be surprised," Katie snickered.

"Mom?" Zachary asked.

"Yes sweetie?"

"What happened to our real mom?" he asked.

"I don't know honey," Katie sighed. "We haven't seen her since the day she gave you and your sister to me. But I'm glad she did because your father and I never would've had you two."

"Do you think she'll come back for us?" Rena asked.

"It's possible but I can't say for sure."

"If she did, would we have to go back to her?"

"I don't think so. Why do you ask?"

"Cause I don't want to go," Rena said almost crying as she held Katie tightly.

"Me neither," Zachary sadly sighed.

"Whoa, whoa, calm down. Where is all this suddenly coming from?"

"Today at school, Leann said because you and daddy aren't our real parents, our real mommy might come back and take us away from you," Rena explained.

"No! That's never going to happen, you hear me," Katie said placing them both off the couch. "Your father and I did a lot to keep you two and no one will ever take you away from us. Remember what your father and I told you? Even if someone isn't your real mommy and daddy doesn't mean they can't be one as long as they love and care for you. Bullies will always say mean things to you but just remember what we always taught you. That's what's important."

"Okay," Zachary and Rena both said.

Katie hugged them both tightly while embracing her tail around them. "I love you guys so much."

Zachary and Rena truly indeed grew up as two healthy young children. The only characteristics they shared with their mother were her soft delicate brown eyes and black hair. Zachary's hair was a short undercut, curly hairstyle while Rena's was spread out down her shoulders. They equally shared a light brown skin complexion, which they picked up from whoever their father was. From their basic appearance, the two truly appeared as twins.

After releasing them Katie said, "Good, so now that today is Friday that means you guys can plan something we can do tomorrow as a family."

"Yah! I want to go to the movies!" Rena cried out.

"I want to play video games with my friends," Zachary said. "We're almost at our high score."

"But first you guys remember who's coming tomorrow," she reminded them.

"Social worker," Rena said.

"Yep, you just make sure to be on your best behavior but act natural."

"Can I show her how me and Markus are doing?" Zachary asked.

"Eh, the social workers always cringe when you guys are rough with the alligators," Katie said walking to the kitchen.

"There's nothing to cringe about. We're best friends, aren't we boy," Zachary said looking at his favorite alligator from across the room.

After all this time, the alligators had finally grown in full size now. They were huge around 11 to 15 ft weighing at around 500 lbs. However, Jerry was still the biggest predator in the family. Unlike Jerry who almost always stays out in the pool, the alligators would occasionally relax in different areas of the house. Yes, they couldn't talk like Jerry, but just as Dylan and Katie explained, they still have a deep connection with them causing the gators to be well tamed. Rena and Zachary appreciated every member of the family but with their child nature, they still had their favorites in the bunch.

Zachary ran over to Markus who was resting comfortably on the carpet then instantly woke up feeling the small child climb upon his back. All the gators (aside from the albino one) had the average color of black mingled with dark blue. Their undersides were also cream-colored but Markus's was bright which made him stand out from the rest. The only movement he made was his scaly eyelid opening as he felt Zachary climbing near his head. He then jumped off of Markus and went in front of his face.

"Come on Markus, open your mouth," he told him. "Open your mouth wide."

Always seeming as if he's bored according to his blank expressions, Markus only took a while until he finally opened his mouth. Once it was wide enough, Zachary placed his head inside, literally lying on the alligator's tongue as if it were a pillow.

"Mom look! Mom look!" Zachary happily cried out.

Looking over from the kitchen, Katie shook her head while smirking. "How many times have I told you how dangerous that is?"

"They won't bite," he told her.

"I know that but their teeth are sharp and I don't want you and Rena to cut yourselves. Do you know how many times your father and I had to rescue and teach you guys to never touch the teeth?"

"Yes mom," Zachary said still lying on Markus's tongue.

"Why do you do that?" Rena said to her brother. "It stinks in there."

"You're just scared," he teased her.

"I'm not scared!"

"Then you do it."

"Mom, Zachary is telling me to go inside Markus's mouth!" she complained.

"Zachary, don't mock your sister to do something she's not comfortable with," Katie said grabbing different pounds of meat from the fridge.

Walking into the kitchen was another alligator. The minute he smelled the food, he came running. He briefly lifted himself on his hind legs trying to get Katie's attention.

"I see you, Iris," she said looking down at him. "Just couldn't wait with your greedy self. Okay, here you go."

Throwing a piece of meat down to him, the gator caught it in a split second then left the kitchen with his reward.

"Greedy ol' Iris," she chuckled. "Okay, who's next?"

"Esma!" Rena happily shouted running to the kitchen with her mother.

"Esma, where are you?" Katie called out then whistled.

A few seconds later they watched another gator that was upstairs the entire time and had to climb down the stairs to meet them.

"Oh I'm sorry Esma, I never would've called you if I knew you were upstairs but it's dinner time," Katie said.

"Can I feed her? Please mommy," Rena pleaded.

"Okay, just remember how I told you to do it," she said crouching down near her, handing a pound of meat to her daughter.

"It stinks," Rena said scrunching up her nose which made Katie laugh.

Once Esma gator came in the kitchen, she witnessed who was holding the meat and respectfully opened her mouth wide.

"Okay now you can put it in there," Katie told her.

Lifting the meat as high as she could, Rena placed the animal protein inside of Esma's mouth. Until she was clear of the kid, Esma respectfully backed away then greedily chomped down on it leaving the kitchen.

"How come whenever we feed them, they act slow but when you and daddy feed them they act greedy?" Rena questioned.

"Cause they know it's imperative to be cautious around you guys," Katie explained as she stood back up and witnessed Zachary still in Markus's mouth. "Zachary that's enough. I always have to end up washing your hair as a result and besides, give Markus's mouth a break."

"Fine," Zachary said leaving the gator's mouth then said, "Okay Markus. You can close your mouth again."

The alligator took a couple of seconds but gradually closed his mouth.

"So who else needs feeding?" Katie said.

"Darren!" Rena shouted.

"Oh, he already ate sweetie. He and Markus both so they're good. Anybody else?"

"Baxter!" Zachary bellowed.

"Oh boy, Baxter," Katie groaned. "We'll be lucky if he'll move his lazy butt at all. Hey Baxter! Come on and get your dinner!"

Rena and Zachary both couldn't help but laugh hysterically.

"Don't laugh," Katie told them. "You try getting lazy Baxter to move."

"He never comes to the kitchen mom," Rena laughed.

"You always have to go to him," Zachary chuckled.

"Ugh, alright let's see if we can at least try to get him to come to the kitchen for once," Katie said grabbing a piece of meat from the counter.

The three left the kitchen heading to the second living room near the front door. And there was Baxter, lazily sleeping on the corner without a care in the world. Apart from the rest of the gators, he was the chunkiest, earning his lazy persona.

"Hey Baxter!" Katie yelled. "Wake up and get your food!"

The alligator only responded by opening his eyelids but didn't budge.

"I'm tired of always bringing your food to you. Get up off your lazy butt and come here!"

Baxter didn't budge, proving his stubbornness.

"Told you he wouldn't move," Rena laughed.

"Sooner or later I'm going to get this stubborn gator to move," Katie complained placing the meat in front of him.

Once the alligator saw the delicious meat, he didn't waste a moment eating it.

"Sure, you're always hungry to eat but you can't even take the time and effort to get up and get your meal like the rest of your siblings," Katie scoffed heading back to the kitchen. "Alright, who's next?"

"Carl!" Zachary shouted.

"Carl, get out here and get your dinner!" Katie called out.

After hearing his name being called, the next member came strolling into the kitchen. However, he didn't look like the rest of his kin. For one, his features were far skinner, so skinny he resembled a crocodile instead of an actual alligator. It was hard to tell them apart when they were small but now that he's fully grown, its apparent Carl was never an alligator this whole time. Baby alligators look just like baby crocodiles when they're infants, so whoever sold them to Dylan and Katie made a terrible mistake. However, that didn't stop the couple from still loving and accepting him as a member of the family just like everybody else. Carl finally came into the kitchen stopping at Katie's feet waiting for his meal.

"Mom, how come Carl's mouth looks skinnier than everyone else's?" Rena asked.

"That's because he's a crocodile, not an alligator," Katie explained feeding him. "Whoever gave him to us made a mistake, cause when they're babies they all technically look the same. We didn't realize it ourselves until he got older."

"Do you think he feels different from his brothers and sisters?" Zachary asked.

"Nah, not in this family. We treat everyone as equals no matter what. Okay, so I guess that's everyone then."

"Mommy, you forgot Diamond!" Rena reminded her.

"Duh," Katie chuckled. "The obvious alligator that sticks out like a sore thumb from everybody else. Diamond where are you?"

"She's probably upstairs in our room waiting for Rena," Zachary said. "She always likes sleeping in bed with her."

"Well she's my best friend," Rena said sticking her tongue out at her brother.

"You only like her because she's white," Zachary brought up.

"She's not white, she's yellow and that's not why I like her," Rena protested. "I like her because she's my friend just like how Markus is your friend."

"Sure that's what you say but I know the truth," Zachary ridiculed.

"Mommy!" Rena cried.

"Alright you two that's enough," Katie reminded.

"Sorry," they grunted.

"It's fine if Diamond is Rena's favorite," Katie stated. "Color doesn't matter in the slightest. Everyone can have their favorites but remember everyone should be respected and treated as equals in the family. We never want anyone to feel left out. Understand?"

"Yes mommy," Rena and Zachary both said.

"If Diamond is upstairs in your bedroom then we'll wait until we head upstairs for your bedtime, then you can feed her."

"Okay mommy," Rena smiled.

"What about Jerry?" Zachary asked.

"He already ate as well. I don't need to be reminded whenever he shouts to be fed so he's always taken care of first before the alligators."

"I wish we could hear him talk like you and daddy," Zachary said.

"No you don't. It may seem cool but trust me, you guys are better off not hearing his loud mouth whenever he's hungry all the time. I'm just proud that he's the only one we can hear. It would be a constant nightmare hearing these alligators talk as well."

"How is it that you can hear Jerry but not the alligators?" Rena questioned.

"I'm not really sure but the majority of us creatures go through it. Most of the time it's usually linked with the first pets we get. Additional pets afterward would mostly remain mute but we still have a great connection with them regardless."

"Do you know any creatures who own a dangerous predator?" Zachary curiously questioned.

"Back home where Dylan and I used to live, his aunt owned five hyenas," she mentioned. "It's been a while since we've seen her so I don't know if she still owns them. My parents also used to own two leopard seals. They didn't own them until I grew into a teenager and ultimately moved out on my own so I don't know if they still have them as well."

"Can we meet your parents and Dylan's aunt someday?"

"Sure, someday. We'll call them and make it a family reunion."

"Mommy, what time is daddy coming home?" Rena asked.

Just as the words left Rena's mouth, right on cue Dylan came in through the front door. "Daddy's home!" he cried out.

19

Dylan was dressed in his usual business attire while carrying his briefcase in his right claw. He noticed Baxter right near the doorway but just ignored him saying, "Pick a better spot to rest in buddy. This is near the entrance."

"Daddy!" Zachary and Rena happily cried out racing over to him.

"Hey guys," he said bending down fully stretching his arms out. The minute they hugged him, he wrapped them into a full embrace. "I missed you all day at work."

"We missed you too daddy," said Rena.

"Oh man, you guys are sprouting. What are you, seven, eight?" he playfully teased.

"We're nine dad," Zachary scowled.

"Nine! Oh man, you guys are already growing up so fast. Well, I couldn't resist getting my little princess and big man special treats," Dylan said pulling out two small gift baskets from his briefcase which contained various treats inside.

"Thank you daddy!" they joyfully shouted taking the baskets from him.

"Can I have some?" he asked.

"No!" they said taking the baskets and ran in the living room with them as Dylan left a playful pout saying, "Aww, what did your mother teach you guys about sharing."

He then walks into the kitchen meeting up with his wife giving her a big hug as well a kiss on the forehead. "I missed you too."

"You're going to spoil them ya know," she said.

"I only do it on occasions, besides we're just giving them the love they deserve."

"Be careful not to overdo it. So how did your meeting go?"

"Great. We settled on a new design and I think it'll help improve the company. I'm glad the project is almost finished because Fridays are usually my off days but since this meeting, I've been working all Fridays these past two months."

"Well, at least tomorrow is your day off. You remember the social worker is coming over."

"Oh thanks for reminding me, I almost forgot. Because remember, we're also throwing a family barbeque later on. Brandon, Shelley, and others will be coming over."

"Yeah, remember how back then it was a big treat going over to Brandon's barbeque that time and now everyone insists always having it here at our place instead," she chuckled.

"I guess it's no secret since we've adopted Zachary and Rena our place is more exciting to come to from other's perspective."

"Yeah with a shark and alligators that won't attack you, I can't imagine why. I told Zachary and Rena they should plan something we all can do tomorrow. We'll have to wait until after the barbeque to spend time with them. Rena said she wants to go to the movies."

"Alright, since we're going to have a full day tomorrow we might as well get lots of sleep tonight. Did Jerry and gators eat?"

"All except Diamond. Rena wants to be the one to feed her," Katie said cleaning up the counter. "Okay kids don't eat all that junk. It's your bedtime time anyway since we have to get up early tomorrow for a busy day."

"Can't we stay up for just five more minutes?" Rena begged.

"No, come on its bedtime," she said clapping her paws.

Grabbing the last piece of meat for Diamond, Katie and Dylan led the kids upstairs to their bedroom. Walking into their bedroom was like walking into a child's fantasy room which has been drastically updated since they've sprouted. It was now a well-groomed environment with a few toys, books, plenty of clean clothes in the nearest closet, a dresser, and a bunk bed that replaced their crib. Lying right alongside the bunk bed on the floor was Diamond, the albino gator. She used to be plain white when she was small but now her layered coat was more of a cream color. Her scaly eyes had the bloodshot feature of pink and red, almost making her cute and unique from the rest. She perked her head up the minute the lights turned on when the family entered the room.

"Hi Diamond," Rena said hugging the crocodilian reptile around the neck. "Are you hungry?"

"Okay sweetie, here you go," Katie said handing Rena the meat.

Just like with Esma, Rena carefully lifted the meat into the alligator's mouth. Diamond happily accepted her food and began chomping away at the animal flesh.

"Alright guys, dress into your pajamas and then go and brush your teeth," Katie instructed. "Your father and I will stay waiting for you in here until you're ready."

Doing as they're told, Zachary and Rena went through their dresser, grabbing their pajamas and dressed into them. Afterward, they left their bedroom heading to the bathroom down the hallway.

"Remember how we thought their crib was the best thing we got for them but by the time they grew out of it, their bunk bed was the next best thing we chose," Katie said staring at the crafted wood frame."

"Yeah, it fits so perfectly and I think we made the right choice," Dylan smiled. "I'm just glad the kids love it."

"Yeah, they almost love everything we do for them. It warms my heart that they appreciate us."

"And that same appreciation is reciprocated with them," he told her.

When the kids came racing back into the room, Zachary climbed to the top bunk which was his portion while Rena's was at the bottom. Once the kids got settled, Diamond climbed into Rena's bed lying right next to her. Both parents then came alongside them. Dylan comforted Zachary while Katie comforted Rena.

"Are you guys nice and comfy?" Dylan asked.

"Yeah dad," Zachary replied.

"Well you guys get some sleep and if you ever need anything, you know we're just down the hall," Katie said.

"Wait mom, can you tell us another story?" Rena asked holding Diamond around the neck.

"Not tonight kids."

"Please!" she begged her.

"Come on honey, it won't hurt," Dylan said.

"Oh right, just for tonight," Katie gave in. "Let me see. Well—once there were two stray cats. A boy cat and a girl cat. They've been strays most of their life, just wandering the streets going through garbage cans looking for their next meal. It was hard for them to trust humans because most people would just throw trash at them and almost hit them on the streets while driving their cars. They would always have to take shelter under cardboard boxes for a place to sleep or whenever it rained. They would usually come across many other alley cats but they were pretty much on their own because to the other felines, they were considered strangers and outcasts. So they were pretty much on their own. Life was difficult for the two cats but they always had each other. As long as they were together, they wouldn't lose sight of hope. Then one day while they were passing by on the streets, a car came out of nowhere and hit the girl cat. An old lady stepped out of the vehicle and was deeply horrified by what she did. The boy cat cried out for his friend. However, the kind and generous old woman helped the girl cat placing her into her vehicle. The boy cat came along too, not willing to let his friend out of his sight. She drove them to the vet in the hopes of saving the girl cat. The entire time, the boy cat worried for his friend fearing he will never see her again. Then to his astonishment, the vet was able to save her. Both were so overwhelmed with joy, the old woman felt it was right by taking them in. She took them back to her place giving them a great home. They no longer had to worry about starvation, running the dangerous streets, or being rejected ever again. The two had to suffer hardship through trials and tribulations but it led them to this moment, where they were now loved and cared for. The end."

"That was nice," Rena smiled truly embracing the story.

"It was okay but I liked the story you told us last time about the misunderstood dragons who fought against the evil superman-like villains," Zachary stated.

"You won't always get the same stories young man," Dylan said tucking him under the covers. "Alright now, it's beddy-bye. Say good night."

"Good night dad," Zachary said as Dylan gave him a kiss on the forehead.

"Sweet dreams," Katie said kissing Rena.

"Good night mommy," Rena said cuddling up against Diamond.

Leaving them by their bedside, the two happy parents watched their children from the doorway for a while before turning off the lights. Katie was even delighted to witness Zachary cuddling his alligator plush toy, a habit he hasn't grown out of yet. The creatures then retreated to their bedroom. Dylan changed out of his suit while Katie waited for him on the bed.

"You know Dylan, it seems just like yesterday when Amber came to the front door and dumped Zachary and Rena into my arms. It's hard to believe how fast they've grown."

"I know what you mean. And then before you know it, they'll be teenagers and then old enough to start families of their own."

"That's what I'm a little worried about. You know no matter how much love you give to a child or raise them, they can still choose their own path in life by getting mixed up in the wrong crowd with the wrong people. And when people usually reach their teenage years their hormones cause them to do the craziest things. I don't want to see that happen to Zachary and Rena."

"Baby, all we can do is give them the best support as much as possible, no matter how bad things get," he said finally joining her on the bed. "Besides, we have been through worse."

"That's true," she said cuddling up against him. "We've come such a long way now and I'm happy with our accomplishments."

"Me too baby," he said fully embracing her tightly.

20

Early the next morning around 7:24 a.m., the family woke up getting themselves ready for a long day, but an exciting one they were looking forward to. The first thing is first. Before they can start having fun, they needed to get business out of the way with the social worker. She said she'd arrive at 8:00 so they wanted to get a head start before she came. Dylan and Katie made breakfast while Zachary and Rena sat at the dinner table waiting for their food and kept themselves busy by playing and texting on their cell phones.

"Kids how many times do I have to tell you no cell phones at the table when you eat," Katie scolded.

"But we're not eating yet," Zachary said.

"You are now," Katie said putting their plates on the table then brought her paw out saying, "Devices now!"

"Yes mom," the two kids groaned handing their cell phones over to her.

"God I swear cell phones are such a distraction these days and I'll be damned if you kids are going to follow in that trend," she said placing them on the counter.

"Mommy's right kids," Dylan said. "They're good for a lot of resources and fun once in a while but they shouldn't be the main focus where they'll always distract you."

"I was just texting our friends about coming over," Zachary claimed.

"You don't have to worry about that because we already texted their parents earlier. Since we're having a family barbeque that means everybody is coming over and we planned it ahead of time. Now eat your breakfast so we can get ready for the social worker."

"I'll go ahead and feed the pets and start getting stuff ready for the grill," Dylan said pulling out all the meat from the fridge. He walked outside to the backyard closing the sliding screen door behind him.

After the kids finished eating breakfast, Katie made sure they were properly dressed and suitably fixed their hair. Not too long afterward, the doorbell rang indicating the social worker arrived.

"Alright kids, remember just like all the other times, be on your best behavior but be yourselves as well. We don't ever want to sugarcoat anything."

Opening the front door, Katie was met with a businesswoman around her thirties, wore short red hair, and a slim figure while wearing eyeglasses.

"Christina, it's nice to meet you again," Katie said shaking her hand while inviting her inside.

"It's good to see you again Katie," she said walking inside then immediately noticed Baxter on the side of the door.

"Sorry about him. That gator is as stubborn as a mule the majority of the time."

"It's okay, as long as they won't bite."

"I'm sure you've read our case file and have determined after several physical visits our exotic pets have yet to harm anyone."

"Yes that's true," Christina said while bringing out some paperwork from her briefcase.

"Can I offer you some coffee or a cold drink?" Katie said leading her in the kitchen.

"Coffee would be fine," she replied.

"Sugar or cream?"

"Cream."

Stepping into the kitchen, Christina witnessed the two kids seated at the dinner table.

"Well hello Zachary and Rena. How are you doing today?"

"Fine," they said.

"That's good. Let's start with your schooling? How are you two doing in school?"

"I signed up for the science fair coming in May because Mrs. Smith says I'm doing a good job in Science. I got an A+," Zachary happily explained.

"That's good. How about the rest of your grades?"

"I'm kinda having a hard time in History and Math but mom is helping me with those," he admitted.

"I go over it with him as much as possible," Katie explained. "His lowest grade was a C- last time but we brought it up to a B at least. I told him if he's ever struggling again, I'll sign him up for torturing."

"Excellent," Christina said writing in her notes. "How about you Rena?"

"I got an A in Science too. I also got an A in Social Studies but I got a B- in Math," she said.

"I go over her homework just the same," Katie said. "She hasn't slipped to any Cs and has been doing great, so I focus more on Zachary."

"That's good progress. Are you two still comfortable with your school? Any trouble with bullying? Do you guys get along with most of the kids?"

"Leann made fun of us because mom and dad aren't really our mommy and daddy," Rena explained.

"Leann?"

"She's a classmate at their school who sometimes gives them a hard time," Katie revealed. "I've talked with the teacher about it and they said they'll take care of her and discuss the issue with her parents."

"Okay. That's a good update with their schooling. What about social structures? Do you kids have a past time activity that you enjoy doing other than playing video games or watching TV?"

"Swimming!" they happily shouted.

"Oh yes, they love to swim," Katie smiled. "Ever since they were little they were fascinated about Jerry and the alligators and how they took to swimming. I believe if it wasn't for them, then they wouldn't be interested in swimming."

"It's a good form of exercise," Christina said. "We had briefly discussed it a few times. How often do you swim?"

"Every day after school, when we finish our homework we swim in the backyard with Jerry and the alligators," Zachary explained.

"And your pets are alright with this?"

"They happily welcome them," Katie said. "They were the ones that helped encourage them to swim when they were timid at first."

"I would like to inspect the house per protocol and then I would like to see the kids in action on how good they are at swimming," Christina instructed.

"Absolutely," Katie replied then turned to her kids saying, "Why don't you guys get dressed in your swimsuits."

While Zachary and Rena left to change into their swimsuits, Katie showed Christina around the rest of the house. Everything seemed childproof and the place was nice and clean. Katie remembers an embarrassing moment a while back when Christina came for the first time. Dylan had inadvertently left a Playcritter magazine lying about. Katie quickly disposed of it before the social worker could spot it. When a furious Katie told an embarrassed Dylan about what could've happened if a social worker discovered any inappropriate material, he swore off of doing that weird habit since that day.

"Due to the extensive size of your home I'm astonished at how impeccable the upkeep is," she acknowledged.

"I guess considering the deplorable conditions we used to live in, we've become basic neat freaks," Katie said.

"Alright, everything looks good around here. So let's go and see the kids in action," said Christina.

Everyone went outside to the huge backyard where Dylan was still getting things ready for the barbeque. Jerry blissfully swam in the pool with the company of Markus, Esma, and Darren.

"Oh, hello Christina," Dylan said respectfully.

"Good day to you too Dylan," she said.

Although that Playcritter incident happened only once long ago, Dylan can't help to think because of his stupid error it could've looked bad on their record. So whenever Christina or any other social worker came over, he would always blush an embarrassing crimson red in the cheeks while somewhat trying to avoid them.

All dressed in their swimsuits, Zachary and Rena immediately jumped into the pool. Christina stiffened a bit seeing two defenseless children swimming in a big pool with a great white shark and three alligators. It seemed scary at first but in almost an instant, she was amazed at how well they were at swimming for their age. Jerry then came alongside Zachary as the young boy grabbed him by this primary dorsal fin. Zachary happily rode him as if he were a professional swimmer riding a killer whale. It was a true spectacle to watch. Rena was then playfully riding upon Darren who came beneath her and swam around the pool.

"This is amazing," Christina said watching the whole event. "It's almost like going to a water theme park and watching professionals on stage with killer whales and dolphins."

"Yeah it does doesn't it," Katie recognized.

"Do they want to become swimmers?"

"I don't know. They truly enjoy it as an afterschool activity and it's good exercise so we're still trying to see if it's something they want to pursue."

"Well so far from everything I've seen, I'm proud to say you and Dylan are still doing a great job as parents. I'm going to inform the judge on what's happened so far but I can guarantee you it's looking great. Keep up the good work."

"Thank you so much Christina," Katie sincerely expressed.

21

About two hours later after the social worker left, the backyard transformed into a pool party. Many family members and friends came over. Balloons, music, entertainment, and plenty of food were present. Zachary and Rena had many friends they made from school throughout their years and were always pleased to have them over. The kids would always get a kick out of playing with Jerry or the alligators since it was always cool playing with real vicious predators that would never attack you. The kids would always climb on top of the alligators by either hugging or trying to ride them. Most of the younger ones would unintentionally roughhouse with them but it was still enough to prove that no matter how physical they were, the gators would still never attack. All the gators were outside with everyone during the party, aside from Baxter who preferred staying indoors. Some of the kids were in the swimming pool playing ball games with Jerry they always found fun and entertaining.

Katie looked over at her friend Shelley. She was proud to know that since she and Dylan adopted Zachary and Rena, Shelley and Brandon have grown really close. So close that they actually got married and eventually had a child of their own. His name was little Malachi. He was only four years old, a bit younger than Zachary and

Rena but still a friend of theirs nonetheless. Katie thinks back to that moment when her friend was distraught over never finding her perfect soul mate, and now it was good to know that Shelley has found someone who truly loves her. Brandon has proven to be a good husband and a loving father, just like Dylan. She eventually walked over to her friend gaining her attention.

"Hey Shelley."

"Hi Katie," Shelley said giving her a big hug. "Another glorious barbeque right?"

"I guess you can say that. So where's that adorable son of yours?"

"Brandon should be out with him in a minute. He had to go to the bathroom. So how did things go with the social worker?"

"It went great like last time. She finally got to see Zachary and Rena in action swimming in the pool with Jerry and the gators. It seemed to bring unease to the social worker but it went along great afterwards."

"Brandon and I are really proud of you and Dylan," her friend deeply expressed. "You've made it through all this and are finally getting the family you deserve."

"I also never would've made it without your support."

Brandon finally came outside with Malachi closely glued to his legs. He wore a toddler's striped t-shirt with blue jeans and a propeller beanie hat on his head making him look twice as adorable. Their son was always a bit shy but everyone was used to it.

"Hi Malachi," Katie squealed kneeling beside him. "It's good to see you again."

"Hi," the nervous kid said hiding behind his father's legs.

"It's okay Malachi," Brandon assured him. "It's just auntie Katie. We've been over here many times before. Remember your friends Zachary and Rena."

"How about you show him some of the alligators," Katie suggested. "It's been a while since he's seen them."

"Would you like that Malachi," Shelley said grasping her child up to her chest. "Would you like to see the white alligator Diamond?"

As Shelley left with her child, Katie continued helping Dylan serve more food to their guests.

"Hey Dylan," said a coworker friend of his named Franco. "With all this attention you guys are getting with adopting your kids and having dangerous predators as pets, you guys can become rich on social media."

"I know Franco, we've been told it over many times before but Katie and I aren't into social media like a lot of people are. That's not the type of life we want to live. It was already big news enough the minute we adopted them but now everyone wants updates on everything we do. We don't like discussing every personal detail of our lives to the world. Besides we don't want to give people the wrong idea of taking selfies with dangerous predators since people here are always taking pictures with our pets. We always have to keep reminding them if they post it, to tell others that the predators rightfully belong to creatures who wouldn't attack anybody. Just one little slipup is all it takes to make us look bad on the internet and we don't want to live like that. It's been a hassle for years and we're sick and tired of it."

"I admire your guys' loyalty," he acknowledged. "Not a lot of people have it in them to do what you guys have pulled off."

"Well you'll be surprised how there are people out there who are strong will-minded and determined," he said.

"Hey Dylan," said a parent from one of the kids playing in the pool.

"Oh hey Mrs. Hatton," he said respectfully as he handed her a plate of food.

"I've been meaning to ask you and Katie something that may seem like a silly question, but how is it that you guys have a shark and alligators that can live in a pool together filled with chlorine," she acknowledged. "I thought sharks could only live in saltwater while alligators live in fresh water like lakes and swamps."

"You're not the first to ask me that. I think it has something to do with our bonding connection with predators. Once we link with them, they're able to withstand any type of living conditions. Since Katie and I like water animals, I guess they're able to withstand any variety of water," he explained.

"He's right," Franco chuckled. "There are some creatures that can keep Arctic animals in the desert region while there are others that keep desert animals in the freezing snow. Whatever magic you guys have, I wish I could get a hold of it."

"It's not magic Franco," Dylan said. "I wish I had all the answers but I don't. I guess it's just how we bond with predators and in the process, it makes them unique above all others and alters their genetic makeup."

As the party continued, the parents carefully watched their children enjoying themselves while they ate their food. Friends and coworkers had casual conversations with each other. As Dylan and Katie sat together, they were glad to see how far they've come and maybe this isn't how they planned their future but how it seemed to turn out ten times better than what they imagined. Right now here in this moment surrounded by friends and family, they counted their blessings truly appreciating what they have.

As the day went on, it leisurely turned nightfall where everyone knew it was their cue to go home. Dylan and Katie thanked everyone along with giving them leftovers for the road. The last individuals to leave were Brandon, Shelley, and their child.

"Thanks again for a wonderful time Katie," Shelley said giving her a big hug.

"It's nothing. You're always welcome here anytime."

Malachi began to become cranky as he cried while his father held him. "I think someone is ready for his bedtime. We better get this little guy home."

"Alright, we'll see ya next time Malachi when hopefully you're in a better mood," Katie playfully said cuddling her face against his.

"Thanks again Brandon and you guys drive safe," Dylan said.

"We will. See you guys later," Brandon said as he left out the front door with Shelley right by his side.

Now that everyone was gone, Dylan and Katie returned to the backyard where their kids were still playing with the pets.

"Mommy, daddy, come in the water with us," Rena offered.

"Haven't you guys had enough for today," Katie said. "Besides I thought you wanted to go to the movies later on?"

"Just for a little bit please!" Rena begged.

"Come on guys, don't make your kids beg you," Jerry said to them.

"Alright, alright but only for a little while," Katie gave in.

Realistically Dylan and Katie didn't need to dress in anything since they generally walk around naked the majority of the time (unless when necessary) but decided to dress in their own swimsuits nonetheless. Once in the water all the alligators jumped in the pool as well, even Baxter finally joined the family.

"Mommy look, mommy look!" Rena shouted riding on top of Carl. She then steadily tried balancing herself standing on her two feet.

"Oh no missy," Katie claimed grabbing Rena before she could fall. "I won't have you and Zachary doing risky stunts like that."

"But we're getting better at it mom," Zachary said. "We promise not to do anything dangerous."

"They are getting better at swimming with Jerry and the alligators," Dylan noticed. "If they want to choose swimming as a goal later in life maybe we can help them get better at it."

Katie reluctantly said, "Oh alright but only when we're around. I don't care if Jerry and the alligators are present. You won't do any dangerous stunts without us monitoring you."

"Yeah!" Zachary and Rena both said.

The happy family partakes in playing with each other in the pool for a good long while. It truly proved how much everyone has grown from their difficult journey. Jerry and the alligators swam around the family while also having the kids ride them trying out new stunts under the guidance of their parents. Dylan and Katie even took turns riding some of the pets themselves while also letting the kids take turns. Jerry ecstatically performed many backflips showing off more of his moves while also leaping from one end of the pool to the other side symbolizing how proficient he was at jumping. Some of the gators represented their own moves as well by rising from the water like a dolphin. Their skillful talents always made for great games such as volleyball which is why kids were always ecstatic of playing with them whenever they came over. They equally made for entertaining videos whenever friends or family recorded them and would get millions of views from people on the internet, although Dylan and Katie weren't keen on that type of stuff. After a decent exercise, the parents eventually retired and took their kids inside. After washing themselves up, everyone got ready to go out and head to the movies. They went to a late-night show and sat down together for a family picture. Dylan sat on a seat from the left-hand side while Katie sat on the right, whereas their kids were in the middle between them. While their kids enjoyed the movie, Dylan took a moment looking at Katie across from him and she noticed. They exchanged smiles then held each other by their paws, content at the thought of another family bonding moment that only increased their relationship further. And by the time the movie was over, the family drove home with Zachary and Rena passed out in the backseat. Returning home they brought the kids to their bed and did their best dressing them into their pajamas. Too tired from a long eventful day, Zachary and Rena remained asleep for the rest of the night. After tucking them in their bed sheets, Dylan and Katie gave them one last kiss before leaving them alone. Diamond strolled by the room, catching the attention of the two parents as they watched her crawl into bed right alongside Rena. Touched by the cute moment the two finally retreated to their bedroom.

"Although today was basically our weekend, it certainly felt like a hard workout day," Katie sighed looking up at the ceiling.

"I feel you," Dylan said resting alongside her as he ran his claws through her red silky hair. "I'm ready to hit the sack. But before we do—how about we end this night with one last party?"

"What if we wake the kids?"

"Please girl, they're out like a light," he said pulling her onto him while he flops down on his back. "Besides, we've always been careful before."

"You're such a daredevil," she smirked.

22

Everyone slept in the next morning after the previous extensive day and felt fully energized the minute they woke up, at least the kids did anyway. Dylan and Katie still felt sore in many areas of their body, especially after the last minute night treat. After everyone had their breakfast, Dylan and Katie decided to keep themselves busy for now by cleaning up while Zachary and Rena played video games together in the living room. They were encircled by Markus and Iris who stayed resting up against the couch while one was being used as a bean bag chair by Rena, although scaly but comfortable nonetheless.

"So you got any plans for today?" Dylan asked Katie who was washing the dishes while he dried them.

"Let's just be lazy for once and relax," she said. "I don't feel like doing anything after the hard week we've had."

"Good idea. How are the kids doing with their homework?"

"Much better. Zachary sometimes still has a problem in History and Math but he's doing a lot better."

"All thanks to you helping him."

"Well, I wouldn't give myself too much credit. I always hated math and did poorly in it as well. The only reason it's easier now because he and Rena are in the fourth grade. It'll get much harder when they move on up to the fifth and sixth grade."

"Yeah, I can understand that. Math really isn't people's favorite subject matter, apart from those geniuses who can ace that stuff like it's nothing."

Their attention is immediately brought to the kids who began shouting after reaching their high score.

"Kids lower your voices please," Katie told them.

The two then suddenly heard a knock at the door. Dylan was about to get it but Katie stopped him saying, "I'll get it. I just finished washing the last dish so you dry the rest."

"Yes your majesty," he teased.

"Watch yourself," she playfully warned him heading to the front door.

When she opened it, Katie felt her heart stop. Her eyes widened in a state of total shock to witness the individual before her.

"AMBER!"

After hearing the name, Dylan placed whatever he was drying down to meet his wife at the front door.

Lo' and behold standing right there on their very doorstep was Amber herself. From the last time they've seen her she was completely unhealthy and wore the perfect depiction of a total crack head. From her appearance now, she wore generic clothes, her hair has grown out a bit and any sign of incoherence was completely gone from her system. Her light brown eyes clearly read stability as if she was a new woman reborn.

"Oh shit. Amber," Dylan said completely dumbfounded.

"Hey Katie, hey Dylan," she said a bit awkwardly. "It's been a long time."

"What are you doing here?" Katie demanded.

"What do you think?" she said.

Feeling as if they've been sucker-punched in the gut, it's right here in this moment that Dylan and Katie felt the family they've fought so hard to build was about to crumble right before them.

"No, no, no, no!" Katie cried out. "You can't just come here and try to take back what you think is yours! You're the one who abandoned them, remember!"

"I admit I was messed up but I've changed my ways and I'm better now," she told them. "They're my kids and you have no right to keep children away from their mother."

"You threw them away! We're the ones who went through blood, sweat, and tears raising them. We gave them love, we took care of them, and we always watched over them. We accepted them like they were our own flesh and blood. We love them," Katie said nearly crying.

"Well they're not yours, they're mine and I deserve to see my kids."

"The courts won't decide with you. We've adopted them in a court of law and they've been ours ever since," Dylan proclaimed.

"And the courts can simply take them away from you too," Amber declared. "The courts usually side with mothers who want to be reunited with her kids. I have a lot to make up for and I want the chance to be with my kids. I will fight to get them back and you can't prevent me from seeing them."

"Amber—you can't do this to us," Katie sniveled. "Do you know how hard we fought to pick up the pieces after you left? You're going to destroy a happy family. Your kids finally have stability and you can't just take that away from them."

"I can give them stability now! Far better than you guys how you're showering them with riches and fame."

"What the hell are you talking about?" Katie inquired.

"I've seen you guys all over the news and internet. You think because you're rich and famous now, you can claim whatever you want. I'm their mother and they don't need that life. I can give them one better than yours."

"We're not rich and famous!" Dylan protested. "Everything we have is because we fought hard to earn it. We don't shower the kids with riches and fame. We give them the proper life structure that all kids deserve. You've been absent from your kid's life all these years and now suddenly you think you can just come to take them away from us!"

All the shouting and yelling caused Zachary and Rena to leave their game and come to the front door with Dylan and Katie.

"Mom, Dad, what's going on?" Zachary curiously asked.

The minute Amber set eyes on her children, she knelt down trying to gain their attention over to her.

"Hi sweeties, do you know who I am?"

"Amber please don't do this," Katie begged trying to hide the kids behind her.

"I'm your real mommy," she straightforwardly told them.

It was now Zachary and Rena's turn to stare completely dumbfounded. Yes, they were always well aware of their estranged mother thanks to Dylan and Katie telling them the truth, but it was never a moment they thought they would have to face her. Unable to speak, Rena tightly held onto Katie's tail while Zachary did the same to Dylan's.

"Did they ever tell you?" she asked them.

"Of course we did. You can rest assure we didn't lie about anything," Katie groaned.

"I deserve my chance with them," Amber said standing back up looking at Katie straight in the eyes. "Let me talk with them."

"The way how you always took advantage of me and Dylan, you don't deserve that chance," Katie growled at her. "You should be thanking us for what we've done for them and instead, you just randomly show up here after all this time and just expect us to hand them over to you. Over my dead body."

"They're my kids," Amber growled.

"They're ours!" Katie retorted staring back at her dead in the eyes as a challenging strategy which Amber ultimately fell victim to.

"This isn't over. I'm gonna fight for them," she maintained.

"Get out of here," Dylan said trying to sound as calmly as possible from all the pent up anger he was now feeling.

Making the right decision to leave, Amber gradually turned around but not before saying one last thing to her kids. "Don't worry guys, mommy will be back for you."

Katie instantly slammed the door shut unable to control her temper from the utter catastrophe that just occurred. Everyone stood in stunned silence for a moment trying to let the unexpected situation process through their minds. Zachary and Rena eventually broke the silence wailing into a frantic state. The two parents did their best to comfort them.

"It's okay kids," Dylan said nearly crying himself. "Everything will be alright."

"Don't listen to anything that woman said," Katie sniveled. "Nobody is going to take you away from us."

23

That night the two distraught parents sat up in bed, still in physical and psychological distress from what they faced today. They couldn't believe Amber could just suddenly appear after all this time and try to take the very kids she abandoned back. If she was going to fight them, it was indeed going to be a hard case. Sure they rightfully won them over but the courts could easily side with the mother believing kids deserve a chance to be with their biological parents. It was all up for debate if Amber really changed her life around. It was possible, but Dylan and Katie had their doubts. Amber was always a troubled person and unwilling to change for the better, even when they tried to help her multiple times. They considered her a damaged case, someone who's too far gone to be saved. If that's true then why on earth would she want the kids? She certainly didn't give a damn about them all this time and just suddenly wants them back out of the blue. Dylan and Katie knew better. Amber was up to something and they weren't going to be duped by her again.

"I can't believe that bitch!" Katie shouted.

"Shhhh! Don't let the kids hear you use that kind of language."

"I'm just so upset! We were getting along so perfectly and now all of a sudden, that tramp comes back and tries to take our kids away from us."

"I've grown fond of calling them our kids too but—realistically, they are still her kids."

"Only biologically. A real parent is someone who's there for their child. They're there for them through thick and thin and try to raise them with the best love and care. They're there for them when they need them the most. To soothe their crying and would never do anything to hurt them. That's a real parent and that's what we've done for them so they're OUR kids."

"You're right baby. They're our kids," Dylan said with his arm wrapped around his wife while caressing her arm up and down. "We fought hard to keep them and we're not going to let her win."

Just then Dylan and Katie were surprised to see Zachary and Rena slowly creep into their room. Their faces were flooded with dried tears representing how much they cried and how distraught they still were just like their parents.

"What's the matter guys, you couldn't sleep?" Dylan asked.

Unable to reply, the fragile kids just shook their heads while wiping the tears from their eyes.

"Come up here with us," Katie said patting her bed cushion.

Zachary and Rena climbed on top of their parent's huge bed where they rightfully cuddled them. Katie held Zachary in her arms while Dylan held Rena.

"Mom," Zachary whimpered.

"Yes sweetie?"

"Is th-that l-lady going to t-take us away," he sobbed.

"NO! I don't care what she said but she'll never take you away from us. Do you understand? We'll always be your parents."

"Daddy? W-was that lady really our real mommy?" Rena asked.

"I'm afraid so," he sadly sighed.

"If she wants us back now then why did she get rid of us in the first place?" Rena cried.

"She's a troubled person kids," Dylan replied. "It was bad what she did but we're glad she did it because then your mother and I never would've had you both. Try to view the glass half full as opposed to half empty."

"Try not to worry my darlings," Katie said kissing Zachary on the head. "We'll take care of everything. We just don't want you to worry so much."

"You guys promise you'll never leave us?" Rena said rubbing her face.

"Never ever," Katie said firmly with determination.

"Mommy? C-can we please stay home from school tomorrow?" Zachary asked.

Considering the grim situation they were all under, Dylan and Katie happily obliged.

"Of course sweetie," she told him. "I'll call your school tomorrow and tell them you're taking a day off for once. I guess we all need to recover from this bleak day."

Tucking them comfortably under the covers, Zachary and Rena slept in the middle while Katie slept on the left-hand side and Dylan slept on the right. Both parents engulfed the kids in their arms keeping them safely snug and secured. While their kids were already comfortably asleep, the two stared at each other for the longest in fear of losing their happy family.

"No one is going to tear apart our family," Dylan whispered to her. "I promise you."

After a nod from his wife, Dylan eventually closed his eyes and went to sleep. Katie however stayed up for a moment. This horrible revelation only brought back more bad memories to her mind. The fear of losing Zachary and Rena brought her back to that very time she and Dylan suffered a great tragedy.

A few years ago after she and Dylan shortly got married, they recently moved into the grim neighborhood which would become their permanent residence for a while. At the time they didn't even have Jerry yet, so the only company they had was each other. One late afternoon, Katie left the bathroom wearing her favorite red bandana beaming with excitement as she waited for Dylan to come home from work. When he finally came in through the front door, she embraced him with a tight bear hug nearly strangling him.

"Easy baby, I love you too but loosen your grip a bit," he said trying to pull her off.

"I'm so excited Dylan! I have wonderful news," she told him.

"What is it?"

Showing him her pregnancy test which read positive she happily announced, "I'm pregnant!"

The words automatically triggered a sensational feeling that nearly caused Dylan to faint. He happily scooped Katie into his arms spinning her in circles around the room.

"Baby, that's wonderful!" he said giving her a kiss after placing her back down on the floor. "I can't believe it. I'm going to be a daddy."

"Yes, we're going to be parents for the very first time and I can't wait."

"If we're going to be parents then we're going to have to work hard to move out of this dump. I don't want to raise our baby in this type of environment."

"Me neither, but it's all we can afford for right now. We'll think of something but right now, I'm just really excited. We're going to be a real family."

"Yes we are," he said giving her a deep lingering kiss. The kiss was so passionate he accidentally fell on top of her as they both slipped and collapsed on the couch together. They comically laughed as they continued kissing and embracing each other.

For the next few months, the two happy soon-to-be parents did everything they could to set up the perfect life for their unborn child. Dylan wasn't working as an assistant investment banker yet. He was still trying to earn his diploma to reach that goal so he worked at a warehouse job at the time. Katie worked at a fast food joint but by the time she started to gain weight, Dylan insisted that she'd stop working. Katie never liked the job but didn't want Dylan to be the only one supporting them. He promised her he would get that diploma soon, but her health was far more important so she eventually quit her job and only focused her time and energy on being a stay at home parent for their child.

Five months into her pregnancy, Dylan came home from work one day with terrific news that he finally got his diploma and would eventually be able to leave the warehouse position and work as a full-time investment banker.

"Oh Dylan that's wonderful!" she said hugging him. "It's like it couldn't have come at a better time too."

"I think we should do something to celebrate."

"Good idea. How about we go out and eat at The BBQ and Burger Steak-Out," she suggested. "It's been a while since we've eaten at a restaurant."

After the two got ready, they left to have a lovely romantic evening together. After making it to The BBQ and Burger Steak-Out, the two had a pleasant meal filling up their empty stomachs.

"Oh, the steaks here are fabulous," Katie hummed savoring the nutritious substance making its way inside her stomach to satisfy their growing child.

"So are their burgers and asparaguses," Dylan commented picking the leftovers in his teeth with a toothpick.

After a silent hiccup from her fill, Katie looked down towards her stomach after feeling it kick. "H-honey, our baby just kicked."

"Really?" Dylan amazingly squeaked looking on with delight. He moved his tail from across his booth reaching Katie's as he gently caressed her stomach with it. "He or she is growing fast. I can't wait until that day finally comes."

"Me too," she beamed with happiness.

By the time they were ready to go, they wrapped up their doggy bags and headed out the door. Dylan drove them back home truly thankful for the family of three they were about to become.

"That was really good," Katie said rubbing her plump tummy. "We should still do it more often once we get settled as parents."

"I agree," Dylan smiled. "You know we still never found out what the sex is. Do you think we should find out or keep it as a surprise?"

"It'll only be a few more weeks now. We might as well wait and see."

"I know you're going to make a terrific mom Katie."

"And you're going to make a terrific dad," she said smiling at him.

Dylan gratefully returned the smile then shifted his eyes back on the road. As he turned the corner after a red light, there was a great big jolt that came out of nowhere. In almost like a flash of lightning, the windows to the vehicle broke into a million pieces while their car was violently shoved aside by a Mercedes Benz. Dylan and Katie were out cold from the unexpected impact. Several minutes had passed before Dylan's vision and hearing came back into focus. As he slowly regained consciousness, he realized he was still in the mangled vehicle as he held his head from the apparent head trauma and briefly looked beside him. There was Katie, in worse shape than he was. She was completely out cold while bleeding from the head and mouth. Dylan rushed to his wife hysterically crying out to her but she wouldn't respond. Her unconscious state brought absolute turmoil to his heart. Katie's troubled husband shakily managed to dial 911 from his cell phone which he struggled to retrieve from his pocket and stayed by her side until help finally arrived, which seemed to take forever. An hour later Katie was rushed into the hospital while Dylan stayed closely by her side till the doctors and nurses told him he had to wait outside the operating room. Full of grief and anxiety, Dylan tried praying for her and his child to be okay. It took hours for the doctors to operate on Katie. Tragically the baby didn't make it. They both lost it before it was even fully developed. For creatures, their pregnancies generally last for 6-7 months, so they would've generally just had a few more weeks before their infant was born. The impact of the other vehicle had instantly killed the baby by crushing into Katie's stomach. She suffered internal bleeding that affected her uterus where she had to be sterilized enabling to save her. When the doctors came back to give Dylan the heartbreaking news, needless to say, the shattered and grief-stricken creature collapsed to the hospital floor and began to wail in despair. He stayed in this distressing position for a long period. When his wife was finally conscious enough to see him, he quietly came in the room as she just laid there on the hospital bed in a way he's never seen her before. It's as if her whole world was just completely destroyed right before her and there was no way of ever getting it back. She didn't make eye contact with him the entire time as she just stared off into space. Dylan slowly approached her then came by his wife's side sitting on a chair right next to her bed. He progressively held onto her paw and in that instant, she pulled him towards her wrapping him in a tight hug, weeping a river of pain. He held her tight never letting go. Tears continued flowing down his eyes but he didn't breakdown knowing his wife was already in an emotional wreck and tried remaining strong for her. They stayed locked in this position for hours unable to comprehend this disastrous event that just destroyed their lives in a split second.

Katie had to stay in bed for two whole weeks to make a full recovery. What the two eventually found out was that a drunk driver collided into their vehicle. He was known as Vincent Blake, a highly respected legal representative, one who was ironically friends with the mayor. Unfortunately, he was under the influence that night and it was Dylan and Katie who had to suffer the price of losing their child. After finding out about Blake's background, there was a good chance he was going to get off without paying any consequences. Desperate for some form of justice, Dylan looked around for the best lawyer to represent them. However every lawyer he came across charged them a heavy price. That was until he came across Chloe Waters. She charged the same price as the rest but for some reason, she said he didn't have to pay full price. Dylan never thought anything of it at the time because he was still full of grief to notice that Chloe had an interesting fascination towards him. She figured if she could represent him then somewhere down the line, she could find a way to weasel her way into his life. When the day finally came, that was the first time Judge Malcolm came to look at the case. With his help and the compelling evidence Chloe had presented to the court, they won. It wasn't a severe punishment though. Vincent Blake was just suspended of his license, had to work community service, and pay a fine to Dylan and Katie without facing any jail time. It wasn't the justice that Dylan and Katie wanted for the price of their child but they felt any form of punishment was at least something better than nothing at all.

For the past few weeks since that tragedy, Dylan finally quit his job at the warehouse and got a position as an assistant investment banker at Lincoln Edward Industries. Before he started working there full-time, he stayed at home with Katie keeping her company. It was a desolate experience to realize not only did they lose their child but Katie wouldn't be able to bear children ever again. Most couples would separate after facing a tragedy such as this but not Dylan and Katie. Creatures like them would endure the most hellish situations just to stick it out in the end. Creatures pair for life the minute they find their mate and take their wedding vows far more seriously than humans do. Katie most of the time just sat in the living room in such a depressive state watching nothing but TV twenty-four seven. Dylan mostly kept busy around the house and would constantly try to comfort her hoping to get her away from the television. Nothing seemed to work, so one day he told Katie he was leaving for most of the day and would be back later. He was gone for nearly ten hours and finally, Katie stopped paying attention to the television fearing something must have happened to him. But to her relief, he came back as she heard the front door unlock. She failed to acknowledge her husband and continued facing the direction of the television.

    "You had me worried for a second," she told him.

    "You have me worried as well, with the way you've been acting lately. But it's understandable."

    "I'm sorry. I know it's been a couple of weeks now but I'm still trying to cope."

    "Uh—I got something that'll probably help cheer you up," he said.

    Finally turning her head around, Katie witnessed Dylan holding a medium-sized tub in his claws. Full of curiosity Katie gets up off the couch and looks to see what he has. Inside the tub was a medium-size great white shark about the size of a cat. Katie looked on in amazement not expecting Dylan to do something like this.

"What's this?" she said.

"He needed a home and I couldn't help to think a pet is something we could use to help us get through our turmoil."

Katie looked to the shark then slowly back at Dylan. She finally cracked a smile after all these weeks and was generous of his thoughtful gesture.

"Oh, Dylan—that's so kind of you but are you sure we can afford him?"

"I think it's worth it. The same finances to take care of him would've been nearly the same as taking care of our child. That is if you want him."

Katie once more looked down at the shark as he perked his head out the water he was submerged in.

"Hey, you guys aren't going to eat me are you?" the frightened predator asked.

"No, of course not," Katie said quite disgusted. "Why would you say that?"

"Cause I purchased him at a sushi buffet market that was eating various types of marine life," Dylan explained. "When I came across this shark in a small tank and realized people were actually going to eat him later on, I had to step up and save him. I felt it was a chance to save at least one life since, since…"

"Shh, shh, shh. It's okay Dylan," she assured him caressing his cheek. "That was a sweet thing you did for him—and us." She then focused her attention back on the shark saying, "You don't have to be afraid. Do you want a home little guy?"

"A h-home?" he said.

"A home with me and my husband. I'm Katie and that's Dylan of course. Do you have a name?"

"I don't know. But my friends used to call me Jerry," the shark revealed.

"Alright Jerry, welcome to our family," Katie said affectionately stroking him across the head.

And that was the moment when Dylan and Katie adopted Jerry. He was indeed a handful but a great member of the family. Nothing could ever erase the horrific tragedy of what she and Dylan went through, but as time went on, they did their best moving by just appreciating life and remaining thankful they had each other. They even decided to occasionally keep going back to The BBQ and Burger Steak-Out, so it wouldn't be stapled as a constant reminder knowing what happened after they left the place. It was one of the healthy mechanisms of moving on.

Katie is finally brought back to the present as she looks down at Zachary and Rena sleeping beside them. It was bad enough to lose one child to an idiot that got off scot-free, so she swore to herself she was never going to let that happen again. Katie eventually ducked her head down and went to sleep with their arms wrapped securely around their kids for the rest of the night.

24

The next day Dylan returned to work while Katie stayed at home with the kids. The doom and gloom expression he represented could only describe how miserable he was. As he nonchalantly sat at his desk, Brandon was quick to greet him from his station.

"Hey Dylan, we want to thank you for a terrific time on Saturday," he beamed.

"Yeah," he casually replied without looking at him.

"Hey, what's eating you buddy?"

"Huh? Oh, uh—you won't believe this but—Zachary and Rena's real mother came back."

"You're kidding," Brandon said almost in shock for his friend.

"I wish. She came on our doorstep yesterday out of the blue and is demanding to take her kids back."

"She can't do that. Can she?"

"I don't know. Although we've won custody of the kids, she's still their mother. She said she was going to try and fight us until she gets them back."

"Well considering her background and how you and Katie took care of those two kids, there's no way in hell she's ever going to have a chance to win them back."

"I truly hope so."

"Do you know if she's ever going to take this to court?"

"I hope not. I doubt she even has a lawyer."

"Well she does now," said a feminine voice that came in the office surprising the two.

"Chloe!" Dylan cried out.

"That's my name," she said walking up to him as he remained seated at his desk. "I've seen you and Katie have made quite a name for yourselves after adopting human babies. Is this a publicity stunt to gain sympathy for your creature's reputation?"

"You're insane Chloe," Dylan growled highly offended. "Everything Katie and I did was for the love of those two children. Nothing has ever been about ourselves. You of all people should know that."

"The courts may not decide with you when they hear you're keeping a mother from seeing her own children," she said handing him a folded paper. "Here you are, a motion to appear in court where you'll release the kids back to their mother. I suggest you and Katie start looking for a good lawyer if you want to win this."

"Wait a minute! Wait a minute!" Dylan cried out standing up. "You can't just randomly do this!"

"I just did Dylan. Oh and forget about gaining sympathy from Judge Malcolm cause he won't be the judge on the bench this time. See you and Katie in court," she smirked walking away.

"Hold on!" Dylan shouted following her out of the office. "Why did you suddenly come out of the blue after all this time just like Amber and are suddenly representing her."

"You of all people should know how desperate you were at a time like that," she said walking down the hallway with Dylan closely by her side.

"It is quite a strange coincidence that after the last time you talked to me, you came onto me. Then you suddenly show up and are representing Amber. If I didn't know any better, I think this is your way of getting revenge because you couldn't get your way with me."

"Don't be ridiculous," Chloe scoffed heading to the elevator as she walked inside. "I'm just doing my job."

"A job you use to your own benefit to manipulate people and abuse your power," he said holding the elevator doors open from closing. "I was entirely grateful that time you helped represent us but not realizing until later what your true intentions were, I feel disgusted. I really hope you're not doing the same thing to Amber just to get your way."

"I'd watch myself if I were you Dylan," she warned him. "You and your wife think just because you were able to adopt human beings gives you brownie points or popularity. You creatures are out of your league and can never measure up to the advancement of mankind. Just one little blemish on your part and your species' reputation can be destroyed in just a matter of seconds."

He began to feel as if he was walking on eggshells, Dylan didn't want to say or do the smallest thing that could now jeopardize their chances of keeping Zachary and Rena. He finally let go of the elevator doors as they slowly closed.

"You really should've taken me up on my offer back at the restaurant," she told him right as the doors closed.

Dylan stood in shock from what Chloe just said to him. How could he have been so stupid to fall for her generosity which seemed too good to be true at the time? His mind shifts to back then as he remembers shortly after the accident, he came to her office unannounced that day. She was just finishing up some paperwork as Dylan knocked on her office door.

"Come in," she said.

The minute Dylan walked inside, Chloe's heart just sank. She always dealt with humans coming in and out of her office on multiple occasions but she never had a creature to come within ten feet of her workplace. Her eyes immediately examined his feature from his attractive skin color down to his unique creature body. He wasn't muscular but he still had a broad chest with a slim feature enough to be eye-catching. Then she looked up into his sympathetic eyes which she could've sworn had tears ready to emerge. Her rational side though gained composure trying to keep things professional.

"Miss Waters?" he said.

"Yes, may I help you," she said placing her paperwork down on her desk.

"Miss Waters, I'm so sorry to come unannounced like this but…" he tried taking a moment to say the words properly without breaking down, "…I'm desperate for a lawyer who can help me and my wife."

"I see," she said folding her hands in a praying position on the desk. "Well have a seat and tell me all about it."

Taking a seat on the chair which was reserved for visitors, he anxiously sat down unable to stop to shaking.

"What's your name by the way?" she asked.

"Dylan. I'm sorry my name's Dylan," he nervously said. "And my wife's name is Katie. I'm sorry I'm just so jumpy and anxious."

"It's okay. Just get whatever it is off your chest."

"Did you hear that story on the news or papers of a drunk lawyer who crashed his vehicle into a creature's car and killed their baby?"

"I somewhat heard of it but—oh! That was you and your wife?"

"Yes. Unfortunately, the guy is going to get off without any type of justice, and my wife and I are desperate for him to pay the consequences of his actions. He killed our baby," the distressed creature whimpered nearly breaking down. "We were about to start a happy family and he wrongfully took that away from us. Because of my wife's conditions, we'll never have children ever again. Please help us. Everyone I've gone to has just rejected me because I can't afford it. I—I honestly don't think it's only because I can't afford it, but—I think no one wants to represent creatures. You came highly recommended when I asked around. I'm basically at the end of my rope."

Chloe carefully studied Dylan the whole time. Rather than focusing on his tragic story, she was just all too interested on how handsome he looked to her. It was very rare and improper for humans to show fascination towards creatures that the creatures themselves deemed as immoral on so many levels. However, there are a few unorthodox humans who still show attractions towards them and Chloe happened to be one of the few. Her long line of relationships usually resulted in her using her profession to sleeping with some of her clients and the Jury just to win her cases. Therefore her relationships always ended in disaster and she cursed all men only convinced they were equally the same. It drove her distaste in men while her new preference drove her to Dylan in particular. She fluttered her eyes at him while slowly exposing her blouse representing an amount of cleavage that should've been enough to warn anybody this woman wasn't someone to trust. Blinded by his own grief though, Dylan simply brushed off any look or gesture she'd given him.

"Well Dylan," she said seductively, "you know considering who you are up against, this is a long shot. I heard Vincent Blake has a lot of friends in high places and this won't be easy."

"I don't care!" Dylan shouted until immediately realizing how he let his temper get the best of him then steadily calmed down.

"I'm sorry—it's just—our baby needs some form of justice. No one should get away with taking a life, especially an infant's life who didn't get a chance to live."

Chloe knew for sure this is someone she definitely wanted to get involved with. However creature's morals run far too deep where they would never mess around with humans, therefore she knew it wouldn't be easy to persuade him so she would just linger by as much as she could pretending to be his friend until she'd finally have her way with him.

"Alright Dylan, I'll represent you and your wife," she smiled.

"Y-you will?" Dylan said fully amazed.

"You're right. No one should get away with this, so considering what you're going through, you only have to pay half price. Consider it my generosity."

"Thank you so much," Dylan deeply expressed while rising from the seat as he shook her hand.

At that moment when he touched her hand, she was absolutely smitten in a way no man has ever captured her heart before. This was a different type of affection no one could explain. She was hell-bent and determined to creep her way into Dylan's life, whether he and his wife liked it or not.

As he stood in the hallway of Lincoln Edward Industries, returning from his flashback, Dylan now realizes how foolish he was for not reading the warning signs ahead of time. He truly regrets walking into her office that very day.

25

Coming home from work after having to deal with Chloe today, Dylan was anxious to tell his wife the unfortunate news. As he walked into the house, he found Katie in the kitchen on the phone.

"Katie, we need to talk," he said.

"I'll call you back Shelley," Katie said hanging up the phone then directed her attention to Dylan. "What is it?"

"You won't believe who came to me today at work."

"Amber?" Katie guessed.

"Worse. Chloe."

"Chloe?!" she bellowed.

"What makes it worse is that she is representing Amber in court to take Zachary and Rena away from us," Dylan said showing her the paperwork.

"I don't believe this!" Katie shrieked snatching the paper from his claws and read it for herself. "That bitch is actually double-crossing us too!"

"It looks that way. She also told me that Judge Malcolm won't be sitting on the bench, so it looks like we're going to be facing a new judge and we're going to have to find a good lawyer to help us."

"Oh you can rest assure I'll do that. She's not going to get away with taking our kids away from us!"

"Speaking of which, where are they?"

"They're in the backyard with the pets. Understandably, they've been in a sour mood all day. I've mostly sat with them on the couch by just consoling them for the past hour or so. I've never seen them so miserable, it actually breaks my heart."

"They're strong Katie, just like us. We've taught them everything we know. Eventually, they'll bounce back."

"I hope so because sadly they're going to be dragged through this crap and I don't want them exposed to too much drama in their lives. They don't deserve that after what their mother has done to them."

"I know but as I said, they're strong. And we need to keep remaining strong for them otherwise they'll truly lose hope."

"You can be sure I will keep remaining strong for their sake. We swore to them no one was going to take them away from us and I'm keeping that promise till the day I die. Now I'm going to start getting on this phone and call a good lawyer."

Throughout the rest of the day, Dylan and Katie mostly kept themselves busy by researching the best lawyer they could find. They might have gotten lucky the first time representing themselves, but they didn't want it to look bad on their record considering Judge Malcolm was a friend they trusted, so they had to do things by the book this time. At least this time they were able to afford a lawyer and Dylan wasn't going to be so naïve like he was the first time around. After thoroughly going through their research, they believe they've found the best one. His name was Gillian Miller, a well-liked legal representative who rarely takes cases if he has a feeling the person he's defending is indeed guilty. From his status, he does right by the books and cares very little about the money. They truly wished they would've come across him instead of Chloe back then but he wasn't even a lawyer then. Still, Dylan and Katie don't know if he's indeed reliable until they talk with him. Katie called him and left messages hoping he would call back. After a little while, he did.

"Hello is this Katie Lloyd?" he said.

"Yes it is. Thank you for returning my call," Katie said putting her phone on speaker so Dylan can be equally involved in the conversation. "My husband is also here with me."

"Okay. I guess it's no secret who you two are. But from what you told me, you said that the kids you've adopted are being threatened to be taken away from you by their biological mother who has come back into the picture?"

"That's right. We rightfully won Zachary and Rena in a court of law nine years ago but their mother and her lawyer are trying to take them away from us."

"I see. Well, it is a tough case, especially if she changed her ways over the years. The judge might sympathize with her if she's truly changed for the better."

"Mr. Miller, you don't know Amber like we do," Dylan said. "She's emotionally damaged from a bad childhood and there were multiple times we tried helping her but she always took advantage of us. She deliberately threw her kids away and we took care of them all this time. We're not saying kids don't deserve a chance to meet and bond with their real mother but to take them away from the very individuals who loved and raised them all this time is downright immoral. We're all they know and if Amber takes them away from us, it will destroy them."

There was a brief moment of silence.

"I haven't met you all in person yet, but from what you've told me and the stories I've read up on, I'm willing to represent your family."

"Oh thank you so much!" Katie exclaimed.

"Come down by my office this week and we'll discuss further details."

"Thank you so much Mr. Miller," Katie emotionally expressed.

"Yes thank you," Dylan said.

After hanging up, Dylan looked to Katie with a bit of positivity. "I believe he'll truly help us. We might have a fighting chance at this."

"It is going to be a challenge but we'll keep fighting no matter how bad it gets."

Much later that night, the family sat down together at the dinner table eating their supper while discussing what was to come.

"So kids, do you know what court is?" Katie asked them as she took a bite of her grilled chicken.

"I heard of it when you sometimes told me and Rena when you adopted us but I don't know how it works," said Zachary.

"It's a place where a lot of important people meet up at a building called the courthouse," she explained. "That's the place where we'll be going to tell a person called a judge that we're keeping you. You guys might also have to be there and your real mom will be there too."

"What do we have to do?" Rena asked.

"Just tell the truth no matter what," Dylan told them. "You never want to lie in court."

"Tell that to Amber," Katie said rolling her eyes.

"The judge and another person will ask you all types of questions," Dylan explained. "Whatever they ask you, just answer everything as best as you can."

"If we do, does that mean we won't have to leave you and dad?" Rena asked.

"Kids we already told you no one is taking you away from us," Katie reminded them. "We're in this together."

Zachary looked below him noticing Markus was right beside his chair looking up at him. Taking a piece of chicken from his plate, Zachary steadily tossed him the meat as Marcus caught it in mid-air with his mighty jaws.

"How many times have I told you no feeding the alligators at the dinner table son," Katie scolded.

"Sorry mom."

Once it was bedtime Dylan and Katie tucked Zachary and Rena in their bunk beds.

"Goodnight kids and pleasant dreams," Dylan said giving them both kisses.

"Goodnight my darlings," Katie said equally giving them kisses.

"Goodnight mommy, goodnight daddy," they both said.

Per her regular routine, Diamond joined Rena on the bed once they were peacefully slumbering. Appreciating the pet's dedication to their kids, Katie bent down beside Rena's bed and stroked the albino alligator across her head saying, "Always look after them."

The two parents then retired to their bedroom. Still filled with anxiety after everything that happened ever since Amber showed up, the two had not genuinely relaxed.

"I can't help worrying so much Dylan," she quivered.

"I know what you mean," he said holding her tight. "But remember what we said. We're going to keep fighting through this no matter how hard things get."

"I only hope that damn Chloe won't brutalize Zachary and Rena up on the stand if they dare drag them into this mess."

"Under these circumstances, most cases do call kids to the stand if they're old enough. They need to get every side of the story so it's a good thing we told them to be prepared for this."

"We might as well be prepared for anything now that we're up against Amber and Chloe both."

26

On Thursday Dylan had finally completed his project at work so he had his Fridays back. And on this Friday, the two parents took advantage of heading downtown to meet Gillian Miller in person after dropping the kids off to school. When they met him in his office, he appeared to be around his mid-forties with short brown hair, wore a petite mustache while wearing a professional black suit.

"Mr. and Mrs. Lloyd," he said extending his hand out to them.

"Yes, I'm Dylan Lloyd and this is my wife Katie Lloyd," he said respectfully shaking his hand. "Thank you for seeing us."

"No problem, please have a seat," he offered them as the two parents sat down on two chairs right across from Gillian's desk.

"So I've gone through your background and you two have a clean record," he said flipping through the paperwork in his folder. "Not even a speeding ticket. I've also looked over all the documents you've given me and it looks like you guys have a pretty strong case. You've gone above and beyond to take care of your kids despite the hardship you were under. I wish there were a lot of law-abiding citizens like you guys."

"So do we. Anyway, thanks for taking our case for us," Dylan said.

"Well don't thank me just yet. Although you guys do indeed have a strong case, the court usually rules in favor of the biological parents if they turned their life around for the better. Do you know if Amber has?"

"We don't know. She seemed coherent than she has been in a long time since the moment we first met her. But we find it hard to believe she's turned her life around considering how well we've known her," Katie explained.

"Regardless, the court isn't going to throw anyone under the bus until proven guilty," Gillian said. "She might gain sympathy from the judge if she has truly made a change. As much as it's probably going to kill you guys, you have to be willing to allow Amber visitation rights to her kids."

"What?" Katie said in repulsion.

"If you do this it might prove how willing you are to still allow their mother to see her kids and gain support from the judge. I highly recommend that you do it but you don't have to if you're not up for it. Are you?"

The two parents looked to each other absolutely reluctant to agree to something that might risk Amber seeing Zachary and Rena again, but had to go through with it if they were going to gain as much support from the judge to keep their kids.

"We don't like it but yes," Dylan said. "We're up for it."

"Excellent. Now the court might call your kids to the stand as well. Everyone will want to hear their side. Whatever they have to say will be crucial confirmation of their rightful place. Even if you guys are against putting them on the stand, it's something that's going to happen nonetheless."

"We are against putting them through the humiliation of a trial but we already discussed it with them so we'll allow them to take the stand," Katie said.

"Alright," Gillian said going through his paperwork again. "I see that Amber is being represented by Chloe Waters."

"Ugh, she represented us a while back when we lost our child to that damn drunk driver," Katie revealed.

"I read about that. I'm sorry that happened to you two. Is there any other reason why she's against you now?"

Dylan remembered what Chloe told him and was afraid if he said anything negative against a woman of her high profile could be lethal on their part. "I guess she's just a lawyer who multitasks on different cases."

"Oh that's bull!" Katie complained. "That woman has it out for my husband!"

"Katie please," Dylan tried warning her.

"What, it's true," she retorted.

"Are you trying to tell me you think Chloe wants revenge on your husband?" Gillian said dumbfounded.

"I don't think, I know," Katie maintained. "I can read a woman's wandering eye and Chloe has it written all over her. Besides the last time I saw her, she tried going out with my husband behind my back."

"That's a serious accusation against someone who's one of the best lawyers around," Gillian warned them.

"Look, none of this has to go on record or threaten our case," Dylan stated. "It's just our own experience on how we dealt with her. Please don't let any of this get out. We creatures already have a bad enough reputation as it is."

"Well I highly doubt that considering since you and your wife adopted your kids, your story has expanded your reputation in a better light," he explained. "I've heard word that other creatures worldwide are backing up your case."

"Really?" Dylan said fully astounded.

"Word has been getting out since the moment you two adopted Zachary and Rena that other creatures have been trying to adopt human kids as well. It's still an ongoing process since you two are considered the first. However, since you guys are now going through this predicament, we need to focus on how we're going to prove to the court you two are the best parents you've established yourselves to be. If there is anything you might think that could damage your case or anything I should know about, tell me now. As your lawyer, I need to know absolutely everything."

"Well just the fact that people still cringe when our kids are around our predatory pets might be something we want to mention," Katie stated. "We've gone over it numerous times with the social workers but after all these years some people still think our pets might hurt our kids. Since the time we've had them, they never injured them. The only bruises our kids ever suffered was from playing rough or falling off of bikes, the normal scars kids obtain every day during their childhood."

"Yes, I see in your record that you own a great white shark and seven alligators. Considering your kids have been okay with them after all this time, then I don't see it as a problem. Still, Miss Waters might use it to her advantage so we want to be prepared for it. Anything else I should know about?"

"Uhh, do you really think we have a shot at this?" Dylan asked.

"I never lie to my clients. I want you two to know I'll do my damn best out there to support you, but just be prepared if it doesn't go in your favor. I've gone through many cases and some of them usually end in disaster. That's just the harsh reality of life."

Taking his words into consideration, Dylan and Katie were now prepared to face this dilemma despite how negative it might turn out.

27

Two weeks later, the moment has finally come for Dylan and Katie to appear in court. They have done their best with prepping their kids for the moment they would have to appear, but they have yet to be called to court. Today while they were down at the courthouse, their kids were being babysat by Shelley while Brandon arrived with the two parents in a show of support. Dressed in their finest business suits, the two anxious parents waited in the hallway with Gillian until they were called in. The news and media were all over this story just like when Dylan and Katie first adopted Zachary and Rena. They were anxious to see what would happen and so were Dylan and Katie, but they weren't going to make a media circus out of this entire mess which they already saw as completely unnecessary. They hated all this attention and only wanted to get back to the normal secluded life they had with Zachary and Rena before Amber first appeared. Still waiting in the hallway, they saw Chloe and Amber walking side by side. Amber gave the two parents a nonchalant expression while the one Chloe gave them was a smug. Dylan held onto Katie's paw as reassurance that they were going to get through this together and they weren't going to be intimidated by the two.

Finally, everyone was called into the courtroom as the two sides took their seats right next to their lawyers. Dylan and Katie were pleased to see their friends and family who came by as support just like when they adopted Zachary and Rena the first time. "All rise! Honorable Judge Devlin presiding," the bailiff announced as the judge came into the courtroom. This time the judge was Devlin Meyers. He was a man around his late fifties to early sixties who wore a thick mustache and beard. His appearance read as someone reasonable but also strict, so everyone knew not to get on his bad side. Dylan and Katie only prayed he was just as understanding as Judge Malcolm was. Once everyone sat back down, the trial began. Chloe first spoke up by saying, "Your honor, Amber Wright comes here before you today to prove she's a changed woman who only wants her kids back. No one is excusing what she did in the past but the court doesn't have the right to keep kids from their biological mother who only wants to make up for the mistakes she's made. She's turned her life around and wants a chance to be with her kids again, giving them the life they deserve."

Katie angrily gritted her teeth taking that as a major insult as if the life they've given them wasn't pleasant enough. When Chloe finished her speech, Gillian stood up announcing his statement. "Your honor, Dylan and Katie Lloyd have been nothing but dedicated parents to these kids treating them as if they were their own children. Upon first appearance from the baby's unhealthy conditions, they've done everything in their power to nourish them back to health and created the flourishing children they are today. The kid's lives are still prospering and they need the only individuals they've known as parents their whole life to get them through it. Their world will be destroyed if they're snatched away from that. These kids need a stable two-parent household which most homes lack these days in society. These two parents just ask of you not to take that away from them when they worked so hard to get here."

After both lawyers said what they needed, the first individual to take the stand was a child psychologist who would give her expertise on the situation. She was first questioned by Chloe.

"Mrs. Smith, is this case uncommon in your profession?" Chloe asked.

"Yes. Most agencies prefer to place a child with their own race, or this case, their own kind," the woman explained.

"So in your opinion, what do you think is best for the children?"

"For them to remain with their kind," she answered.

"No further questions," Chloe confidently smiled as she returned to her seat.

"Mrs. Smith," Gillian questioned next, "does your organization put racial politics above the child's own personal wellbeing?"

"No, we simply place different racial kids among different races but our resources have shown that children are far better off with their own kind instead."

"With all due respect Mrs. Smith, you can't speak for the children who think differently about knowing what is best for them."

"That's true but the principles are what's most important. Children can't function properly if they don't know their roots. It sends them to a downward spiral knowing they've been living a lie. Sometimes it's not the best opinion but it's usually in the child's best interest to return to their biological mother."

The following witness called to the stand was the county's child protective services social worker Christina Ferrari.

She was first questioned by the Lloyd's representative counselor Gillian as he approached the witness stand.

"Miss Ferrari, from your heightened efficiency as one of the county's designated social workers overseeing the Lloyd's case for a number of years, are Dylan and Katie adequate parents?"

"According to the results of my frequenting the Lloyd residence, over the years I found no evidence of neglect or other abuse and found their home to be quite tidy and inviting. They are model examples of what ideal parental figures should be," Christina answered with a warm smile.

"No further questions." Gillian turned to the defendant's table to take a seat.

Chloe began her line of questioning by inquiring, "So, Miss Ferrari, nothing was found out of the ordinary with every visit to the Lloyd residence throughout their guidance of the human children for nine years is that correct?" She sarcastically emphasized the word guidance.

"That is correct," Christina calmly replied.

"Is it also true you aren't the only social worker to survey the Lloyd case these past nine years?" Waters asked as-a-matter-of-factly.

"Yes that also rings true, however, I have reviewed all past documents and made sure that past visits were accurately charted and up to date," Christina professionally replied.

"Are you sure? Because it was found that five years ago there was a period of interchanging social workers from the spring to the fall—and records indicate some filing may have been glazed over or even altered." Waters sneered as she glanced over at Dylan.

Caught off guard, Christina paused before answering, "That wouldn't be possible."

"How so? I have the documents from that time frame right here in black and white." She stated as she held up the files for the bailiff to present to Judge Devlin.

"Those files should be accurate per protective services policy," Christina slightly stammered.

"Well those documents in question were overseen by a George Withers, Bailey Smith, Daniel Cummings, and Samantha Kuznetsov from the spring to the fall and their thoroughness was least to be desired. Almost expeditious and superficial, if you ask me."

Christina was speechless and dropped her head in defeat.

"No further questions." Waters gave a tight-lipped artificial smile as she trotted to her seat.

Amber was the next individual to take the stand as she was being questioned by Chloe.

"Amber, can you tell us a little bit about your past?"

"Both my parents were drug addicts," she sadly explained. "My dad abandoned me when I was just two years old and my mom abused me every chance she got. One time she threw boiling water at me and that's when the police finally came and took her away."

"I'm sorry that happened to you Amber," Chloe said. "Did you feel safe when they finally took your mother away?"

"No. When they sent me to foster care, I still felt as if I was abandoned. No one loved me or ever took care of me the way a real parent is supposed to. I always had to look after myself. When I was finally old enough to be out on my own, I got a job but admittedly turned to drugs. It got worse until eventually I got fired. Just like my parents, I guess I became what they were."

"Tell us what happened when you got pregnant with Zachary and Rena?"

"I foolishly slept around because I didn't care about myself or the guys I had sex with. When I found out I was pregnant, I didn't have enough money for an abortion so I decided to have them. I was influenced by too many drugs to care what I was doing and fully regret the decisions that I made."

"How did you get involved with Dylan and Katie?" Chloe asked her.

"We used to be neighbors in the same apartment building. A boyfriend I was seeing during that period used to beat me all the time. One day he beat me so bad he left me for dead then ran away. Dylan and Katie came next door after hearing all the commotion and found me. They called the ambulance to take me to the hospital. They even called the cops who later arrested my boyfriend but—they eventually let him go because I decided not to press charges. When I was released from the hospital, Dylan and Katie told me I could stay with them so I wouldn't have to worry about my boyfriend coming back to beat me again. He did ultimately come back, always threatening Dylan and Katie to release me back into his custody but they weren't intimidated by his threats. Unable to get through to them, he eventually gave up and moved on somewhere else. After staying with them for about three weeks, I left on my own."

"Why would you do that when they helped you so much?"

"I felt ashamed. It was my fault my boyfriend came back since I didn't press charges against him. Besides, it was the first time anyone has ever shown me appreciation and kindness and I didn't know how to react to it. I eventually moved in with a friend in the same apartment complex just across from Dylan and Katie. I tried keeping in touch with them regularly. Knowing the good individuals that they were, I knew they would take care of my kids. I was in no shape to take care of them or be a mother so that's why I left them with Dylan and Katie."

"And what makes you think you're a better mom to take on two kids you've never known and completely abandoned?"

"I've been clean now for three years. I got a job, I go to church every Sunday and turned my life around for the better. When I watched Dylan and Katie on the news and social media with my kids, it was as if they were making a mockery about them with their popularity. I don't want that life for them. I want to make up for the mistakes I made and give them the proper upbringing I was never given. I'm only asking for a chance to be the mother I never got to be."

Chloe finally finished her line of questioning and allowed Gillian to speak next. He walked towards Amber on the stand saying, "We are all sorry Amber for what you went through during your childhood."

"Thank you," Amber said looking away shamefully.

"But you think you're better now?"

"Yes, I know I am."

"Are you currently single?"

"I have a boyfriend I've been seeing. He's a great guy and he says he'll help me with the kids if I win them back."

"We've already seen your past relationship in men weren't exactly the healthiest. In some cases, women are drawn to physically abusive men because it's all they know. Are you sure you're not going to follow that same trend again?"

"I've learned my lesson about men in the past. I'm not going to put myself through that again, or my kids."

"If it doesn't work out, are you capable of raising two kids by yourself?" he questioned.

"Yes, I know I can do it."

"Realistically, it's best for kids to be raised by two parents instead of one which is why society is pretty messed up as it is with so many parents separated. You don't want to set that bad example for your kids do you?"

"No! I know Katie has always had Dylan but no one is perfect in relationships. I have made terrible mistakes in the past with men but I'm not going to let that happen again."

"Were you doing drugs while you were pregnant with your kids?"

"A little—but the moment they started growing in me, I immediately stopped," she regretfully answered.

"That could've led to major health problems for your kids. Tell us, if you knew you were so destructive when you were doing drugs and wanted to have an abortion the minute you found out you were pregnant, then why didn't you use protection? It's easy and cheap, more so than buying drugs."

"I was young and stupid."

"Did you plan on abandoning them to Dylan and Katie?"

"No, not at first. I tried to take care of them for the first week I had them, but it was harder than I thought. They were always screaming and crying and I just couldn't take it. I just had to get rid of them."

"Did you plan on coming back for them?" he asked.

"No. I just had to get away. I had to get away from the neighborhood, I had to get away from the people. I had to get away from everything," Amber admitted.

"So you ran away."

"Yes!" she shrieked.

"And now after all these years, you think just because you changed your life around you can take your kids back without facing any consequences?"

"I've already faced the consequences for my actions," Amber angrily remarked. "I'm their mother."

"Who deliberately abandoned them the first chance she got," he pointed out. "Your kids didn't matter enough to you if you were so desperate to get rid of them and not come back after all this time."

"I was troubled and messed up. I just want a second chance."

"Tell me something Amber, has everything always been about you?"

"Objection!" Chloe shouted.

"Overruled," the judge said. "Please answer the question Miss Wright."

"Has everything always been about you?" Gillian questioned again.

"What do you mean?" Amber said.

"From what I've heard, you never even thanked Dylan and Katie for taking care of your kids after all these years. Even when they took care of you after your boyfriend left you for dead, you were quick to abandon them. They said whenever they gave you money to help, you just used them for more drugs. And how do you think this is going to affect your kids? Have you ever thought about what this might do to Zachary and Rena, taking them away from the only two people they've known as their parents? Everything has just been selfishly about you."

"I'm only thinking about my kids," Amber maintained. "They deserve to be with their mother."

"What about Dylan and Katie? After all they've done for you, don't you have the humanity to care about what this is going to do to them or your children?"

Amber had no good explanation to give and was too ashamed to answer. It's true she never once thanked Dylan and Katie for anything and was now regretting it.

Gillian finally finished his questions and both sides were done with Amber. Up next was Dylan who sat on the stand as he was being questioned by Gillian first.

"Dylan can you give us a little information about your background?" he asked.

"Well, I grew up in Cleveland, Ohio with both of my parents. They raised me well but I sadly lost them at the age of seven due to a drive-by shooting. It was a traumatic experience that still haunts me to this very day, but I didn't want to steer in the wrong direction since my parents raised me with enough common sense. The only recklessness I've done was by joining a heavy metal rock band to get through the pain. I might have dressed and looked like a punker, but I never caused any trouble always remaining civilized. I lived with my aunt most of my childhood who raised me with love and care. One day during my sophomore year in high school, the building was performing musicals on stage from various musicians and that's when I met Katie for the first time. She was part of a separate band but when we combined our music we became inseparable. Ever since that moment, that's when we became girlfriend and boyfriend. After graduating high school, we got married and moved out here to California. Because it was too expensive we decided to sadly settle in one of the poorest living conditions in the projects. I planned on getting my diploma for becoming an investment banker which is why we moved out here since there was a job opportunity. I did get it, but it was during that tragic event when Katie and I lost our child. I worked seven long years at my job to get my family and I where we're at now. Everything I've done was always through hard work and with Katie helping me every step of the way."

"Sounds like you've been through a lot too. Tell me something Dylan, if that horrible accident hadn't occurred and Amber still came to you and Katie with Zachary and Rena, would you have turned her or her kids away?"

"Never," Dylan firmly claimed. "We would never abandon children or people who need help. If Katie and I haven't lost our own child, we still would've happily accepted them in the family nonetheless."

Gillian finished his questions as Chloe made her approach next. Dylan stiffened up a bit as he could sense the woman trying to make him nervous.

"Tell me something Dylan, do you think it's wrong to keep a child from its real parent?" she asked.

"Katie and I feel no kid should be taken away from their parent unless they deserve it. No kid deserves to be abused or neglected by the hands of the very people who are supposed to love and protect them. I think every child knows those who love and care for them would rather want to flourish in that atmosphere more than anything."

"Are you perfect?"

"No, of course not. Everybody has their flaws."

"Do you think you make a better parent than Amber does?"

"I don't try to compare myself. I only try to do my best."

"Don't you think the children are better off with their own kind than being raised by creatures? Don't you think this will confuse a child and jeopardize his or her stability disabling them from functioning properly in society with their own kind?"

"We've raised Zachary and Rena to the best of our ability and informed them at a young age that they are indeed humans and we're not their biological parents. We taught them to act and be just like all humans. They're around humans every day in school, with our friends and other people daily. We're still teaching them but after all this time, we believe they got the message."

"Still you should know regardless of the situation, you're not humans. You're cartoon creatures different from our own culture who can never understand what it's like to be a human. Therefore, you can't defend the fact no matter how many times you teach Zachary and Rena to act like humans, you'll never know because you're not us."

Dylan admittedly didn't know how to answer the tough question and paused nervously for the first time.

"Do you feel keeping Zachary and Rena is replacing the very child you and Katie lost?" Chloe questioned.

"Objection!" Gillian stated.

"Overruled," the judge said.

"No!" Dylan shouted. "Keeping them was never replacing the child we lost. Nothing will ever replace what we will never have, but that doesn't mean we don't mind giving love to kids who deserve a chance at happiness."

"Do you regret getting in the car that night knowing it would've led you to this very moment?"

Trying to control his temper which suddenly boiled inside of him, Dylan calmly said, "The only thing I regret is encountering that drunk driver who crashed into us. You should know that far better than anyone Chloe since you did represent us before."

Hoping she hit a nerve, Chloe finished her questions with Dylan but not without smirking before she left and didn't go unnoticed by Katie. Last but not least to take the stand was Katie who was first questioned by her lawyer.

"Katie, can you tell us what you went through after that accident that caused you to inadvertently lose your child?"

"It was like someone just ruptured a vast hole in my heart," she sadly expressed. "My body might have recovered but I never did emotionally. It broke my heart when the doctors told me I would never have kids ever again."

"I'm sorry you had to go through that. Have you and Dylan ever considered adopting?"

"I don't know. It's hard to adopt creature babies because our kind doesn't give up their children. To adopt human babies has been a serious debate by the system for years because of our reputation. We didn't expect to take care of babies until Amber came and forced them into my arms that very day."

"How did they appear when she first gave them to you?"

"They were in bad shape from dehydration and emaciation. We would've called child protective services on her but we've called them numerous times in our neighborhood on occasions. The authorities hardly came in the horrible district we used to live in, even the cops. So Dylan and I did the best we could to provide for them ourselves. We were financially strained, going through financial difficulties and we were even on the verge of being evicted from our apartment but we continued taking care of them regardless of the situation."

"Were you tempted to return the kids to their mother?"

"Unfortunately, yes. We agreed to help babysit the kids just to be there for them since she was in no condition to take care of them. I warned Amber to clean up her act and if she didn't, we made the decision to call CPS on her. But the day we came to return her kids, that's when she ran away. That's the moment we decided to keep them. If we had turned them in, it would've just been another form of abandonment and we didn't want to put them through that again."

"Are you happy with Zachary and Rena in your life?"

"More than I have been in a long time. Those two kids have helped heal the broken heart in my soul. Taking them away from me and Dylan would just destroy us more than the first time. We've helped them get through a lot as they have for us. We're not perfect but we try to give the best love and care that kids deserve."

Gillian finally finished as Chloe now came to question her. Katie gave the woman an apparent glare, but not enough to be intimidating as she was trying to look civilized in court.

"Tell me Mrs. Lloyd, do you trust Amber?"

"Sorry I don't."

"Why not?"

"She was always an individual who relapsed and took constant advantage of us. We saved her life, protected her from her abusive boyfriend. We gave her food, shelter, and money, but it always ended the same way. One day I had enough of her games and finally told her unless she goes to rehab and help herself, I wouldn't support her anymore. I even escorted her to the rehab center and waited for her to walk inside. But she never did. She just ran off and then expected me to give her more money for drugs the very next day. I'm not saying people don't have a chance to change for the better, but after all the drama we've gone through with her, it was enough to never earn my trust."

"Do you think the life you're giving Zachary and Rena is far better than a life their own mother can't give them?"

"No life is perfect. But Zachary and Rena are nine and they're still growing. We don't want them taken away from the only life they know. You don't know what that does to a child to have their world suddenly flipped upside down. It destroys that little spirit in them which is supposed to be thriving and full of life. I don't want that spirit destroyed. You just can't be absent in your kid's life, you just can't! They'll take that to heart for a very long time and it will destroy them."

"Did you ever tell them the truth about their mother?"

"Of course we did. We would never lie to them."

"Do you really think your environment living around vicious predators is the proper setting for vulnerable children?"

"Our pets have never attacked anybody. The only individuals our shark attacked were intruders who tried breaking into our apartment. Zachary and Rena love our pets and they love them. They're part of the family."

"How can you assure an accident won't happen? I mean kids have been attacked by far less worse things than what you and Dylan have."

"If an accident occurred then it would've happened by now. If you just look at the posts and videos that our friends and family insist posting on social media, it shows how gentle our pets are. They've been with them for nine years never to harm them or anybody else. Our kids suffer minor bruises like any normal child from small accidents but nothing was ever intentional and especially not by our pets."

"Should it concern you that this is possibly a bad influence to give your children the wrong impression that all predators are harmless. This could lead them to believe that all predators aren't dangerous and literally put their lives in danger if they happen to run into one."

"No!" Katie cried out.

"This isn't only a bad impression on your kids, but all the countless children you have come over your residence. You're generally giving them a bad message as well."

"We've told our friends countless times that the predators we own rightfully belong to us and not to put their lives at risk around other unknown predators," Katie clarified.

"Kids will be kids. You can't reassure them of their safety because of your incompetence being around predators who won't hurt your kind. Your influence on keeping predators could cause a bad impression on their growing minds. This is exactly the main reason why society deems you creatures as unfit to be raising vulnerable human beings. Realistically if you and Dylan were out of the picture, your shark and alligators would've killed Zachary and Rena a long time ago. Is that true?"

Katie refused to answer as Devlin had to intervene by saying, "Please answer the question Mrs. Lloyd."

"No," she quietly replied.

"Can you say that louder," Chloe stated.

"No!" Katie shouted.

"How can you say that for sure if you creatures are out of the picture?"

"Because realistically if Dylan and I were out of the picture, then our shark and alligators would be in the wild where they truly belong. So Zachary and Rena wouldn't be in any danger."

The apprehensive creature annoyingly shifted in her seat, indicating how much Chloe was getting under her skin. Giving her own personal smug, the calculating lawyer continued to press further.

"Tell me Katie, I mean Mrs. Lloyd, did you breastfeed Zachary and Rena?"

Catching her by surprise, the female creature stood frozen for a moment not realizing the question would ever transpire and took a moment before answering. She first looked over to Dylan and her lawyer while showing a sign of guilt knowing this was something she should've prepared for.

"Did you ever breastfeed Zachary and Rena?" Miss Waters repeated with a confident grin.

"Yes," she shamefully confessed.

"Isn't that an act of already trying to claim the kids as yours when they rightfully didn't belong to you during that time? Seems to me like you were trying to acquire the kids as your own, knowing that children bond with their mother through breastfeeding as a first imprint."

"You're wrong," Katie almost shouted desperately trying to control her volume. "Amber was on all types of drugs so God forbid if she even breastfed them which would've led to major health problems."

"And your milk is far superior to humans," Chloe said pacing the floor back and forth.

"Yes it is," Katie said with confidence. "Our milk contains minerals, proteins, vitamins, and much more healthy nutrients, everything that Zachary and Rena desperately needed at the time. I never wanted to breastfeed the kids already knowing they rightfully belonged to Amber but they were in such dreadful shape, they needed that libration. Because of my milk, it helped spring them back to life into the healthy kids they are today."

"Do you think all this attention with you guys adopting the kids is your way of gaining popularity to win your case?"

"Of course not! I don't like all this attention, especially for our kids. People automatically come to us wanting to know every detail about our life, but we try to keep it discreet. We don't lie about anything but we also try to keep everything restrained. Dylan and I don't like the social media life and just want a normal family structure."

"Do you know how hard it is for a mother who can't connect with her biological child if forces are keeping them away from her?"

"I've gone through that horrific scenario every day of my life since that accident," Katie growled. "Amber chose to have children without taking precautions and then neglected them. She made her choice and knew what she was doing. She got rid of them. I never would've done such a horrible thing. I still remember the very last words she told me before she abandoned Zachary and Rena. She said, *"Who are you to tell me what to do with my life! You're not my mother. This is my life and I choose to do what I want with it!"* I admit she was on drugs during that moment, but even so, it proved she didn't care enough to change for her kids."

"Yet, you're unwilling to allow the kids to see their own mother because you're stuck in the past of what she's done. Are you sure your judgment is not clouded by past events?"

"My judgment is just as clear as day. I'm not unwilling to allow the kids to see or spend time with their mother. I just don't want her to take them away from us. After all we've done for them, it was out of love. We always loved them like they were our own."

Chloe has accomplished what she set out to do by inflicting more pain upon them, bringing up the past and putting them in this position. Saying all that she needed, she finished her questioning. After hearing both sides of the story, Judge Meyers concluded the hearing for the day. He told Dylan and Katie they needed to bring their kids in court tomorrow so they can finally give their side of the story. When that happens, the judge will make his final decision on who will get full custody of the kids.

28

Later that night, Zachary and Rena were already dressed in their pajamas while sitting in the living room downstairs on the floor with Markus, Iris, and Esma. Dylan and Katie sat on the couch trying to go over the case with them for the last time. When they left the courtroom earlier, the two couldn't help but feel betrayed by the system all over again. The questions Chloe drilled on them greatly affected the emotional creatures to the core. They were just two parents trying to get on with their lives and didn't want to be put through this drama anymore, but were willing to face it just to keep their kids.

"So do you two remember everything we've gone over?" Dylan announced.

"Tell the truth no matter what," Rena stated.

"That's right," Katie said. "It might seem scary at first but when the people ask you questions, just answer as best as you can."

"After it's over, will we find out if we'll be able to stay with you and dad?" Zachary asked.

His words had stricken Dylan and Katie straight to the heart. They know the judge will make his final decision after the kids give their testimony. It could go either way and the thought of losing them was devastating.

"Y-yeah, we'll all s-soon f-find out," Katie sadly stuttered.

Anxiously fearing the worst after seeing the look of worry in their parent's faces, the two children immediately embraced them.

"It's okay mom," Rena told her. "Don't be afraid."

Appreciative of the fact her child was trying to encourage her caused Katie to nearly break down crying as she embraced them tighter.

"It's okay kids," Dylan assured them. "We need to remain strong for each other."

"Like remember that story I told you about the two cats," Katie reminded them.

"Yeah," they both said.

"The two cats remained strong and despite how grim their situation was, they eventually made it alright in the end."

"But that was just a made-up story," Zachary pointed out.

"Stories are good sources of motivation," Katie brought up. "It depends on how you look at it. There's usually a meaning behind everything. Understand?"

"I guess so," Zachary sighed not fully comprehending the message.

"We all should hit the sack right now and get ready for tomorrow," Katie said.

"Before we do, let's pray," Dylan stated stretching his claws out.

Everyone happily concurred as they held hands together in a circle saying a moment of prayer to the Lord in the hopes of keeping their family together. Either way it goes, they were still going to fight for their kids till the very end.

After the family got the rest they needed, everyone was up bright and early the next morning. Dylan and Katie dressed Zachary and Rena in their finest clothing then headed down to the courthouse. When they made it there, they waited in the hallway with Gillian Miller again until they were called inside the courtroom. When Chloe came strolling by with Amber, the desperate mom tried taking a moment to talk with her children.

"Oh you guys look so cute," she said bending down near them.

Zachary and Rena reacted by hiding behind Katie's big tail.

"Still keeping the kids from their mom I see," Chloe sarcastically mocked.

"There's no need for harsh criticism Miss Waters," Gillian strictly warned her.

"Can I at least see them?" Amber asked.

Katie looked down at her kids who aggressively shook their heads no.

"I'm afraid they're not comfortable seeing you just yet," she told her.

"Only cause you brainwashed them," Amber angrily remarked standing up.

"Don't make a scene Amber, not in front of the kids," Dylan advised her.

"My kids," Amber retorted as she rudely walked away with her lawyer.

"Ugh, both those women are really pushing my buttons," Katie growled.

"It's almost over baby," Dylan assured her briefly massaging her shoulders. "We need to be as calm and civilized as possible."

"He's right, so are you guys ready for this?" Gillian personally asked them.

The two parents looked toward their kids and asked, "Are you guys ready?"

The only reply they gave them was a positive nod. After one last hug, Dylan and Katie boldly walked into the courtroom while Zachary and Rena stayed outside with a security guard until they were called to come in.

"All rise! Honorable Judge Devlin presiding," the bailiff announced as the judge appeared taking his seat. Once everyone was seated and Devlin was ready to proceed, they first called Zachary to the stand. He anxiously entered the courtroom as all eyes concentrated on him. He generally didn't know if he was going to make it to the stand trying to take his precious time hoping not to trip and make a fool of himself. The timid kid nervously shook in his seat as all attention was focused on him. But looking across the room at his loyal parents who smiled at him gave him the confidence he needed. After breathing a big sigh, he knew he was ready. He was first questioned by Gillian who tried to talk as lightly as possible not wanting to make the boy any more nervous than he already was.

"Zachary, what is your full name?"

"M-my name is Zachary Lloyd and I'm nine years old."

"Do you know who your real biological mommy is? Biological is the person that gave birth to you."

"No," he said.

"You were told who your real mom is, isn't that correct?"

"Yes I know that lady over," he said pointing in Amber's direction, "is the woman that had me and my sister in her stomach but I don't know her. She was never around. My real mom and dad are over there," he said now pointing in Dylan and Katie's direction.

The two parents couldn't help but nearly cry, trying to hold back their tears. Amber on the other hand was fidgeting the whole time feeling like this case was going to backfire on her. Chloe herself even had to admit once it came to the kids sticking up for Dylan and

Katie was major destruction on their case. If she were clearly thinking with her head straight on her shoulders, she would've bribed the judge to win her case. However, Devlin wasn't one of those individuals who was corrupted or easily persuaded by money, so winning this case was a fifty-fifty shot. Chloe just casually looked on while Amber looked over to her for support but didn't get any.

"Zachary, do your mom and dad take real good care of you?" Gillian continued.

"Yes. They always feed us," he began to explain. "They always read stories to us. They help us do our homework. They take us to school. When we're sick, they always stay with us until we got better. They sometimes let us sleep in bed with them when we're scared or have a bad dream. They're always there for us and I don't want any other parents but them."

"What about your real mommy? Would you want to spend time with her?"

"No. If she loved me and my sister then she wouldn't have thrown us away. I would rather stay with Dylan and Katie who I'll always see as my real parents."

The courtroom beamed with pleasurable sighs after hearing everything Zachary had just said. Amber felt a sharp pain trigger her heart after hearing what her son just said. She was so blinded by getting them back, she didn't realize how emotionally dedicated they were to Dylan and Katie. Feeling enough has been said from him, Gillian took his seat as Chloe now began her line of question.

"Zachary, were you ever hurt while your mom and dad weren't or were watching you?"

"Uh—one time I hurt my knee from falling off my bike and hit my head from running into the table," he said. "Dad always helped put band-aids on my cuts."

"So you were never hurt by your pets?"

"No. Mom and dad always told us to be careful around them because of their sharp teeth. They never hurt us because they're our friends."

"Okay. Maybe you were never hurt by your pets but you still got hurt nonetheless. What about your real mommy? Wouldn't you want a chance to get to know her?"

"Not really."

"You know she loves you and she's really sorry for what she did. She just wants a chance to do right by you and your sister. Don't you want to give her that chance? I think we already know who you'd rather be with but how can you know the type of person your real mommy is if you're unwilling to spend time with her?"

Zachary adorably shrugged his shoulders saying, "I don't know but I feel if she ever loved us she never would've threw us away."

Chloe finished her questioning with Zachary. It already wasn't looking good for Amber but the last one to now take the stand was Rena. However, when she entered the courtroom, she was more terrified than her brother.

"Step forward child," Devlin announced.

The fragile girl couldn't make it pass the aisle as she stood frozen once all eyes set on her. Crouching down on her knees, she could feel the pressure of anxiety grip her little spirit unable to get up. Witnessing the frozen state her daughter was in, Katie looked towards the judge hoping he would allow her to encourage Rena.

"Your honor, may I?" she spoke up.

"You may," he allowed.

Katie quickly left her seat and headed down to her timid daughter as she crouched near the floor.

"Sweetie, are you okay?" Katie softly spoke to Rena while helping her up.

"I—I never did anything like this before," she sniveled holding on tightly to Katie's fur. "I'm scared."

"I know you are sweetie," Katie whispered while kissing her on her forehead. "I told you it might be scary at first but once you go through it, it won't be so scary anymore. Your father and I need you to be strong for us sweetie. Can you do that?"

After the encouragement from her mother, Rena slightly nodded as she received a hug from Katie. Her hugs were always soft and warm due to the fact her fur was always well-groomed and smooth making it a satisfying reward, just the remedy that Rena needed. She then held on to her mom's paw as she slowly led her down the aisle to her seat on the stand. She was still nervous but not as much thanks to Katie's support.

"Are you sure you're comfortable with doing this child?" Devlin asked her.

Rena responded to the judge by nodding. Knowing the discomfort Rena was already under, Gillian approached her gently.

"Hello Rena," he kindly said to her.

"Hi," she spoke softly.

"Can you tell me who your real mommy is?"

"She's over there," Rena said pointing at Katie.

"And who's that woman over there," Gillian said gesturing towards Amber.

"She's the lady that had me and my brother in her stomach but she's not our real mommy," Rena said.

By this point, Amber nearly broke down crying unable to take this turmoil.

"Do you like living with your parents?" Gillian asked.

"Yes. Because mommy and daddy love us the way a mommy and daddy are supposed to. They always took care of us and we don't want to leave them."

"Rena, don't you want a chance to get to know your real mommy?"

"Not really."

"Why not?"

"Because she threw us away," Rena said nearly crying.

Seeing the poor girl nearly break down, Gillian stopped his line of question and looked towards Chloe hoping she'll have the decency to be mellow on the child. Breathing a long sigh before standing, Chloe finally approached Rena.

"Rena, you know your real mommy had it rough growing up?"

"I know. Mommy and daddy told us."

"Did they teach you and your brother about forgiveness?"

"Yes, but they said we had to make our own choices. I forgive her for what she did but my choice is to stay with mommy and daddy," she revealed.

"Rena you know your real mommy loves you too, right?" she asked her.

"I don't know."

"How can you and your brother know that if you don't give her a chance?"

"Because if she really loves us then she wouldn't be doing what she's doing," Rena expressed. "Bringing us here is mean and it's hurting our family. Zachary and I are happy and if she takes us away from mommy and daddy then she doesn't really love us." The little girl then turns to the judge crying tears weeping, "Please don't take us away from mommy and daddy. They're all we know and we love them."

Enough was said after Rena's statement. It solidified everything. Even Chloe knew she couldn't question her any further and just took her seat right next to a distraught Amber. Devlin kindly told Rena she may leave the stand and head outside the courtroom with her brother. Once Rena left, Devlin flipped through all the paperwork on his desk before making his final decision. Dylan anxiously held onto Katie's paw as her leg rapidly jumped up and down. Amber looked on in suspense unable to take the judge's slow pace. Taking off his eyeglasses he finally spoke saying, "In both parties like this, the case is never easy. What we have is a mother who's made a change for herself only wanting to be reunited with her kids while we have two parents who have gone above and beyond to take care of these kids like their own children. Both of you have been through a lot during your lifetime and surprisingly came out strong in the end. I rightfully believe children deserve to be with their real parents but in a case such as this, it makes me think otherwise. I always think in the best interest of the child and what's right for them. After hearing their side of the story, it's clear that these kids love the very individuals who raised them with a lot of love and care. It was very evident from what I witnessed with Katie comforting Rena. They truly have a deep bond."

"That was clearly for show to win their case!" Amber angrily protested. "They set all this up and brainwashed my kids!"

"Miss Waters, control your client!" Devlin scolded. He then looks to Amber saying, "Miss Wright, I've been a judge on the bench for a long time and I can clearly tell the difference between a show and how people may attempt to deceive me to win their case. That was not a show."

Angrily admitting defeat, Amber was wise not to interrupt the judge again as she allowed him to continue.

"Getting back to serious matters, I sympathize with what you've gone through and I admire how you're finally making a change for the better. But it's unpleasant how you randomly just come trying to obtain custody of your children without thanking the very creatures who have helped you and raised them due to your past mistakes." He then looks at Dylan and Katie saying, "I've heard and read everything about you two. I don't approve of some of your methods such as keeping dangerous predators, but you guys have proven that they never attacked anybody, aside from that intruder you mentioned and your kid's safety has not been jeopardized by them. I looked through your kid's records seeing how well they're doing in school and are even great in sports such as swimming. You guys were also given positive evaluations from social workers despite some small hiccups from their offices. I admire how much love and care you gave these kids who needed it the most."

After setting down his paperwork he takes a big sigh and says, "Your counselors have proven strong cases on both sides and I'm genuinely divided between the two. However, in court, we sometimes fail to overlook the situation from the child's point of view and who they're comfortable living with. I want everyone to know this court has clearly heard them. Despite what I've seen from both cases, I'm going to decide with the kids on this one. I'm granting Dylan and Katie to keep custody of Zachary and Rena."

The courtroom clapped and cheered with excitement from their supporters. It was the same overwhelming feeling they felt after adopting Zachary and Rena. The two happy parents couldn't help but stand up and hug each other with exhilaration. Amber noticeably showed nothing but grief while Chloe unceremoniously just rolled her eyes.

"I only recommend that you two will give Amber visitation rights to see her kids," the judge stated. "A mother deserves a chance to be in her kid's life regardless."

"Oh yes your honor," Dylan replied. "Until our kids feel comfortable enough, we'll allow her to see them."

"Very good," he says then looks to Amber saying, "Give your kids more time to adjust before they'll be comfortable to visit you. This was already too much for them to take and they need as much stability as possible. Don't squander your good fortunes. This is possibly your last chance. Just be thankful they're alive and well living a prosperous life. That's the best gift you can be thankful for." Raising his gavel mallet in the air, he bangs it by saying, "In the matter of this hearing, this case is closed."

Dylan and Katie were so happy they even hugged Gillian for representing them.

"Oh thank you so much Mr. Miller," Katie deeply expressed.

"It was my greatest pleasure supporting you two," he said extending his hand to them. "This will certainly increase my reputation where I'll possibly have more clients who'll want me to support their cases, both human and creature alike."

"We should pay you double for your efforts!" Dylan blissfully said shaking his hand.

"No need," he smiled. "You guys just continue taking care of those two kids. You're good people."

"Creatures actually," Katie chuckled.

"Later," Gillian happily said as he left the courtroom while carrying his briefcase.

Chloe briefly came by saying, "You guys might have won the battle but you haven't won the war."

"Good day to you too Chloe," Dylan scoffed narrowing his eyes at her.

Walking away with her nose high in the air, Chloe gradually left the courtroom, not the least bit affected by losing the case. Amber however was greatly affected by this whole ordeal. Blinded by her ignorance and selfishness throughout her years of drug abuse, she realized she never accepted or was apprecative of all the good Dylan and Katie had done for her. Her arrogance however continued to cloud her judgment only wanting her kids back with her where she believes they truly belong. She knows the only way she'll get to see them now is if she'll gain Dylan and Katie's approval, which she knows will take a long time to earn considering what she's put them through. Standing up from her seat, she progressively walked towards them until they gave her their full attention.

"All that matters to me are my children," she told them.

"They matter greatly to us too Amber," Katie firmly declared.

Her eyes shifted towards the ground unable to look at them face to face. "I realize you two will need time after what I've put you through but—when can I see them?" she asked.

"It's going to depend on them," Dylan said.

"Alright then, here's my number," she said handing them a piece of paper with her number scribbled across. "Please call me the minute they're ready."

Katie took the number but wasn't the least bit comfortable going through with this. Amber nearly destroyed their family and could've gotten away with it. She was just hoping Zachary and Rena will take all the time they needed before they'd agree to meet her. Already feeling awkward from the brief silence the two parents were giving her, Amber made her quick retreat leaving the courtroom.

"Well honey, we did it again," Dylan smiled at his wife.

"Thank God we did," she said. "It's still an uphill battle but at least Zachary and Rena still belong to us."

Heading outside the courtroom the two parents happily embraced their kids who were anxiously waiting for them.

"Mommy, do we get to stay with you and daddy?" Rena asked in her mother's arm.

"Yes dear, you and your brother are staying," she smiled kissing her.

Filled with tears of joy, the children contentedly hugged their parents back as the family was soon surrounded by their friends and the media.

29

That night the family celebrated at home with a few of their friends and family who came over to eat while they continued to discuss the case. Zachary and Rena played with their friends in the living room while also heading outside to the backyard at the same time. As Dylan brought out more soda cans on the kitchen counter, Brandon came up to him saying, "Dylan, Shelley and I are so proud of you and Katie."

"Thanks, Brandon," he smiled with pride.

"I think you won the judge over when Rena became paralyzed and Katie had to come to her rescue. That really made it a done deal."

"I hated seeing Rena break down like that," Dylan scowled. "It did probably help our case, but I don't want to dismiss Mr. Miller for his decent work on supporting us. He played a big part in helping us win our case too."

"Whatever you say. Well, I'm glad you won because I've been dying to discuss this with you after the case. How come you never told me you and Katie used to be in a rock band?"

"Oh, well that was so long ago," he brushed off.

"Damn Dylan, if I ever have known I would've pushed you into playing some music. You've got to play us something."

"Brandon, Katie, and I haven't played anything in a long time. I doubt we still have it in us," he explained opening a can of soda and poured it in a cup for one of his guests.

"Nonsense, it's like riding a bicycle, you never forget," he said. "You gotta play us something. How about as a celebration for winning the case?"

"Brandon I probably would but I'll have to go through all my old boxes searching for my guitar and I don't feel like doing that right now. Maybe some other time."

"Killjoy," Brandon pouted. "But I'm not going to let up until I hear you play something someday."

"Congratulations on winning," Shelley says to Katie lifting her glass in the air.

"Thanks, for a minute there I was terrified of losing them," Katie expressed.

"I'm glad the judge was able to see all the hard work you and Dylan have done for them. Still, I can't help feeling sorry for Amber. When I heard about her childhood, no wonder she ended up the way she did."

"And Dylan and I tried helping her every way we could numerous times. We felt sorry for her too but when people clearly don't want help, what's the point of putting your time and effort into them. They have to help themselves to get better."

"When are you going to allow the kids to see her?"

"I don't know. Not any time soon but we're leaving it up to Zachary and Rena. We just hope when it happens, it won't become a mundane exercise. It was bad enough after everything she put us through and we don't want another repeated life cycle of that crap."

"Well, the most important thing is that you and Dylan still have the kids."

"Yes and I pray it'll stay that way."

As the party died down, the family thanked everyone for their support and bid them farewell. The last ones to leave were Shelley, Brandon, and their child Malachi. They carried their sleepy child to their vehicle and waved good-bye to their friends. They promised they would get together like this again but felt it was fair for the two parents to take time recovering after the case they just went through. Although they won, going through a trial was a traumatic experience that only kept reminding them of the first one they went through after losing their first child. As they walked back into the living room, they watched Zachary and Rena happily playing with Markus, Baxter, and Diamond on the carpeted floor. They were truly blessed to still keep their happy family together almost nearly having it ripped apart.

"I'm going to thank the Lord every day for moments like this," Katie grinned extensively.

"Me too," Dylan said cementing the moment by taking out his cell phone and took a few snapshots while also recording for a few seconds.

"Hey mom, dad!" Zachary called out riding on top of Markus. "Uncle Brandon says you guys used to play in a rock band."

"Oh, I can't believe he told you that," Dylan embarrassingly said.

"Can we hear you play something?" Rena asked as she rested herself on Diamond's scaly body.

"We're not so sure we're still good at it," Katie admitted.

"Please!" Zachary begged.

Just then Jerry squeezed half his body through the sliding screen door and said, "Hey, you two forgot to feed me!"

"Oh sorry Jerry, we've had a long day," Katie said going to the fridge getting out the meat for him.

Although Zachary and Rena couldn't hear Jerry speak, they always acknowledged him whenever he came around. "Hi Jerry," Rena said getting up from Diamond and strolled over hugging him.

"Hey there you little runt," the shark remarked. "Glad you and your brother are here to stay. I remember that day you guys were so small and screaming and crying all the time. After I protected you from that asshole intruder, I rocked you back to sleep. Man how time flies. It seemed just like yesterday."

"What's he saying mommy?" Rena asked.

"Oh he's just saying how small you and Zachary used to be," Katie explained bringing the meat over to him. "And he protected you guys from an intruder."

"When?" Zachary asked fully astounded having to hear it for the first time.

"It was when you guys were really small so you wouldn't remember," Dylan clarified. "It's when we used to live back in that horrible apartment building."

"Bad people used to break in our place all the time but Jerry always scared them away," Katie said dropping the meat in Jerry's mouth as he ravenously chomped it away.

"He's a good guard shark," Rena gleefully beamed while giving him a much bigger hug.

"Aww kid, you're turning me into mush," Jerry said embarrassingly although his clear shark expression couldn't show it. "So what were you guys talking about before I interrupted?"

"The kids just wanted to hear us play music," Katie said.

"Oh yeah, whenever I asked about that poster you used to have hanging up on the wall, you mentioned you used to play in a band," Jerry remembered. "I'd like to hear you guys play something too."

"We haven't played in years," said Dylan. "I don't think we're that good anymore."

"You won't know until you try," Zachary mentioned.

"You know what Zach, you're right," Katie said then turned to her husband saying, "Why don't you try searching for our old guitars? They should be somewhere stored in the attic."

"I don't really see the point but alright," Dylan reluctantly gave in as he left heading upstairs.

"It's about time," Jerry said. "Now you and Dylan can relive your childhood."

After a couple of minutes of searching through the attic, Dylan came across two old electric guitars they haven't touched upon in years. They were about 24 inches long with a gloss finish although it was hard to tell from all the dust they collected over the years. Dylan's guitar was a Charvel Star design that was black with red lightning stripes. Katie's was a Flying V design that was dark/light blue with radiant lightning bolts. Touching them brought Dylan back to the first moment he met Katie and couldn't imagine how relic items as these were forgotten about when it was a vital memory to their past. He was glad everyone talked him into bringing these musical instruments out. Bringing them downstairs to the family, Katie was also amazed to witness her old friend which led her to meet Dylan. After cleaning the dust off of them, everyone was able to get a clear image of the equipment that once brought Katie and Dylan so much joy.

"Cool, did you guys used to play these," Zachary said holding Dylan's guitar.

"Yeah, I guess we did," he said.

"You two are pathetic!" Jerry shouted. "All this time you guys had those things sitting away and never played anything ever since!"

"Hey it was part of our somewhat rebellious ways growing up," Dylan scowled. "When we moved out here we had to put away childish things and focus on more serious matters. And you know all the things that set us back."

"Yeah, yeah, I get it," Jerry irritably groaned. "Now play something already!"

"Play something mom!" Zachary cried.

"Yeah play something daddy!" Rena also cried.

Pressured by their family, the two parents looked to each other slowly smiling. They both held the guitars in their grasps as it brought them back to the very first time they met.

30

Even in school, he stuck out among his fellow students being one but many of very few cartoon creatures that dwelled there. It was during Dylan's sophomore year in high school as he walked down the hallways of Calvin High while wearing a black leather jacket and sucking on a lollipop making him look like the school bully. However, as he continued walking, he immediately halted looking across from him at the real gang of school bullies. They equally wore the same black leather jackets as him but manifested brutal personas and at the moment were tormenting a student who tried escaping their clutches. They ridiculed him constantly making him trip and threw his school books everywhere. Nearby students warily tried walking in the opposite direction not wanting to get involved or hoping they wouldn't become their next victim. Just when all hope seemed lost for the vulnerable student, Dylan came to his rescue.

"Hey that's enough!" he intervened.

"Well, well, well, if it isn't Dylan to the rescue again," said the first bully.

"Why are you always spoiling our fun Dylan?" the third bully whined.

"I told you guys for the hundredth time to stop tormenting the other kids," Dylan scolded as he helped the student up. "This is why I don't hang out with you guys."

"Too bad," said the second bully. "You'd make a great intimidating sidekick with you already being a creature."

"Sorry about that," Dylan told the student as he helped him with his books. "I'll try to keep a lid on them."

"Thanks," the terrified student squeaked as he rushed as quickly as he could to get out of there.

"You can't keep a lid on us," a fourth bully scoffed. "You may not be part of our gang but we don't have to do a damn thing you tell us."

"I can easily leave the band," he threatened. "You guys know without me, your music will fall apart. I only ask that you'll ease up off the other students or you can find somebody else to replace me."

Knowing this was true, the bullies reluctantly had to agree. Dylan was one of the best musicians who supported their band and it's because of him, why their music was very popular and well known (at least around the neighborhood and school). Besides, they didn't want to go up against someone such as him with his quick moves, sharp teeth, and claws that can easily impair them in a split second.

"You know something Dylan, you really are a son of a bitch," the first bully said shaking his head.

"So you always tell me," he said rolling his eyes.

"Since you had to bring up the band, you are going to show up after school?" the third bully reminded him. "We're supposed to be going up against another rock band that's joining the music program for the school."

"Yeah, I didn't forget. It'll help benefit the school if we all win the contest."

"Correction, us," said the first bully. "We're the ones who are going to win it."

"I think everyone's involvement will help win the contest," Dylan said. "We're not the best."

"Yeah well when we cream the other band, we'll remind you that you said that," the first bully remarked as he and his posses began to leave. "Be there 3:15 sharp."

"Whatever," Dylan scoffed.

Exactly around that time after school, the assembly was in an uproar with most of the students gathered for the music ready to be performed on stage. One band had already played their music first as the students eagerly waited for the next group to arrive. Behind the stage curtains, Dylan got ready with the rest of the bullies who got their instruments together. As they bickered and complained, Dylan just stood there as he held his prized possession in front of him. It really got him through a lot after facing the death of his parents. It was his basic coping mechanism as he fantasized countless times of just sitting up late at night playing with his musical instrument on a recliner. Playing different themes and melodies that would just randomly come to his head was a soothing experience to block out the negativity of demons that taunted him from the absence of his parents. He was thankful the minute he picked up the Charvel Star guitar as a new best friend who helped him survived and to not follow the path of corrupt temptations.

"Earth to Dylan!" one of the bullies yelled at him.

Snapping out of his daydream, Dylan scowled at the bully who said, "You ready or what? We're about to go up against the other band."

"Yeah, yeah I'm ready," Dylan said placing his guitar around him while also putting dark sunglasses on.

"You better be, because we're about to kick some ass," said the first bully.

Once the curtains opened up, Dylan and the other bullies finally caught sight of their rival band just sectioned on the opposite side from them. Then that's when it happened. Taking his sunglasses off, Dylan's eyes fixated on Katie for the first time. Her feature was still the same, aside from her hair positioned in a punk, spiked hairstyle with lots of hair gel while also wearing a black leather jacket. Cupid's arrow had instantly struck his heart at that moment by just staring at her. Engrossed by love, Dylan didn't realize the music had just started and instantly got on track. The whole time he played, his eyes never left Katie but she didn't notice him yet. She was too busy focusing on her own music to perceive him. As always Dylan has come through really helping bring the music to light. The heavy metal rock music really drove home, making students rise from their seats clapping and singing along. The head bully sang through a microphone leading the music as the vocalist and after their portion was finished the other band did the same. The auditorium cheered with excitement once more proving the music always was invigorating. As the band began to slowly depart, Dylan stayed put, still in fascination of Katie's presence. Something then gradually began to develop inside of him. Looking down at his guitar, which was also his musical companion, it's as if the instrument was driving him to play something. Steadily moving his fingers against the strings, he automatically started to play. And in that moment, that's when Katie finally turned around to notice him. He brought the music up a notch really gaining her attention. It's as if he was trying to draw her nearer him with the music he was performing and it was working. Getting into the rhythm, Katie progressively began to play her guitar joining in. Both sides of the band looked at their guitar players in bewilderment. The show was over and yet they were still playing. The audience equally knew this but couldn't help listening to the two. The music was an engaging rock melody and eventually began to buildup sucking them in. Bringing up the speed, the music compelled them together like magnets. This caused the two to hypnotically advance towards one another until they eventually touched tails, resulting in the connection they suddenly shared. Their tails were in sync and appeared to have a mind of their own as they intertwined almost dancing as the two continued playing at the same time. Dylan twirled Katie across the stage with his tail as she did the same with him. She eventually held him low with her big bushy tail looking down upon him as if she were about to kiss him. Dylan's heart just sank with overwhelming love, already knowing this female creature was determined to be his. Nearly getting lost in his deepest desires, Katie flung him back up swerving him across the stage. Coordinating his moves, Dylan began to play in a way he's never played before. His fingers were flying across the strings of his guitar and as a result, smoke began to emerge from the strings and his fingers. Everyone in the audience screamed with excitement from the mind-blowing music that brought them to a place they've never experienced. Katie helped Dylan finish the final touches as it brought the music to a grand finale. The audience cried out with exhilaration clapping and cheering like crazy. The prior music they played was nothing compared to what Dylan and Katie just performed right now. Although this music wasn't part of the contest, it truly solidified the result of the school winning the contest. When the curtains finally went down, Dylan and Katie looked at each other steadily trying to catch their breaths. Noticing that his fingers were slightly smoking, Dylan embarrassingly blew them as Katie couldn't help but chuckle. After waving them off once the smoke subsided, he extended his claw to her saying, "Hi, I'm Dylan." She shook his hand replying, "I'm Katie."

After that moment the two became inseparable. They instantly became girlfriend and boyfriend truly in sync with one another. They always played their music as the perfect duo and helped other rock bands within or outside their school. Until the two had their own place living together as a couple, that's when Dylan developed the bad habit of collecting Playcritter magazines, where the desperate creature fantasized many days and nights until he had Katie as his mate. Alas, he carried that bad habit for a long while until it was eventually broken thanks to Zachary and Rena's adoption. By the time they got married, Dylan and Katie felt their music was sometimes a bit overwhelming, favored most during their rebellious streak. Sometimes it unintentionally attracted a boisterous raunchy crowd much to their dismay. This is the reason why Dylan would sometimes proclaim their music to be more or so recklessness in their youth. So they finally decided to move on with their lives putting away their black leather jacket attires and focus on more serious matters. Katie even got rid of her punk haircut and allowed it to flow down her back. When moving out to California, Dylan remembered packing the guitars away in a large box. He looked down at the items regarding them as close friends. Without them, he probably never would've met Katie the way he did and truly appreciated her in his life. He thanked the musical instruments promising he'll come back to them again one day. Unfortunately, that day never came when he and Katie faced a lot of hardship ahead of them. Now in the present, he truly regretted how he disregarded his old friend, becoming a mere relic of the past.

31

As if they were reliving the moments they did back then on stage, Dylan and Katie held their guitars close to their chests gearing up to play something. Like magic, it automatically came to them. They first played something calm and simple trying to gradually absorb that rhythm that dwelled deep inside of them. Zachary and Rena amusingly watched while sitting on the floor with the gators. Jerry started to get irritated and shouted, "Come on! Bring it up a notch!"

As if on cue, Dylan and Katie began playing exactly the way they used to back then. The music was engaging and stylish, truly making it significant. Dylan began to play harder as Katie followed in suit.

"Now that's more like it," Jerry remarked in contentment.

Zachary and Rena amusingly cheered and clapped truly astounded to hear their parents play like this. It astounded the two as well not realizing they were still good at this after all these years. Plagued by the music, Dylan eventually jumped on top of the couch really showing off his moves. The two children gleefully squealed unable to take the excitement. Katie brought him down with her tail as if wrapping him in a vice grip. After she swerved him away, he gave her a look that read, "I'll get you for that later." The two parents continued playing bringing the music level up until they reached their climax. The ending was well worth it from the sudden urgency of playing music they thought was something that died from their spirits long ago. Zachary and Rena couldn't stop jumping up and down excitedly as they embraced their tired parents on the floor.

"Not bad, but I heard better," Jerry commented, but realistically enjoyed it.

"Thanks for the critique Jerry," Katie said rolling her eyes.

"That was so cool," Zachary said truly impressed as he took his dad's guitar. "Can we play too?"

"Sure son but it's going to take a long time before you get at the level of your mother and I," Dylan remarked.

Three hours later, Zachary and Rena were already put to bed while Dylan and Katie were in their bedroom.

"I can't believe we never brought the guitars out after all this time," Dylan remarked leaning his head against the headboard while his arm was secured around his wife.

"Thanks to Brandon who brought it up," she mentioned. "We should start doing it again as a regular activity. That is, not to the extreme. I don't want to give Zachary and Rena the wrong idea about negative music."

"I think we know better to do what's best for them," he said then looks at her with a seductive look. "And now that our family is back together, we never got a chance to have our own celebration."

"Oh I don't know," she giggled playing dumb. "I think we celebrated enough."

"Not nearly enough," he said positioning himself on top of her. "Remember that moment I saw you on stage and I played that tune to get your attention. And we wildly played endlessly until we had the whole school relishing at our feet. We played and danced until we ran out of energy—just like sex."

"You're comparing the first time we met to sex?" she amusingly smirked.

"What else would you call it? The way we were deeply in sync with each other. The music was the wave of pleasure while the dancing was the seductive moves."

"I guess you make a good point," Katie grinned embracing her large tail around Dylan to bring him close.

"So do you agree?" he said getting ready to enter her.

"Yeah, now bring that music back to my system," she smiled granting him access.

Happily obliging to his wife's request, Dylan forcibly drives himself inside of Katie. The immediate bond always reinforced and increased their passion for each other. It was a fervor sensation at its highest that no one could ever comprehend and it's what made them genuinely inseparable. He then clutches her breasts, massaging them while constantly licking her across the face like a cat affectionately licking its fur. Katie responds by clutching him by the hips immediately intertwining her tail with his to keep him from using it to enter her again this time. He begins passionate and slow teases before he sets the real commitment to her inner desires. She moans from the now burning sensation developing within her. He now increases his speed driving harder inside of her causing Katie to cry out, "Oh God Dylan, please don't stop." He equally feels the same marvel like a fire of affection burning through his veins. Between excessive grunts, he can't help but to keep going pumping her with his fluids at an aggressive pace. Both their minds race only focusing on pleasing the other which is a common routine they happily engulf every time they connect. The high point of ecstasy was gradually approaching much to their dismay, but both held off as long as they could until they were completely out of energy. Katie's grip tightened around Dylan's tail indicating the pain and pleasure she was now undergoing. She can't help containing herself as the claws extend from her paws scratching him across the back. It might have been painful but Dylan gladly accepted the pleasured fury he brought from within her. Her grip tightens even more causing Dylan to drive harder and harder until finally, he ejaculates releasing an overwhelming euphoria causing both to cry out. Their spark once more was something like a miracle within itself which deepened their link by the minute. By the time she lets go of his tail, hers is just as skinny as his from all the sweat and tightening. He collapses on top of her fully exhausted and eventually rolls over allowing more room for her to breathe. Dylan looks to Katie's disheveled hair and sweaty fur which although messy still turned him on to his highest fervor.

"I truly believe that passion was the same as our music," Dylan says between pants.

"I agree," she says.

"You know, I'm starting to run out of excuses to tell the kids why I have scratch marks on my back," he comments.

"Just tell them what you've always been saying as an excuse," Katie brushed off. "That one of the gators accidentally jumped on your back wanting to be fed. You accidentally scratched your back too hard. Or just put on a t-shirt."

"If you say so," he smiles scooting alongside her. "I guess I'm just always hungry for you. You're like an appetizing banquet I keep craving for and can never get enough of. By the time I'm full and you satisfy my hunger, I just wait around until I'm hungry again waiting for my next meal."

"Well you know since we've had Zachary and Rena, we always had to be careful," she reminded him. "Remember that one incident they came barging in on us unexpected. Good thing they didn't see anything but you don't know how embarrassing that was."

"Yeah and then little Zachary accidentally jumped between my legs really spoiling the moment," Dylan laughed remembering himself. "They were like three years old at the time. They then asked to sleep in with us so we couldn't finish up until the next day."

"That was a night we truly won't forget," she chuckled.

"But realistically we've done a good so far along with everything else," he said affectionately licking at her breasts.

"I swear you're so horny. Give a girl a chance to recover first," Katie partly chuckles pushing him away.

"Fine," he pouts. "Let me know when my next order is ready to be picked up."

32

The two happy parents were very blessed to still retain custody of Zachary and Rena, however as the week went by, Amber started becoming a constant nuisance by calling twenty-four seven. Katie kept informing her they would call her when the kids were ready but the determined woman wasn't having any of it. As much as Dylan and Katie hated it, they still had to keep their word to the judge and allow Amber a chance to meet her kids. Coming to an ultimate decision, they told Amber they'll talk it over with the kids and let her know as soon as possible.

Now that is was Friday, the two parents thought this was the best time to discuss the issue with Zachary and Rena. With Dylan having his Fridays back, he decided to pick them up from school today. Katie waited for them to return as she tended to Jerry and the alligators outside.

"So, you and Dylan are actually going to allow your kids to see their biological mother?" Jerry said from the pool.

"We don't have any choice," Katie said feeding each gator their pound of meat. "The judge ordered us to and we don't want any more of this stress on our part. I still dislike Amber but as much as

I hate to admit it—she probably needs a chance to reconnect with her kids."

"Just be very careful," Jerry warned her. "I remember every time you brought that woman to our apartment, she was nothing but trouble."

"She was. I'm only hoping for her kid's sake she has made a change for the better."

"You never know with humans. I at least know with creatures like you and Dylan, you guys have unconditional passion for commitment. You stick to your words wholeheartedly."

"It's just in our nature I guess. Some humans are different however. Not all humans are the same. I mean look at our friends Shelley and Brandon. They've stuck with us after all this time and they became a wonderful couple and have a beautiful baby boy. It's just that when you're around crappy humans most of the time, it's hard to accept that there are still some good ones."

"I'm surprised hearing you talk like that after all the struggles you and Dylan went through with Amber. She didn't make it easy on you."

"It wasn't just her. It was that tramp Chloe. Ungrateful bitch backstabbed us and went to trial plotting against us."

"Wasn't she just doing her job?"

"There's more to this woman," Katie scoffed. "I believe she's after my husband."

"Are you sure you're not overreacting just a little bit?"

"Don't talk to me like that. We know people like that and homewrecker is written all over this woman."

"Well if what you say about her is true, then someone with her reputation will get caught sooner or later, especially with her profession."

"I hope so because unfortunately Dylan and I can't do anything about it. If she so much as says any bad accusations towards us, then it's our asses that burn. We don't want to risk losing Zachary and Rena because of a tramp like her. She already came this close to taking them away from us. It's just part of her game to make us suffer."

"All because she likes Dylan," Jerry couldn't help but chuckle. "Just when I thought humans couldn't get any weirder. Well if she's the unethical one then why is that no one would believe you and Dylan."

"Jerry, what world are you living in? We creatures are looked down in society and no one is going to believe us when Chloe has a big reputation as a lawyer. The best thing we can do is back off."

"Now you and Dylan are the stupid ones. After all this time, you guys have made a name for yourselves. You're practically famous now. Who's not going to believe you?"

"You're always going to have haters in this world," she replied.

Their conversation ended when she heard Dylan come in the door with their kids.

"We'll continue this conversation later," she told him. "We're going to have to talk to Zachary and Rena now."

As Katie opened the screen door to greet her kids, some of the alligators all came inside to greet them as well.

"Hi guys!" the kids happily cried dropping their backpacks down and cuddled them.

"Kids remember I told you not to throw your backpacks on the floor when you come in," Katie scolded.

"Sorry mom," they both said.

"Why don't you guys sit with us in the living room for a bit," she said. "We need to talk."

The family of four walked into the living room as they sat on the couch together.

"Kids remember when we told you Amber wants to meet with you," Katie reminded them as she kept her arm around Rena.

"I don't want to see her," Zachary firmly declared.

"Me neither," Rena agreed.

"We know guys but Amber really, really wants to meet with you," Dylan said.

"I don't care. I thought you guys won the case so why do we still have to see her," Zachary argued.

"Because the judge says we still have to allow you guy's visitation rights with her," Katie explained. "Like it or not sooner or later, you guys are going to have to reconnect with your real mom anyway."

"We're still not ready yet," Rena claimed.

"We can't keep delaying this you guys. Amber has been calling all week and she won't let up until you meet up with her," Katie said. "Just have a casual meeting with her and if you're not comfortable then you don't have to see her again for a while."

"So if we just have a little meeting with her, then we don't have to see her again," Zachary made clear.

"That's not how this is going to work guys. Regardless she's going to be in your lives one way or other," Dylan stated.

"Ugh, fine," Zachary relented. "Let's just hurry up and meet her so we can get this over with."

"Hey now, none of that," Katie said a bit firmly. "I know how reluctant you guys are of meeting her but just give her a chance. We couldn't give you guys all the details but we always told you she had it rough growing up. Just be thankful you had us to give you a better upbringing. Give a little bit of that love we gave you back to her."

"And remember what we told you kids about forgiveness. You guys said you forgave her, so how about proving it to us."

Zachary felt extremely reluctant to give Amber a chance, but Rena was more willing to give it a try.

"Okay mom," she said. "We'll do it."

"That's my girl," Katie said kissing her on the head. "How about my big man? Are you going to give it a try?"

Zachary stubbornly didn't answer as his father had to nudge him. "Answer your mother Zach."

After taking a gruff, the young boy scoffed, "Fine."

"Change that attitude of yours young man," Dylan scolded. "We didn't raise you and your sister to act like that."

"Sorry mom, sorry dad," he said remorsefully.

"Fair enough," Katie accepted. "Now that it's settled, I'm going to call Amber and tell her you're willing to meet her."

As the day went on it was now nightfall and the family sat down together at the dinner table eating their meal.

"So kids, after talking with Amber today she's agreed to meet with you guys tomorrow since it's your day off. She's coming here around 10:00 to pick you up and she's going to take you to the neighborhood park," Katie explained.

"You mean alone," Zachary said a bit worriedly.

"You won't be alone," Dylan said. "You'll be with Amber."

"What are you Zach, scared?" Rena humorously teased.

"No, I'm just—I just don't trust going with Amber alone," Zachary revealed.

"She's your mom, I don't think she'll do anything stupid," Katie said but then couldn't help thinking of that same moment when Amber abandoned the kids to her. "At least she better not," she murmured under her breath.

"Can one of you at least come with us?" Zachary pleaded hoping they would agree.

"Sorry buddy but it's only supposed to be you, Rena, and your mom for some alone bonding time," Dylan clarified.

"Please stop calling her our mom," Zachary quivered. "I'm not used to calling her our mom too. She's just Amber for now."

"Okay fair enough," Dylan happily concurred.

"Come on, until me and Rena feel comfortable being around her can we at least bring one of the alligators with us?" Zachary begged once more.

"Oh—I don't see why not," Katie allowed. "We walk the gators around the park numerous times. If you take one of them with you, it shouldn't hurt."

"I'm taking Diamond," Rena claimed.

"Of course you are," Katie said playfully pinching her daughter's nose.

Dylan takes a look at his son seeing the worry look on his face. "Hey big man, what's eating you?"

"Nothing," he grumbled.

"Come on, out with it," he pressed.

"I—I just don't trust Amber," he admitted. "She was so eager to get rid of me and Rena when were just babies. And then when she comes back after all this time, the first thing she does it try to take us away from you and mom. That's not someone I'm ready to be around."

"I can understand," Dylan said gently stroking his son's back. "It's going to take a long while for you and Amber to get used to her."

"How long?"

"Everyone is different. Sometimes it takes months, even years. But eventually, you'll find a way to truly forgive her and move on from this. It's the best closure you can give to yourself and her."

Zachary wasn't sure he entirely understood what his dad just told him but decided to go along with it anyway.

33

Next morning, the Lloyds woke up early to get ready for Amber's arrival. Everyone was on edge, aside from Rena who decided to give her biological mom a chance. Zachary was still unwilling to go through with it but knew he had no choice since he was being forced by mom and dad. He felt a little relieved that he was bringing Markus along while his sister was bringing Diamond but still couldn't shake the thought of being in the presence of the very woman who almost came close to ruining their lives.

"Kids, are you ready yet?!" Katie called in the hallway getting their jackets out of the linen closet.

"Almost mom," Rena said trying to clip the body harness leash on Diamond's back which they always use to walk the alligators with.

"Mom, how long are we staying with Amber?" Zachary called back as he held Markus who walked ahead of him already secured in his body harness.

"Maybe an hour or two depending," Katie said coming back in the living room with their jackets in her arms. She didn't like the idea of her kids being alone with Amber either, but felt better they would be in the company of their alligators who wouldn't let anything happen to them. "Do you kids have your cell phones with ya?"

"Yes mommy," they both said.

"Good. Whenever you guys go out, especially with Amber, always keep them with you," she said helping put their jackets on.

"I will," Zachary promised.

Katie bent down to her son's level looking at him face to face with a serious look. "You're smart Zach. You're wise to be wary of Amber but don't be rude. Just ask the questions you feel need answering. Some of it may not make sense and it may hurt a lot but you'll get through it. Remember how your father and I always taught you to be strong."

"Yes mom," he said taking her words to heart.

"You're my growing big man. And I'll always love you," she said hugging him.

Hearing a knock at the door, they knew Amber had arrived. She released Zachary, still terrified at the thought of having her kids in the presence of this woman. Despite being their biological mother, and once a troubled person, Amber seemed to only care about no one but herself. Katie had reached a point of no return and there was no backing away from it now, so she knew it was best to get it over with. Dylan joined his wife and kids in the living room as they all headed to the front door. They opened it to find a well dressed and eager Amber waiting for them. She wore a fashionable light brown pencil skirt suit, her hair was wrapped in a bun and her feet were donned with colorful flats. If the family didn't know any better, they'd think she's trying to truly impress the kids with her feature.

"Hi kids!" she cried out.

"Hi," they muttered not sure what to make of her.

Amber nearly jumped out of her skin after witnessing the gators beside each of the kids. They didn't help the situation by growling at her.

"I hope you're not bringing those things along," she said distrustfully.

Zachary angrily scowled at Amber retorting, "They're not things. They're our friends! And we're bringing them along or we're not coming."

"Zachary, remember what I told you," Katie said then looked to Amber saying, "Listen Amber, I don't trust you with the kids. We agreed to let you see them when they were ready and they still aren't. The only way they'll go with you is by bringing their pets along. They do it all the time so don't worry about it. Just go along with it for their sake."

Hesitant to be part of this stupid charade, Amber knew she just had to suck it up if she was going to spend time with her kids. "Fine Katie," she said narrowing her eyes at her. "Well come on kids before we waste any more time."

Zachary and Rena first looked at their parents for their approval.

"It's okay guys, go on," Katie said.

"You'll be fine," Dylan assured them.

After their parents' okay, the two left their property with Markus and Diamond closely beside them. Amber stayed in the middle as she led the kids to the park. The two parents kept their eyes on them until they disappeared down the block.

"I'm so worried Dylan," Katie shivered holding on tightly to her tail.

"They'll be fine baby," Dylan said hugging her. "They got their cell phones and they got Markus and Diamond with them. They'll be fine."

"Not with that woman. Zachary was probably right not to trust her. We taught them about forgiveness but what if we're the ones that never really forgave her?"

"Then that's something we're going to have to work on," he says then grabs her by the tail saying, "Since the kids are out, how about we have a little bit of fun?"

"Really, at a time like this!" she said looking at him like he lost his mind. "You're actually thinking of sex while our kids are in the presence of that woman!"

"You need someone to loosen you up to get all this stress off your shoulders," he insisted coaxing her up into his arms carrying her straight upstairs while closing the door behind them with his tail.

Amber and the kids strolled down to the park in a jittery state. For Amber, it was being around vicious alligators that could snap at her at any minute. It was obvious for Zachary and Rena where they weren't comfortable being in her presence. After a long awkward drawn-out silence, Amber attempted to break the ice by saying, "Do you kids want some ice cream?"

"I don't care," Zachary replied.

"I do," Rena said.

As they entered the park there was an ice cream truck parked near the sidewalk.

"You kids wait here while I'll get you some," Amber instructed leaving them for a quick sec.

Rena looked at the sour look on her brother's face and said, "Remember what mom and dad told you."

"I know," he said with a gruff.

"Then you better change your attitude or they'll find out."

"That depends on what Amber has to say."

After reuniting with them, they all found a spot on the lush green grass with a blanket that Amber brought with her. After spreading it out they all took a seat on it. Some of the neighborhood kids who were familiar with the family bringing the alligators out on walks couldn't help but to stop by and start greeting them. Amber was greatly annoyed by the constant children who kept showing up due to yearning for time alone with her kids but unenthusiastically allowed it. After a bit, the neighborhood kids slowly dispersed, it gave Amber the moment she'd been waiting for.

"I can't believe how big you two have gotten," she commented.

"Yeah, it has been nine years," Rena said licking her ice cream.

"Yes it has," she replied.

"Why did you decide to come back for us after all this time?" Zachary questioned.

"I had to get my life together. I was going through a hard time when I had to leave you kids with Katie and Dylan. I didn't want that life for you. So it took me a while but I'm finally back."

"You tried taking us away from mom and dad," Rena pointed out.

"Because I'm your real mommy," Amber said offended.

"Not to us you're not," Zachary remarked. "You left us. Mom and dad are the ones who took care of us so they're our real parents."

Unable to argue with her kids who rightfully knew what was best for them, Amber paused for a minute staring completely dumbfounded. "Yeah, I got that. They did take care of you and it's understandable why you would feel so close to them. But I'm still your mother and I think I deserve a second chance."

"We know. Mom and dad told us but it's just going to take us a while," Zachary said patting Markus beside him.

"I don't like the fact you're around those predators," Amber remarked. "It's not professional, nor safe."

"We've been with them for years," Zachary said. "They would never hurt us."

"The fact remains, people shouldn't be around predators. Do you know how many stories there are of people getting attacked because it's unnatural to own a dangerous animal? Yours might be different because you live with creatures who tamed them, but I wouldn't take that chance if you guys were living with me."

"Maybe that's one of the reasons why we enjoy being with mom and dad because their lifestyle is different and unique," Zachary said. "It's not normal."

"Being just like everybody else isn't so bad."

"Well to me it's dull and boring," Zachary remarked. "Mom and dad always taught us that being different is always a great thing, to be unique from everybody else."

"Oh, what the hell have those creatures been teaching you," Amber muttered under her breath. "Look I realize you need more time to adjust. I was hoping that tomorrow we could do something fun and catch up."

"Like what?" Rena asked.

"My boyfriend who I've been living with has really helped me get back on my feet and he set up something that we can do together. I was told that you guys like swimming so he got tickets for us to go on a yacht."

"A yacht?" Zachary said curiously.

"I've never been on a yacht before," Rena said.

"It'll be lots of fun," Amber said. "What do you guys say?"

"Can our mom and dad come?" Rena asked.

"I'm afraid not because my boyfriend didn't get tickets for them. It's only supposed to be for us so we can have more time to bond. It'll be a great way for us to start on something that can turn into a positive activity."

"I don't want to go without mommy or daddy," Rena maintained.

"Me neither," Zachary said.

"Listen kids, we don't have a lot of time left and this is something that needs to be decided now. I promise you it'll still be fun without Katie and Dylan. Please just give me a chance to be the mother I never got to be."

The two children stared at each other not sure to go along with it. But as compassionate as Rena was she said, "Okay."

"Good!" Amber said excitedly.

"I don't know," Zachary somewhat refused.

"Come on Zach, it'll be fun," Rena said.

"I said I don't know!" he argued.

"Well you still have all of today to think about it," Amber said. "Just give me your decision as soon as possible. I promise you it'll be the adventure of a lifetime."

After Zachary and Rena had spent all their time with Amber, she returned them back home. She mentioned the yacht to Katie which the uptight creature was clearly against and bluntly refused her offer by telling her no. Needless to say, Amber was downright upset with Katie's response but figured it was really up to the kids who would make the ultimate decision.

During their customary family dinner that evening, Katie was still going off about the cruise idea.

"The nerve of that woman," Katie argued placing a spoonful of potatoes on her plate. "Did she actually think we were going to go along with it?"

"I said okay mommy," Rena mentioned. "I've never been on a yacht before."

"No honey," Katie argued. "It's too spontaneous."

"I don't like it either," Zachary said.

"But mom, I thought you told us to give Amber a chance," she reminded her.

"You did say that honey," Dylan said to his wife.

"Shut up, you're not helping," she growled at him.

"She said she just wants to spend time with us and have a good time," Rena said.

"Unless we're coming too then no," Katie insisted.

"She said she only got tickets for me and Zachary. Please mom, I really would like to go on a yacht," Rena begged.

"I said no," Katie claimed. "Finish your food."

Angry from her mother's reluctance to allow her to go on a yacht, Rena irritably threw her fork on the table making a loud clanging noise then excused herself.

"Rena!" Katie shouted as they watched her head upstairs.

"She really wants to go on that yacht," Dylan acknowledged.

"Oh, ya think," Katie snapped rolling her eyes.

"Well, I'm glad we're not going," Zachary commented eating his food. "Rena is just going to have to find something else to do."

After the family finished their dinner, Katie went upstairs to her kids' bedroom to find Rena crying soft sobs into her pillow. She rested alongside her in the lower bunk gently massaging her arm.

"I'm sorry honey," Katie spoke softly. "I know how much you would like to go on that yacht. It's just when you're a parent, your kids' safety always comes first above anything else. Your father and I had you all this time and this whole situation is scary with Amber coming back into the picture."

"I'm a big girl now mom," Rena told her.

"Yes, yes you are," Katie acknowledged. "You and your brother both are. I remember the first time how scared Dylan and I were when you took your first leap into the swimming pool. I thought I was about to have a heart attack. Although we were there watching you, so were Jerry and the alligators. Jerry helped you and your brother up while you guys held on tight. Then Dylan and I took a hold of you and your brother. I didn't think we would ever let you guys go. You two cried for a bit but when you got the hang of it, you just couldn't get enough of the water. From that moment I knew you guys were strong. When you're a parent, all you care about is protecting them and keeping them safe from this scary world. But the truth is, your kids will never frolic or thrive in life if they don't get out in the world and experience it for themselves. That's just part of growing up."

After wiping the tears from her eyes, Rena turns to look at her mom face to face. "I only want to try something different mom. You said it yourself, we won't know how the world works without experiencing it for ourselves."

"I know. You really want to go on that yacht don't you?"

"Yes mommy, I really do."

Katie took a moment gazing at Rena only wanting the best for her. Still not favoring the situation, Katie reluctantly said, "Okay."

"Really?" Rena said excitedly.

"Yeah," she smiled.

"Thank you, thank you so much mommy," Rena cried giving her a tight hug.

"Okay, okay, but your brother is not going to like it."

"Well, he doesn't have to come if he doesn't want to."

"No Rena, if you're going on this yacht then your brother is coming with you. You two have to stick together through thick and thin."

"Like that story about the cats you told us about."

"Exactly," Katie smiled pleased with the thought her daughter remembered the metaphorical story she told her. "If you're doing this, then you promise to be on your best behavior and not to do anything stupid."

"Of course mommy."

"And you'll keep in touch with your father and I at all times?"

"Yes mommy."

"Alright, I'll call Amber tomorrow and tell her you guys are going," she sighed.

34

The next morning Dylan and Katie helped their kids pack their backpacks to take along anything extra they would most likely need on the yacht. Zachary was unwilling to have fun on this trip but promised his mom he would watch over his sister. It was going to be hard, especially since it was only going to be him and Rena. They couldn't bring any of the alligators along with them this time, so Zachary wasn't looking forward to this trip in the least. Katie was still just as worried as ever but tried reassuring herself it was going to be okay. As she was fixing the sheets on their bunk bed, she came across Zachary's alligator plush toy. She couldn't help but cuddle it close as if this was the last time she was going to see her kids for a while. Dylan came into the bedroom finding his wife standing emotionally alone.

"Baby, are you okay?" he asked.

"I—I don't know. I'm just worried about the kids. What if they get hurt? What if Amber doesn't keep an eye on them? What if the boat gets lost? What if…"

"Enough with all this negativity," Dylan stated firmly. He held her by the arms looking at her nose to nose. "Our kids are smart and know better to look after themselves. They have their cell phones to contact us and I made sure to activate international roaming so no matter where they're located we can always keep in contact as well as GPS to track their every move. We'll keep in touch with them and they'll keep in touch with us. You gotta have a little faith in them."

"I trust them wholeheartedly. It's Amber I don't trust."

"You said it yourself, we'll never get pass this if we don't move on and forgive her," he said softly caressing her long silky red hair. "We can't live in distress like this whenever the kids are with her."

She hated it when Dylan was always right, but she had to admit that she said those very words herself. After staying silent for a few seconds she finally confessed, "You're right. You're right. It's going to take a while to get used to this but we're just going to have to accept it."

"Mom! Dad!" Rena called from downstairs. "We're ready!"

"Just like when they were babies, we needed to stay strong for them," Dylan said. "So let's go show them how much faith we have in them now and that we'll continue to remain strong for them."

Taking heed of her husband's comforting words, Katie strongly wised up and went downstairs where they both met their kids in the living room who were saying good-bye to some of the alligators.

"Too bad you guys can't come with us," Zachary said comforting Iris, Carl, and Darren. "We know you would love it."

"Maybe next time we'll talk Amber into bringing you guys with us," Rena said hugging Baxter and Diamond.

"Fat chance," Zachary groaned. "She doesn't even like them living with us."

"So do you guys have everything you need?" Katie asked.

"Yes mom," Rena said standing up properly positioning her backpack over her shoulders.

"Let me just make sure you have everything you need," Katie said unzipping Zachary's backpack rummaging through it.

"I'm pretty sure I do mom," he said.

A knock finally came at the front door. Dylan answered it seeing Amber nearly dressed the same way as she was yesterday.

"Are my kids ready?" Amber requested.

"Yes, OUR kids are ready," Dylan firmly stated.

Before Zachary and Rena stepped outside the house, they hugged their parents.

"You guys will be alright," Katie said hugging Rena while Dylan hugged Zachary. "Make sure to call the minute you guys get there, and anytime you feel like contacting us."

"I will mom, I promise," Rena said.

"You look after your sister now, you hear me," Dylan said to Zachary briefly ruffling his hair.

"I will dad," Zachary said straightening his hair back into place.

Once the two kids said their good-byes, they left the house heading inside a vehicle waiting for them near the sidewalk. The two parents stared heavily at Amber as she did the same to them.

"You better watch over them," Katie strictly ordered.

"They're my kids," Amber maintained. "You had them all these years. Now it's my turn to have my time with them."

"Just don't let anything happen to them," Dylan begged. "They've never been on a yacht before."

"Why would I let anything happen to them? I'm their mother," Amber scoffed.

"So you keep telling us," Katie moaned.

"I already gave you the details of the dock where we're departing," she told them. "The kids will call you when we make it there."

Amber then left the two worried parents without a moment's peace.

They watched her head inside her vehicle as she started the car. Their kids waved to them from the car window as they drove off leaving the area.

"I can't believe we let them go," Katie shivered.

"Just have faith honey," Dylan said massaging her shoulders. "Try not to let this anxiety get to you."

"Ugh, this is going to be harder than I thought," she complained walking back inside the house.

It was quite a long drive to the yacht but Amber eventually made it to their destination. After leaving the vehicle, the kids stood in awe to witness the sailboat for the very first time. Right next to the docks sitting in the water was a medium-sized yacht, a very luxurious one with enough room for at least fifteen or twenty people. As they slowly made their way to the dock, Zachary and Rena watched Amber run into the arms of a man they've never seen before. He seemed around the same age as Amber with short light brown hair and lovely blue sapphire eyes. He wore a cruise line attire to match for the perfect occasion.

"Well, well, well," he said looking down at the kids. "I'm glad you guys could make it."

"Kids this is my boyfriend Josh," Amber happily told them. "He's the one to thank for us going on this vessel. He was the one able to afford this yacht."

"Really?" Rena said fully amazed.

"Yeah well with money like mine, you do quite well with yourself over the years," he said with pride. "So I heard you kids like to swim because there's a swimming pool on deck and a little kitchen where we can serve you the best food."

"I can't wait," Rena happily squealed.

Zachary however was still melancholy about the whole situation, but at least tried to pretend to enjoy himself. "Yeah, sounds like fun."

After everyone got properly introduced, the four individuals gradually boarded the sailboat. Rena took great pleasure in searching through the yacht to find at least seven different cabins with small cramped windows. Some of the rooms might have been tight on space but they were at least comfortable and luxurious. Zachary tried his best remaining behind an excited Rena as she ventured through the different rooms.

"This is so cool!" she cried out.

"Rena will you stop running for a minute," Zachary shouted. "I need to call mom and dad letting them know we've made it here."

"Too bad they can't be here with us," Rena said placing her backpack on a bed in one of the rooms they temporarily took residence in.

"I know," Zachary said bringing out his cell phone dialing their number. After just the first ring, the phone was picked up. "Hi mom. Yeah, we're here. Yeah, I'm here with Rena. Okay. Okay, I'll tell Amber. Alright, I'll call you back in a little while. I will mom. I love you too. Bye."

"Kids where are you?!" Amber shouted from down the hallway.

"We're in here," Rena called back.

Coming into the bedroom, Amber displayed a bitter expression. "Don't run off like that without me knowing!"

"Sorry Amber," Rena said apologetically.

"Start calling me mom," she says. "That's who I am!"

"We're not used to you yet," Zachary made clear. "I told you yesterday it's going to take us a while."

Slowly calming down, Amber shifted her attitude back to a relaxed state. "Okay, I'm sorry," she said taking a seat next to Rena on the bed. "So do you like this room?"

"I guess so," Rena says a bit timid after the way Amber went off on them.

"Do you want it?"

"Yeah."

"Okay then, this is you and your brother's room," she announced. "Just don't go into any of the bedrooms because they're occupied."

"Great," Rena said feeling a lot better. "When can we go swimming?"

"In a little bit," Amber said. "For right now, the boat is about to take off. When we're out to sea then you guys can probably go swimming."

"I can't wait!" Rena cried out.

"Yeah, neither can I," Amber smiled.

35

After the yacht was set and ready since everyone was now onboard, it slowly took off leaving the docks. Amber brought Zachary and Rena out on deck near the swimming pool, as well as the ship's control panel where Amber's boyfriend was managing the steering wheel. The other only individuals aboard the sailboat were the housekeepers and cooks. The yacht took them further out to sea where the two children were able to witness the city getting smaller from afar while the water stretched far out wide. It was a mesmerizing experience the two deeply enjoyed and thought this was a good idea after all. The ocean was bright and beautiful with its inhabitants of fish and other marine life such as whales who would occasionally surface from the water showing off their gifted moves. It reminded Zachary and Rena of Jerry and really wished he could be here to see this. After taking in the sights, Zachary and Rena had permission to now swim in the pool as they changed into their swimsuits. Ironically the pool wasn't as big as the one back at their house but it didn't matter to them. They still had fun regardless. Amber herself was impressed by how good her kids were at swimming. It's almost as if this was destined to be their profession. It truly made a part of Amber punch herself in the gut for missing out on a big part of her kid's life. There was so much more to them that Dylan and Katie have prospered in such positive conduct over the years. A part of her was grateful, but at the same time, a part of her was still jealous unwilling to accept cartoon creatures raising her kids. After running out of energy, the two children called it quits for the day and got dressed back in their usual clothing. By then the evening stars began to take shape and the kids were told by Amber to return to their chosen bedroom where she'll have dinner shortly served to them.

Rena went running down the hallway nearly bumping into one of the ship's crewmember just passing by. She came into her and Zachary's room where she found him sitting on the bed just casually flipping through the channels on the TV with the remote.

"Zach what are you doing?" she said coming in.

"What does it look like I'm doing? I'm just trying to watch something on TV," he said impassively.

"Why are you sitting here watching TV when there's so much stuff we can do on this ship instead?"

"We already went swimming. Now I'm finished."

"Why do you have to be so negative? We came here to have a good time."

"No, you came here to have a good time. I never wanted to come," he argued.

"I just wanted to give Amber a chance and try something new for a change," Rena said trying to climb on the bed right next to him.

"Fine, as long as it doesn't involve me," he said emotionlessly turning his attention back to the television.

"Why are you acting this way when Amber is trying so hard to earn our love," Rena scowled. "Mom says people deserve a second chance and that's what we should do for Amber."

"I don't have to do anything for Amber after what she did to us!" Zachary retorted. "A mom should never throw her kids away no matter what. I'm not ready to give her a chance just yet. I still don't trust her."

"You're wrong."

"Maybe but it's my choice," he said turning back to the TV once more.

"Fine!" Rena said upsettingly at her brother's stubbornness. "I'll show you how wrong you are, then you'll be sorry."

With that Rena exited the room leaving Zachary alone with his thoughts. "Whatever," the irritable sibling groaned.

Rena traveled down the empty hallways of the yacht searching for Amber. She was hoping if she could get her and Zachary to talk, then maybe there would be less tension between them. After traveling around for a bit she thought she heard her on the second floor. Coming across one of the rooms, she heard Amber inside possibly talking with her boyfriend. Just as she was about to knock on the door she overheard, "We finally did it!" Not sure of what they were talking about, Rena decided to listen in on what they were saying.

"It took us long enough but we finally did it," her boyfriend said pouring a bottle of champagne in Amber's glass.

"Yes we did. It's just smooth sailing from here on out," she smiled kissing him deeply on the lips as they sat together on their bed.

"Not just yet," he told her sitting up. "We still need to head across the border. Once we make it to Mexico, we won't have anything to worry about. If they even try to come looking for us, it'll be like hunting for a needle in a haystack."

"You don't know how hard it was to just sit here watching Dylan and Katie raise my kids after all this time. Playing the good girl act by getting a job and going to church on Sundays literally made me sick to my stomach. I don't know why you couldn't just pay me instead?"

"Hey, we had to make it look good. Now you can kiss that job and going to church good-bye forever."

"But going to court was a big waste of time since I didn't even win custody of my children," she argued.

"Like hell it was. We agreed that was our first plan on getting your kids back, and if that didn't work, then we'd resort with phase two on kidnapping them instead. You may not have gained custody of them, but it sure felt good bringing those two assholes to court just to humiliate them. And now that you got your kids back, this is the most justifying pleasure of all."

"They certainly didn't have a clue," Amber chuckled. "The only reason I was able to convince them was because Rena was so gullible wanting to come along. But I know when the kids find out, they're not going to take this news very well."

"Heh, who cares what they think," he said turning her over to kiss her. "You are their mother and like it or not, they're going to have to get used to it either way."

As the two engaged into a passionate kiss, Rena who overheard everything felt nothing but absolute betrayal and terror at the same time. She couldn't believe how naïve she was. All she cared about was giving her biological mom a second chance. Now feeling nothing but hurt and treachery, all Rena could do was cry in soft sobs. Her mind raced at a fast pace while her heart felt like leaping out of her chest from this new trauma which now threatened her and her brother. Understanding the danger she and Zachary were in, she quickly ran all the way back to their bedroom. When she made it inside she slammed the door shut causing Zachary to jump from fright.

"Geez! What's your problem Rena?"

"Shhhh!" Rena quietly whispered crawling on the floor beside the bed.

"What's the matter with you?"

"Zachary, you were right," she cried.

"Right about what?" he said crawling on the floor next to her.

Clutching her legs against her chest, Rena softly cried on her knees unable to control her emotions. "I'm sorry Zachary. I should've listened to you."

"What are you talking about?" he said trying to comfort her.

"I—I—I just heard Amber and her boyfriend. They said they're taking us away."

"What?!" Zachary said a bit puzzled.

"They said they're taking us to Mexico away from mommy and daddy. They're kidnapping us. They also said if I wasn't so gullible then we wouldn't be here. This is all my fault."

Zachary consoled his baby sister hugging her tight as she wept a pool of tears. "Don't cry," he said delicately. "This isn't your fault Rena. The only thing we can do is call the police."

"No please call mommy and daddy first, then call the police," Rena begged.

"Okay, okay, I will," Zachary said going to his backpack pulling out his cell phone dialing the number.

After two rings, Katie picks up the phone. "Hi Zachary, are you two having fun?"

Zachary puts the phone on speaker so she can hear them both. "Mommy! Please help us," Rena cries.

Picking up on the scared tone in her child's voice, Katie immediately panics saying, "Whoa what's wrong sweetie? What's going on?"

"Mommy you were right about Amber and I'm sorry," Rena couldn't stop crying.

"Mom, Rena said she overheard Amber and her boyfriend say they're taking us to Mexico," Zachary stated.

"Well that's what you do on a yacht honey, you travel the world by sea…" Katie tried desperately to rationalize with young Zach after all her nerves had been rattled the entire day.

"No mom, you don't understand, they're kidnapping us!" Zach almost broke down in tears.

"What?!" Katie screamed. Hearing the shout from the other room, Dylan came running beside his wife.

"Kids! Kids are you okay?" Dylan cried out.

"Daddy, please come and take us home," Rena wept. "I want to go home."

"Don't worry guys, we're coming for you," Katie assure them. "Can you give us the name of the boat you're on so we can tell the police where to find you?"

"We didn't see a name mom," Zachary said. "The boat we're on is just white."

"You mean there's no name on the yacht?" Katie shrieked.

"Please mommy, daddy, just come and get us," Rena frantically cried out.

"Don't worry kids, we're going to come and get you," Dylan tried his best calming them.

"Until we do you guys just hang tight," Katie instructed. "We're going to call the police and come down there ourselves."

The door to the bedroom was suddenly slammed open by Amber and her boyfriend. The two terrified children dropped the cell phone to the floor holding on to each other tightly as the two adults approached them.

"Who are you talking to?!" Amber demanded.

Unable to answer, the two kids just stayed locked in a firm embrace not knowing what Amber or her boyfriend planned on doing. Amber looked to the floor hearing Katie's voice from the phone screaming, "Zachary! Rena! Answer me!"

Before Amber could pick it up, her boyfriend retrieved it instead.

"Hello! Hello! Zachary, Rena please answer me!" Katie bellowed.

"Hello Katie."

"Who is this?!"

"Don't you remember me? It's Vincent Blake," he revealed.

The two creatures stood dumfounded feeling both their stomachs drop after hearing this shocking revelation.

"I know how you guys must feel about me, I mean after all I was intoxicated that night behind the wheel," he casually said. "I was just having a bad day that night. You guys may have lost a child but I lost my status because of you two. I was doing well with my career until you two had to drag me to court and spread my name all over the papers. You don't know how excruciating it is, always having to take the bus and catching Ubers! Doing shitty community service for five damn years! The mayor cut ties with me and everyone in my law firm shunned me, barring me from my practice… I was an outcast! I was treated like shit thanks to you two. My reputation was ruined. Going through the hell that you guys put me through might as well have been prison. I decided to bide my time and make sure you guys suffer the same way as I have. After seeing the popularity you two had gained for yourselves after adopting these kids, I'm the one who contacted Amber. It's because of me why she wanted to get back into her kid's lives. I'm the one who helped her get clean and find a job to obtain the reputation she needed to win her kids back. It was also I who contacted Miss Waters. Why do you think it was she who represented Amber in court?"

Right on cue, Chloe came in the room as well revealing she was a passenger on this yacht all along. She came alongside Vincent and briefly held the phone in her hand saying, "Hello Katie. Hello Dylan. I guess the gig is up. It was fun while it lasted."

Taking the phone back to talk, Vincent continued on, "As I was saying, we decided it would be best to keep you two worried and guessing what happened to your kids but now that you know the truth, it's probably best this way. It's worth the same satisfaction to know how I defeated you and you'll be able to suffer the same humiliation as I have. You should've known better than to mess with people like me."

"You son of a bitch!" Katie yelled. "If you so much as touch our kids we'll…"

"You'll what Katie," Vincent snickered. "By the time you call the police or coast guard, we'll be long gone. We already got a head start all day and we're in the middle of the ocean. My yacht is unlicensed so no one would be looking for us. By the time the police do find our boat, we'll be in Mexico. I wish I could see the look on your guy's faces as we relish in the comfort of defeating you. It might have taken all this time but it was well worth it. Sayonara my dear Katie. See ya Dylan."

After hanging up Vincent destroyed Zachary's cell phone. Amber then went through Rena's backpack and destroyed her cell phone as well. The three adults looked down at the two frightened children just chuckling to themselves from the victory in which they relished.

36

Now faced with a new threat of an old nemesis, Katie and Dylan were petrified out of their minds for Zachary and Rena.

"AHHHHHH! FUCK!" Katie screamed hysterically. "How could I have been so stupid? I should've known!"

"Katie none of us ever would have known Vincent was behind this," Dylan said grabbing the cell phone. "I'm calling the cops."

"Screw the cops, I've got to get over there right now!" Katie cried about to race across the room until Dylan stopped her.

"Katie listen to me, I know you're worried and so am I but we still have to call the police," he said.

"What are they going to do? You heard what that asshole said. He said by the time we get the police or the coast guard over there, it'll be too late."

"That may be but they still need to know."

"How? They're not going to believe us against a well-known attorney who's been plotting against us with our greatest adversary after all these years. Besides they'll just say it'll be their word against ours."

"Not after they hear what Vincent has to say for himself," he said showing Katie the minute Vincent answered the phone Dylan cleverly pressed record. Vincent's entire confession was being told and it was enough evidence to back them up.

"Great thinking baby," Katie said giving him a quick hug. "But I'm sorry, I'm not just going to sit here until the cops show up. I want to find my babies."

"And we will," he assured her. "Here's what we'll do. I'll call Shelley or Brandon seeing if one of them could come over. I'll tell them what happened and to call the police showing them the evidence on the cell phone by leaving it here. We'll go look for Zachary and Rena ourselves."

Very much liking the idea, Katie happily agreed. They suddenly had the alligators coming near their feet as if they were informing them they wanted to come also.

"What? You guys want to help us find the kids too?" Dylan said.

The alligators responded by opening their mouths and growling. Oblivious to everything that has just happened, Jerry shoved his upper body through the sliding screen door shouting, "Feed me!"

"Not now Jerry!" Katie snapped. "Zachary and Rena have been kidnapped."

"What the hell are you talking about?" he said thunderstruck.

"It turns out that their so-called mom has planned on kidnapping them with the help of that no good Chloe and Vincent!" Katie revealed.

"Chloe and Vincent? As in the same Vincent who was the drunk driver that killed your guys' baby years ago?" Jerry said taken aback.

"Yeah, they're all in on it and they took Zachary and Rena away on a yacht," Katie said. "We're going to find them right now."

"Well then count me in too," Jerry said squeezing his whole body through the screen door.

"Jerry you can't come too," Dylan said.

"Hey am I part of this family or not!" he retorted. "I love Zachary and Rena just as much as you guys do. I remember how small they were when you guys left me to babysit them at that time. I protected them from that burglar and I want to protect them again. I always swam with them in the pool, keeping them from drowning, helping guide them, lifting their spirits. And that's a bonding experience I will never have again without them. This is not up for debate. I'm coming with you."

After hearing Jerry's determination, there was no way Dylan and Katie were going to refuse his request.

"Okay then, I guess we're all going," Dylan says to everyone.

Eager to get their family back as safe as possible, everyone scurried out to their vehicle parked outside in the driveway. Dylan drove on the driver's seat while Katie sat in the passenger's seat. All the gators were cram jammed in the backseat while Jerry was sticking out in the trunk barely fitting in.

"Oh crap, I hope this will be a short trip," Jerry complained barely managing to get comfortable.

As Dylan drove he gave Katie his cell phone to call Shelley and Brandon telling them about everything while they left Katie's cell phone at home as evidence for the cops. While the family rushed as fast as they could do the docks, Zachary during this time was trying his best to comfort his crying sister. Ever since Vincent got off the phone with Dylan and Katie, Rena couldn't stop tearing up.

"Will you shut that damn kid up!" Vincent shouted strolling back and forth around the small room.

"She's just a little girl," Amber told him. "Why don't you calm down."

"Don't tell me what to do," he said threateningly pointing his index finger in her face. "All my life, people have been telling me what to do. Well no more."

"No one is telling you what to do baby," she said placing her hands on Vincent's cheeks. "You just need to relax a bit."

"The only reason I tagged along with you guys is to see this plan play out since we were all in on it," Chloe declared. "You know by the time you guys reach Mexico, we go our separate ways and you pay me what you owe me. I'm not looking for a fugitive life in a different region. I still got my reputation which greatly sustains me."

"Not if Dylan and Katie tell the cops you were in on this," Amber pointed out.

"No one is going to believe them," she brushed off. "I'm one of the most prosperous lawyers around here with a lot of connections. Why do you think I come highly recommended and got away with winning so many cases in the past?"

"That would make two of us if it weren't for Dylan and Katie ruining my reputation," Vincent scoffed. "Don't worry, by the time my money pulls through, I'll give you your final payments. It should be ready by the time we reach Mexico."

"Please take us back home," Rena tearfully cried.

"You guys are never going back to Dylan and Katie," Amber exclaimed. "I'm your mother and you guys will start listening to me from now on."

"You're not our mother," Zachary scowled upsettingly.

"You're going to have to start teaching them brats some manners," Vincent proclaimed rolling his eyes. "I'm not going to be staying with you if they're going to be this complicated."

"Don't worry baby," Amber assures him. "They'll learn their lesson."

"Good, cause we still got a long way to go and I'm hungry," Vincent said leaving the room with Chloe.

Amber looked at her kids not feeling the least bit guilty for kidnapping them, believing they were her personal property, but still couldn't help feeling sorry for how distressed they were. "I'm going to get you guys something to eat. You stay here and don't cause any trouble."

Once she left the room, Rena continued crying against her brother's shoulder as he continued consoling her.

"Rena it'll be okay," he told her.

"I want mommy and daddy," she sniveled wiping her nose and the tears away from her eyes.

"And they'll come for us," he assured her. "They won't stop until they find us."

"But what if they don't?"

Fearing just the same thing, Zachary quickly rummaged through his backpack hoping there was something useful. Other than his clothes, he equally found his alligator plush toy. Not remember packing it, he figured Katie must have put him in there without his knowledge. Just the thought of his mother thinking of him this way while he studied his favorite toy gave Zachary the encouragement he needed.

"Remember what mom and dad always told us. To remain strong. Like—like remember that story mom told us with the two cats?"

"Yeah," she sniffed. "I told her the same thing yesterday."

"Before I didn't quite understand but now I do. Mom said stories are good sources of motivation and we have to be those two cats now. It may be rough but as long as we stick together, we'll get through this mess."

"But what if mom and dad won't find this boat and we're too far away for them to find us?"

Zachary stands up and looks outside for a moment seeing they were still in the middle of the ocean. It was hard to make anything out at night but from Zachary's perspective, he could've sworn he saw land further away. It was nearly impossible for anyone to swim from this distance, but if they kept going in this direction, Zachary believed he and Rena could make it to shore.

"Well, we're going to have to jump," he told her.

"What? No!" Rena objected.

"Listen Rena, we both know how good we are at swimming. We swim with Jerry and the alligators all the time. I know we could do this."

"But we're in the middle of nowhere."

"No, look," Zachary said bringing his sister up to look out the window. "I think that's land over there. We'll wait until the boat gets closer then when the time is right, we'll jump and swim to shore."

"I don't know," Rena shivered.

"If we want mom and dad to find us, then we're going to have to try and get away," he explained to her. "We need to do this together and be strong, for mom and dad. Will you try?"

Sensitive Rena was terrified more than anything but was willing to try as long as they had a fighting chance of getting back to Dylan and Rena. "Okay. Okay, I'll try," she said taking a hold of her brother's hand tightly.

37

Finally making it to the same docks Amber took off with the kids from earlier, Dylan and Katie had arrived parking their vehicle near the area. The docks were empty and isolated. No one was around, not even a boat or coast guard insight which is precisely why Vincent and Amber solely chose this dock in particular. The only sound that could be heard was the water being gently rocked back and forth against the pier.

"Damn it!" Katie screamed. "Not even a boat is here for us to take. What are we going to do now?"

"What are you two waiting for," Jerry said leaving the trunk and hobbled his way to the pier until he dropped into the water. "Hop on."

"What? You're expecting us to ride you?" Dylan said.

"How else are we going to catch up with them? Now get on before we lose them for good," Jerry ordered.

Unwilling to argue with their pet shark, the two anxious parents hopped onto Jerry's back and held on tight to his primary dorsal fin. Right as Jerry took off, the alligators immediately followed in suit. They jumped into the water and swam alongside Jerry at a fast pace. The desperation to get their family back has caused the shark and gators to swim rapidly like they never have before. Even Dylan and Katie had to hold on tight from slipping or falling off. They knew they had to catch up as much as possible from all the daybreak they've wasted not knowing how far they could be.

"Are you sure you can keep this up Jerry?!" Dylan shouted. "We might have a long way to go!"

"You guys just hang on and don't worry about me," he proclaimed. "You two just lookout for any signs of boats ahead."

Back on the yacht, Zachary and Rena tried their best to bide their time waiting for the right moment to escape. Until then they were being watched by the servants and cooks, who turned out to be Vincent's bodyguards. They warily watched them in their bedroom until Amber came back with a tray of food. She excused the guards as she set the food down on the bed ordering her kids to eat.

"I'm not hungry," Rena said.

"Come on now, you kids need to eat," Amber insisted.

"After everything that has happened, do you really think we're in the mood to eat anything," Zachary stated.

"Fine, whatever," Amber said rolling her eyes. "I understand you kids dislike what I'm doing but what you need to realize is that I'm your real mother and you belong to me. No court order should justify who you should stay with or who should raise you. And I'll be damned if I'm going to let you guys be raised by some damn creatures. You guys are my own flesh and blood, my family!"

"A mom is someone who is always there to take care of their kids and who loves them," Zachary made clear. "You never did any of that."

"Look here damn it!" she yelled losing her temper as she rammed her hand on the tray. She then pulled up her shirt revealing something to them that possibly no one knew of, other than Dylan and Katie. She revealed a severe red-pinkish scar leaving an everlasting reminder of the day her mother threw boiling water on her. She suffered severe damage to her skin which could've led to life-threatening issues but luckily survived through it. "This is the harsh truth of reality!" she shrieked covering herself back up. "I had a screwed up childhood with parents who didn't give a shit about me. No one is perfect in this world and you can't expect me to be so ideal just like Dylan and Katie. Life isn't full of sunshine and roses and white picket fences. This is the real world! It's cruel and it's ugly so wake up! I deserve my chance of happiness in this hellish existence and by God, I'm getting it. You two are the only things I have left in this world and no one is going to take that away from me. You two belong to me, understand!"

Zachary didn't say anything as Rena started to whimper crying a bit. Losing her temper once more seeing this conversation wasn't getting them anywhere, Amber got up tossing the tray of food all over the floor.

"Fine!" she shouted leaving the room. "Eat it on the floor for all I care, at least tried."

When Amber left the two kids alone, Rena looked at her brother saying, "Mommy and daddy would never treat us like this. Why is she so mean?"

"Because she just told us," Zachary said realizing the root of Amber's problems. "Her parents were mean so she is too. I actually feel sorry for her. But I don't want to turn out like her. I want to choose to be different because mom and dad raised us with love and care." Getting up he looked back towards the window. "We're still a little far away. We gotta wait a little longer."

"I hope we'll be able to make it," Rena prayed.

"We will," he said confidently.

Zachary was still young just like his sister but, indeed, Dylan and Katie's determination had truly rubbed off on him over the years. And he was putting it to good use by gaining enough courage to help him and his little sister.

A little bit later the two children were forced to leave their bedroom and head back on deck with Amber and Vincent while Chloe was somewhere else within one of the cabins. Zachary and Rena nervously held hands as they sat on beach chairs watching the two adults drink to another bottle of champagne.

"I can only imagine the pain and suffering of what those two freaks are going through right now," Vincent chuckled amusingly while embracing Amber around her waist.

"Yeah, they're probably calling the cops right now and are going out of their minds," Amber giggled.

"A justifying revenge I've been looking forward to," he said kissing her around the neck. He could genuinely feel the buzz impacting his state of mind, feeling empowered and driven. "Pretty soon we'll be living the high life while we'll watch those two on social media going over the grief of their two lost kids."

While they chattered in their drunken state, Zachary kept his eyes towards the water. He possibly saw their chance coming and whispered over to his sister saying, "When they're not looking, we're going to have to jump."

"Now?" she whispered back to him.

"It's now or never," he said.

"To the human race!" Vincent happily shouted raising his glass of champagne in the air.

"To the human race!" Amber repeated. "And damn all those creatures to hell."

"Amen to that," he humorously chuckled.

Figuring he and Amber were watching the kids, Vincent didn't bother telling any of his guards to monitor the children. Zachary witnessed how drunk the two adults were getting as they paid less attention to them. Since none of the bodyguards were around to watch them, Zachary quietly took his sister by the hand walking over to the railing, the only thing that was separating them from falling off the ledge of the yacht. Zachary helped his sister carefully climb over the railing first, then shortly followed her. Their hearts began pounding against their chests as their feet balanced on the ledge looking below at the rough waves from the sailboat's motor. It was absolute tension, keeping them from making the right decision to jump. Rena shook her head doubtful if she was able to do this.

"I can't do it," she cried.

"Listen to me Rena, we got this okay," he swore to her. "Remember that first time we dived into our swimming pool. Ever since then, everyone always told us we were good at swimming. We can do this."

The confidence from her brother was enough to reassure her a little, although she was still utterly terrified. "You promise you won't let go."

"Just like in mom's story, I'm not leaving your side," he promised her. "Now let's do this."

"Okay," she said gripping his hand.

"Here we go," he said. "One, two…"

"Kids! Get down from there!" Amber shouted finally catching sight of what they were about to do.

"Three!" Rena shouted as she and Zachary jumped into the cold awaiting ocean.

The two adults watched in horror as the children leaped from the yacht dropping directly into the water below.

"Son of a bitch!" Vincent shouted as he and Amber ran to the railing where the kids jumped from.

They worriedly looked over the edge to see if they could spot the kids resurface from the water but there was no sign of them.

"We gotta go and jump after them!" Amber frantically cried.

"We're not jumping," Vincent angrily declared clutching her by the arm.

"We can't just leave them!"

"I'll get my men to go after them," he insisted as he called out his bodyguards on deck. "Turn this boat around! We need to circle the area where they jumped."

One of the guards took control of the ship using the control panel to turn it around. They circled the same location but couldn't find any signs of Zachary or Rena. One guard turned on the searchlight attached to the yacht in case of emergencies. They continued scanning within the same area but still couldn't locate them.

"No sign of them," one guard shouted.

"Jump in after them!" Amber screamed with hysteria.

Putting on lifejackets, two guards jumped into the water doing their best in search of the kids.

"I don't understand," Amber cried. "How could they do something so stupid?!"

"Maybe they take the same traits from their mother," Vincent remarked. "We all know how screwed up in the head you were."

"You bastard!" Amber angrily reacted by viciously slapping him across the face. "Don't ever talk that way about me or my children again."

"Your so-called children just put a damp on our plans," Vincent said painfully restraining her by the hair. "We won't only be fugitives on the run, we'll be wanted for kidnapping and possibly murder. I'm not going to jail over this because of your dumb ass kids trying to commit suicide. Now you either get your shit together if you want to find them alive."

In pain from his constant pulling, Amber timidly shook her head in compliance.

"Good," he said finally letting her go. "Oh and Amber, if you ever hit me like that again—I'll kill you."

After that sinister warning, Vincent walked off leaving the vulnerable woman alone. Standing paralyzed in fear not realizing how unpredictable this man truly was, she was now starting to regret this whole situation.

Further away from the yacht, Zachary and Rena were able to swim a great distance to safety. At first, it was challenging from the first jump. They were practically sucked into the boat's steel propellers making it nearly impossible to escape from. The suction underwater was a strenuous struggle which felt like being sucked into a giant vortex. For a moment Zachary tried getting his bearings together once the countless bubbles cleared from his sight. Finally spotting a clear opening, he and his sister forcefully swam away from the dangerous propellers. It was a scary close call but keeping true to his word, Zachary held tight onto Rena's hand the whole time and aggressively pulled them both away to safety. The kids first watched as the sailboat passed them, then carefully ascended to the surface. Fresh air filled their lungs after holding their breath for what seemed to be an eternity, and the two aggressively used their best skills to paddle away.

"Swim Rena, swim!" he declared while out of breath.

All their hard work and training was evident as it helped them get further away from Vincent and Amber where they wouldn't be able to find them. Until they were tired out, the desperate children kept swimming until they reached ashore nearby.

"Good job Rena," Zachary said as he swerved his arms and kicked his feet into overtime. "Just keep going."

"I will," she replied keeping up with him.

While the two children were trying to flee with their lives, Dylan and the others were just a couple of yards away and had miraculously found their way to the yacht.

"I think we found them!" Jerry happily shouted.

"Good job Jerry," Katie told him through splashing waves. "I just hope we're not too late."

Dylan carefully leaned near the water and told the alligators, "Guys. Spread out and survey the area." With that order, the alligators separated from the group, branching off in different directions.

"Jerry, get us as close as you can near the boat," Katie directed.

The shark kept up with his swift velocity until he was able to get Dylan and Katie close enough to the yacht. Once he did, the two spotted a rope from the dock bollard that was the perfect object for them to use enabling to board the vessel. Katie wrapped her arms securely around Dylan's neck staying glued to his back while he clutched onto the rope. As he held on tight, Jerry was finally able to fall back trying to regain his strength from all that hasty swimming he's done for the past hour. Dylan and Katie were able to sneak on board without being noticed thanks to the ruckus still taking place after the kid's absence. As he climbed his way over the railing, Katie first hopped on the yacht then carefully helped Dylan over. Unaware of the children jumping ship, the two parents' sole mission was to find Zachary and Rena.

"What are we going to do if we find them?" Dylan whispered.

"If? When we find them, we're going to get them the hell out of here," Katie whispered back in a harsher tone. "That's what we're going to do."

"I know but we're out in the middle of nowhere and even if we do get the kids out of here, do you honestly think they can take this long journey back? And who knows what we're going up against on this boat?" he said worriedly.

"Dylan, the way I'm feeling right now after these assholes abducted our kids, I'm in no mood for negotiation," she scowled at him. "I don't care who or what we're up against, but we're getting our kids back regardless of the situation. Do you understand me?"

"Yeah sure baby, whatever you say," he said timidly.

"Now here's what we'll do, we'll split up and search all over this ship for them," she instructed. "Then we'll meet up back here in this exact spot."

"Wait honey, I thought splitting up was a bad idea… especially in thriller and horror movies," he quietly commented.

She gave him one last look as an annoying expression then simply rolled her eyes disappearing down the hallway.

"Well, it suddenly feels like a thriller movie to me," Dylan shrugged his shoulders as he went in the opposite direction.

He carefully walked down the empty hallways trying to remain inconspicuous. He warily searched at the multiple doors that had small windows to them trying to peek inside one of them. A guard who suddenly came running in his direction would've seen him if he hadn't swiftly dodged into the next room by quickly opening the door. Staying crouched down against the floor until the guard moved on, he stayed quiet and motionless. After a bit, he was able to gradually perk his head up scanning the window from the door. He didn't see anyone and presumed the coast was clear. Dylan carefully clutched the doorknob about to open the door, until a blunt object struck him across the head from behind, rendering him unconscious. If he wisely looked behind him this whole time, he would've realized it was Chloe's room he was in. Shocked at Dylan's presence, she grabbed the closest object which was a small statue and used it as her weapon.

"Well, well, well," she chuckled looking down at an unconscious Dylan right next to her feet. "Look who happened to show up in my room."

38

Unaware of Dylan's predicament, Katie continued searching the hallways on the second floor. She carefully peeked into the first door she came across. Finding nothing but an empty room, she carried on further down. After opening the next door, she found the room that Zachary and Rena were staying in. She immediately noticed their backpacks on the floor and entered the room. Cautiously closing the door behind her, she ran over to the bed looking underneath it.

"Zachary, Rena," she whispered. "It's mommy. Are you guys in here?"

Next, she checked the nearest closet but still found nothing. She felt her heart break after no such luck of finding her kids. She then bent down near their backpacks looking at whatever items they have left. She recognized Zachary's plush alligator toy she packed earlier as it pulled on her heartstrings. The sensitive creature felt her emotions fluctuating as she held the toy in front of her face crying tears of pain. It was the same pain she felt when she and Dylan lost their baby that horrific night. To make matters worse, they were dealing with the very perpetrator who did it, feeling like déjà vu all over again. He already took one child from them. She'll be damned if he'll take Zachary and Rena from them as well. Breaking free of her emotions, Katie suddenly heard footsteps coming down the hallway. Thinking fast she squeezed her way underneath the bed. It was tight but she was able to fit. The only problem was her tail since it was bigger but she was able to squeeze it in with her. She couldn't see who it was as the footsteps entered the room but recognized the voices as Vincent and Amber.

"Stop blaming me for all this!" Amber shrieked. "I never knew they would do this!"

"You should've kept a better eye on them," he retorted. "You are their mother."

"I was distracted and so were you. How was I supposed to know they'd jump?!"

Katie's heart leaped up to her throat after hearing this news. She couldn't believe Zachary and Rena jumped off the yacht. She had to fight all the strength within her to keep herself from crawling out from under the bed and attacking her rivals right then and there. She mentally prayed over and over to the Lord for her kid's safety. She had faith knowing how well they are at swimming and hopefully Jerry or one of the alligators will find them, but overall she still couldn't stop worrying about them.

"It's funny how well Dylan and Katie took care of them after all this time, yet when they're around you, you can't keep a hold of them," Vincent mocked.

"So is this your game," Amber said crossing her arms against her chest. "Just to sit up here and criticize me of how I raise my children."

"If we're able to find them through some dumb blind luck, what makes you think you could watch them going forward once we make it to our destination?"

"This time I'm sure," she makes clear although it wasn't enough to convince him.

"Yeah, whatever Amber," he scoffs.

"I mean it Vincent!" she yells. "I'm not going to be as reckless as I was before."

"I need another bottle of champagne—and a beer," Vincent casually said shoving Amber aside to leave the room.

"Don't walk away from me!" Amber shrieked following him. "My kids could be drowning out there and all you could do is drink at a time like this!"

Once the two were gone, Katie finally came back out. "Those idiots are so screwed up in the head, they can't watch their own asses. Now my children are lost out there. God, I pray Jerry or one of the alligators will find them. I got to find Dylan and tell him what happened."

When Dylan finally came to, he found himself in a room which almost seemed pink with a red texture. Feeling sore due to whatever hit him across the head, he reached over to rub it but was suddenly restrained. Looking at his claws, he realized they were handcuffed to the headboard of the bed he found himself lying on. He looked on in terror trying to pry himself free, but couldn't get loose all while discovering his feet were handcuffed as well. His mouth was equally muzzled with a belt, mostly on the side where he couldn't open it wide enough but was still able to speak.

"Hey what is this?!" his cries were muffled.

"So I see you're finally awake now," Chloe said poking her head from the bathroom across the bed.

"Chloe! What the hell are you doing?!" he shrieked.

"I've been looking forward to this moment for a very long time," she wickedly smiled coming out from the bathroom.

Dylan's eyes widened in horror to witness the devious woman dressed in nothing but a black bikini. The bra was a skinny strap micro triangle bikini top while the panties were a skinny dipping strap thong. The image of a siren who was seductive and tempting but not enough to deceive Dylan. It turned his stomach in disgust to witness what she was about to attempt.

"Chloe, whatever you're about to do, you better put those sick delusions back into that psychotic head of yours," he growled. "I won't tell anyone what you're about to do if you'll just let me and Katie get our kids back."

"You're right because you won't tell anyone about this," she remarked casually making her way over to him on the bed.

"I can't believe you're actually thinking of doing something this sick while my kid's lives are in danger because of you people!" he shouted. "How could you guys do this?"

"Rejection is the one thing we don't take too well to," she said. "No man has ever denied me in bed. I guess that makes you the first. I promised myself until I got you where you're at right now, I wouldn't let you go."

"Chloe! I am not a man! I'm a creature! We creatures don't go screwing around with you humans. It's immoral, depraved, and along with the levels of bestiality. Half of you humans are sick thinking this is okay which it's not. This is not the way God designed things. You humans just twist his program to your own benefit and turn it into a disease which is why the earth is so messed up."

"I don't care about your moral lectures. All I care about is what I want. The truth is Dylan, you can keep fooling yourself believing if you do the right thing you'll come out alright in the end, but we live a world that doesn't care about honesty anymore. You're the one who's always been messed up and delusional."

"There's no use convincing people like you. You're already too far gone. Now I'm not going to tell you again Chloe, let me go! I'm not going to lie here and play these sick sex games with you while my kids are God knows where!"

"Sorry Dylan but this time you don't get to tell me what to do. I would've had my way with you a long time ago if you and your wife weren't so difficult all the time."

"What do you mean?" he said confused.

"Oh take a hint you clueless dork," she scoffed rolling her eyes to the ceiling. "You couldn't even catch any of the signs from the first time you met me. I only took your case to get closer to you. All those times I called you after the case was over wasn't even an indication. Hell that time I was finally able to get you to go out and eat with me, I planned on drugging you."

"You what!" Dylan yelled in shock.

"I would've gotten away with it too if it weren't for that bitch you call a wife to show up and ruin everything."

"You take that back!" he retorted.

The conniving woman chuckled amusingly at Dylan's hopelessness to get away. "You look so cute, even when you're angry. I know I'm going to enjoy this."

"I doubt that," Dylan sighed in defeat throwing his head back against the pillow. "You humans just don't learn."

"Oh I'm about to learn a few things alright," she said crawling directly on top of him. His body shivered from Chloe's flesh making contact with his. Thinking it couldn't get any worse, she took the apprehensive creature by surprise giving him a deep kiss right on the lips. Dylan reacted by snatching his head away from her spitting in disgust.

"It's strawberry flavor. You don't like it?" she grinned.

"It's you I don't like," he growled at her. "Don't you understand I'm only dedicated to my wife! I'm not attracted to humans, especially sick delusional people like you!"

"Sick," she chuckled. "I'll show you just how sick I can be. So, where's your package?"

"Hidden where you can't find it," he scowled looking at her directly in the face.

Smoothly running her hands up to his chest, she worked them all the way down between his legs then squeezed tight. "Ahh, there it is."

"Don't do this Chloe," he cringed. "Creatures of my kind just won't work with you humans."

"Try me," she smiled squeezing him tighter. "I'm up for new things. I want to experience your creature's wild side."

"You really want to know?"

"Give it to me," she insisted kissing him on the lips.

"Let me go and I'll show you."

"You don't think I'm that stupid do ya? You're just going to have to improvise."

"Okay, you asked for it," he said.

Luckily she didn't restrain his tail, so he was able to move it which was hidden underneath his body this whole time. It moved near Chloe's backside removing her panties. He watched the aroused state she was now in, expecting something beyond her wildest dreams. His tail slowly raised itself in the air and aimed high. Like an arrow, it directly inserted itself inside of Chloe's butthole. He used it the same way as a pleasurable experience when connecting with his wife, however for Chloe, instead of feeling arousing pleasure as she expected, she felt as if a knife had just penetrated her insides. Widening her eyes in shock, the senseless woman screamed her head off in severe pain.

"Get it out! Get it out!" she shrieked.

"I told you so," he said releasing his tail from her. "As I said, you humans never learn."

Chloe fell off the bed still screaming in pain as she curled up on the floor like a round donut. Katie who was wandering the hallways heard the scream nearby. She came directly into the room after recognizing the voice belonged to Chloe.

"Katie, thank God," Dylan said in relief.

"What the devil is going on around here?" she said bewildered by the whole situation seeing Dylan restrained on the bed while Chloe was partially naked crying on the floor.

"Chloe tried having her way with me," he said. "I guess she had to learn the hard way."

"Stupid bitch, I outta..." Katie growled attempting to lunge and attack the defenseless woman but was stopped by Dylan.

"Katie no! I think she's already learned her lesson. Besides, we should save our energy by looking for the kids instead."

Katie reluctantly agreed as she found the keys to the handcuffs and set her husband free. "Don't you humans know it just doesn't work with you and us? What did you do to her by the way?"

"As much as I hated it, I only stuck my tail up her ass," he revealed.

"Haaa! You're just lucky he only used his tail cause you don't want to know what it feels like to have us inside of you."

"Yeah," Dylan said rubbing his wrist from where the cuffs were tightened. "We feel the same pleasure when we make love with our kind but if you humans even attempt to try with us, it feels like your insides are being destroyed. That's why it's immoral. If I were you Chloe, I'd wear diapers for a while and sit on pillow hemorrhoid cushions before you'll fully recover."

From the massive pain she was still struggling with, Chloe only responded by saying, "Son of a bitch."

"That's what you get for coming between me and my husband," Katie remarked as she watched Dylan run straight to the bathroom. "Where are you going?"

"I'm going to wash my tail!" he cried out.

39

It might have been a long swim, but Zachary and Rena had finally made it to the closest shore nearby. Tired and exhausted the two children collapsed on shrubs of grass around the shoreline. The area they came across had multiple trees exhibiting the region as a wilderness. Excessively fatigued to care where they were at, Zachary and Rena continued relaxing a bit trying to catch their breaths.

"We did it Zach," Rena inhaled and exhaled.

"Yeah, I told you we got this," Zachary said a little relieved.

Finally taking a look at their surroundings, the two children had no idea where they were.

"Where are we?" Rena questioned.

"I don't know," Zachary said standing up. "But if we're going to find a way to get help, then we better continue on."

Zachary held onto his sister's hand as he helped her up. The two were about to journey into the woods until they heard a random noise that spooked them.

"Shhh! Did you hear that?" Rena whispered.

"I think so," Zachary said vigilantly.

The two kids carefully tried not to make any noise but the tension of the dark woods in this type of atmosphere was enough to put anyone on edge. Hearing the sound of twigs breaking and snapping, Zachary and Rena cautiously stood still as the hairs stood upon their backs. After a moment of silence, the kids could swear the only sound they heard was their beating hearts. Before taking another step, the culprit turned out to be a random alligator. Nowhere was this alligator related to their family, it was indeed a wild one and it had every intension on attacking the two vulnerable kids. Rena frighteningly fell backwards unable to get back up as the vicious predator made his way towards her. Zachary tried pulling her up but by then the alligator was already upon them with his mouth wide open. Closing their eyes preparing for the worst, they couldn't even predict what happened next. Another random alligator shot directly in the path of the kids and clamped his mouth directly on the wild gator. Opening their eyes in astonishment, they were surprised to see it was Markus; their alligator. In the nick of time, he came to their rescue as he wrestled against the other alligator.

"Markus!" the kids happily shouted.

From behind them another random wild gator slowly made his advance to the defenseless kids. He approached them from behind believing he could take them off guard, however, Diamond who equally came to shore rushed into the alligator battling him. Iris, Carl, and Darren shortly followed along joining in the fight. The gators wrestled in a twirl brawl flipping their bodies all over the place until the wild gator gave up. It was a strenuous, gruesome battle but both sides were equally matched so it was a confrontation that would most likely result in plenty of scars and bruises. Markus ultimately dominated the other alligator he was battling by keeping him pinned to the ground and once he was in a lockjaw position,

Darren then equally joined in by helping finish him off. The oblivious wild gator was outmatched by what started as two now turned into three clashing against him. Finally realizing they were outnumbered and up against alligators that weren't anything like them, the wild alligators made their quick retreat running back into the water. Relieved and utterly grateful that their pets came to their rescue, Zachary and Rena immediately gave them plenty of love and affection.

"You guys saved us!" Rena happily shouted hugging Iris and Diamond.

"Thank you guys," Zachary said appreciatively petting Markus, Carl, and Darren. "You don't know how happy we are to see you."

"Markus, Darren, Iris, Diamond, and Carl are all here," Rena counted. "But I don't see Esma and Baxter. Where are they?"

Zachary scanned the area hoping to spot them but they weren't anywhere to be found. "I don't know. If they're here then maybe mom and dad are too."

"Oh I hope so," Rena said. "So what are we going to do now?"

"We're going to continue looking for help and hopefully find someone who will call the police," Zachary stated. "Now that the alligators are with us, they'll protect us from any other danger. Come on."

Following her brother, the two siblings walked deeper into the woods with the alligators staying close by their sides.

Back on the yacht, Katie and Dylan left Chloe's twisted sex chamber and made their way down the hall.

"What do you mean Zachary and Rena jumped?" Dylan cried out after getting this information from his wife.

"I heard Vincent and Amber say that they jumped," Katie clarified. "I swear when I get my claws on those two I'm…"

"Now Katie, before you go off doing something stupid, let's only focus on getting our kids back."

"Don't you think I'm fully aware of that!" she growled at him. "That's what we're trying to do, only we're being thwarted by these damn humans. How do you think I felt catching you in there with that bitch Chloe!"

"I'm sorry Katie, it was my fault because I should've watched my back more carefully," he said with remorse.

"Ugh. Dylan don't apologize," she said placing her paw on his cheek. "You were the one that was the victim. But one good thing to come out of this is that she'll think twice before messing with creatures like us again."

"Oh I think she'll do more than think twice," Dylan grinned. "I might have downright ruined her sex life."

Carefully arriving up on deck, the two parents didn't spot anybody. They carefully scanned the area and noticed the searchlight was still on pointing in the direction of the water. Dylan looked over at the control panel noticing no one was there so he decided to take control. Katie grabbed hold of the searchlight hoping to spot her children within the midst of the dark, vast ocean.

"Zachary! Rena! Where are you?!" she cried out.

"Nowhere to be found," said a familiar voice behind her.

Turning around, Katie was faced with a 45-millimeter pistol in her face with Vincent as the culprit. After witnessing their greatest rival pointing a gun at his wife, Dylan frantically cried out, "Katie!" Before he could rush over to her, he was stopped by Amber who tripped him with her foot and wielded a knife as her weapon of choice.

"I wouldn't try anything stupid if I were you," she warned him.

Shortly after, Vincent's bodyguard emerged on deck too.

"Where did you guys come from?" Katie scowled.

"My yacht, my boat," Vincent clarified. "This is one of my prosperous savings from my glorious years. I designed this yacht to have many different compartments."

"Whatever," Katie said rolling her eyes. "Someone with money like yours has plenty of connections to do dishonest things. How much did you pay these guys to do your dirty deeds for you?"

"Watch it missy. You do realize I'm the one who's holding the gun here," he warned her.

"So this is what it's come to," Katie yelled as Dylan came by her side. "After what you did to us years ago, you actually had the balls to kidnap our children!"

"Stop calling them your children!" Amber yelled. "They're mine!"

"You lost that privilege the minute you abandoned them and tried taking them away from us again!" Katie shouted pointing her index finger at her. "And look what it's led to! You don't deserve to be their mother."

Amber angrily scowled, ready to lash out at Katie but somewhere deep in the back of her mind, she knew she was right.

"Creatures like you make me sick always being the goody-two-shoes with your positive nature and morals so deep nothing can break you," Vincent claimed. "I want you guys to suffer the way I suffered once my reputation went down the drain."

"You want us to suffer!" Katie shrieked. "You son of a bitch! You have the nerve wanting to make us suffer after you already succeeded in that aspect after killing our baby! If anything, you got off easy. You have no idea what you put us through and you're doing it all over again. Humans like you don't even have morals. You're the exact opposite in every way possible."

"Katie don't piss him off," Dylan told her hoping Vincent wouldn't pull the trigger.

Instead, the deranged man just chuckled amusingly. "I like you guys. I find you so entertaining how your principles won't allow you to alter to the slightest corruption. You're literally in a world of your own. But you have to understand in this world with us humans when you step on the wrong toes, you're going to have a shit storm ahead of you."

"Then bring it on," Katie challenged. "I'm not afraid of you!"

"You should be," Vincent said as he signaled one of his bodyguards to seize Katie.

"Let her go!" Dylan shouted as he was equally restrained by two bodyguards.

"As you wish," Vincent replied.

Right on cue, the bodyguard tossed Katie overboard as she splashed into the water.

"Katie!" Dylan hysterically screamed.

"Now she can join your children and pretty soon you can join them too," he said walking closer to Dylan roaming alongside the railing. "You guys will be the perfect happy family you always wanted."

"You bastard!" the anxious creature retorted. "You won't get away with this."

"It's funny how you heroes always say that," Vincent sneered pointing his gun directly in Dylan's face getting ready to pull the trigger. "Cause I already have."

Savoring in his sweet revenge as he slowly squeezed his finger on the trigger, the next thing Vincent knew was catching sight of a random alligator that rose from the water and chomped directly on his arm. He was the perfect target for Esma since he was close near the railing. Thanks to the alligator's leaping skills, she was able to lunge herself high enough to reach him. The unexpected attack caused Vincent to fire but luckily it didn't hit anybody. Shouting in agony, Vincent was forcibly dragged from the ship directly into the water as Esma pulled him under.

"What the hell was that?!" one of the guards shrieked.

Dylan saw this as his chance and fought off the guards. A few of them were martial artists but luckily Dylan had a few moves of his own and used them to his advantage, like using his claws as knives and his tail as a whip to defend himself. Amber became so terrified after everything that had just happened, she immediately retreated to the control panel and tried controlling the yacht. She looked out in the water witnessing Vincent struggling with the alligator and drove the sailboat in his direction. Hoping she wouldn't hit him, she tried maneuvering the yacht beside him hoping he would make it. Nearly hitting Esma in the process, the gator released Vincent retreating from the area. He managed to take hold of the rope on the side with his good arm since his right arm was now mangled considering what Esma did to it. He's just lucky she didn't take the whole thing off. Struggling with all of his strength, Vincent tried pulling himself back aboard the yacht. Amber then spotted Katie up ahead. If she had any decency, especially after everything that had occurred, then she would've tried to help her, but instead, she pushed the panels into overdrive hoping to run her over. The yacht came into Katie's direction not allowing the creature enough time to retreat. Amber looked on hoping to get it over with, fearing if she didn't go through with it now, then she would never have the nerve to do it again. However, she was violently knocked aside along with everyone else on the yacht before she could carry out her evil scheme. It was thanks to Jerry who knocked his body weight against the sailboat. Regardless, he still couldn't match the same size as the yacht so ramming up against it took a lot of energy out of him. The shark then steadily swam up to Katie as she grabbed a hold of him. He then flung his body the way a shark would pounce out of the water to catch its prey, only he tossed Katie in the air with his tail as she soared through the sky until she landed back on the boat. Conveniently she landed in the same spot as Amber knocking her over in the process. After catching their breaths, Katie angrily glared at the petrified woman.

"Listen Katie, I—I...," Amber nervously stuttered.

"Save it Amber. I saw what you were about to do. You're just the same as Vincent. Cold, calculating murderers."

"No, please don't call me that," Amber cried. "It wasn't supposed to be this way!"

"Well, how did you think it would turn out Amber! No good was going to come out of this anyway."

"I—I just wanted my children back," she wept.

"Your delusions have done nothing but cloud your judgment. I wanted to give you a chance Amber, deep down I really did—but after this, I don't know what to think of you anymore. Can't you ever think about anyone but yourself! You put Zachary and Rena's lives in danger! That's something I can't ever forgive you for."

The weight of guilt had finally dawned on Amber, feeling like an actual blow to the face. Amber's vocal cords were paralyzed and all the vulnerable woman could do was only look at Katie with nothing but absolute shame and remorse. Katie would've loved more than nothing to give Amber a good beating, but figured she wasn't even worth it. She honestly didn't want to stoop down to Amber's level. She could already read the guilty conscience in her eyes and decided to leave her alone allowing her guilt to weigh more heavily on her. Katie then looked across the deck spotting Vincent who just crawled back on the yacht. He now was an exception she wouldn't mind beating to a pulp. As he witnessed the infuriated female creature making her way towards him, Vincent quickly opened one of his hidden compartments and slipped inside.

"Come back here you coward!" Katie screamed scratching at the wooden floor.

As she tried finding her way inside the compartment, she was violently snatched by one of the bodyguards pulling her by the tail.

"Ahhh, let go!" Katie yelled trying to break loose.

The bodyguard aggressively pulled her away from the compartment preventing her from trying to get to Vincent. He jerked her closer to him standing near the railing of the sailboat which was the perfect opportunity for Baxter who was nearby. He rose from the water and clamped his jaw on the man's leg. Releasing Katie's tail, the bodyguard cried out trying his best to hold on to the railing but the strength of Baxter's lockjaw strapped around his leg was enough to make anybody let go. And there he plummeted into the water with Baxter, dragging him down below. After rubbing her tail a bit, Katie looked around her to notice that most of the guards were already unconscious from Dylan who was tired from the intense brawl. Now it was just Vincent left to deal with. She crawled over to Dylan lying on his side who was obviously out of breath.

"Dylan! Dylan are you hurt?" she cried shaking him.

"I don't think so," he groaned.

"Remind me to thank Baxter for finally getting up off his lazy butt and helping us," she remarked.

"Are you alright?" he said thankful that she got back onboard safely.

"Yeah, thanks to Jerry. What about you?"

"These guys were a lot tougher than they look," he replied. "I'm not used to fighting."

"I know you're tired but we're not out of the woods yet," Katie said forcing him up on his feet. "We still gotta find the kids and take care of Vincent.

40

Traveling further through the woods, Zachary and Rena didn't think they would make it out of there but eventually came to a clearing. The first thing they spotted was a small house that was pretty rundown but possibly inhabited.

"Look Rena, a house!" Zachary shouted.

"Do you think someone's home?" she questioned.

"We won't know until we find out. Come on."

The kids were a bit wary and still drenched, but didn't waste a moment running up to the house. They aggressively knocked on the door hoping someone would answer it. To their astonishment, someone did answer, but the random stranger had a shotgun ready to fire.

"Get off my property!" the older man yelled.

"Please don't hurt us," Rena cried hiding behind her brother.

"Kids! What the hell are you doing out here," he said putting down his weapon.

"Please help us," Zachary begged. "There are these bad people after us. They kidnapped us and we escaped but we think they might still be after us."

The man immediately noticed the alligators around them and got spooked. He was even about to slam the door on their faces, until he slowly recognized the group. "What a minute—are you guys those kids that live with those creatures as parents?"

"Yes, yes that's us," Zachary said.

"I watch you guys on Youtube all the time!" he happily beamed. "Of all the places I would never expect you to show up on my doorstep. This is amazing."

"Could you please help us?" Rena asked.

"Sure come on in," he offered. "My name's Tom by the way."

"I'm Zachary and this is my sister Rena."

"I know. I watch your videos. And your parents are Dylan and Katie Lloyd. And you have seven alligators and a great white shark." He took notice that the alligators forced their way inside his house refusing to let the children out of their sight. He then had to ask, "They won't bite, right?"

"No—unless someone is trying to hurt our family," Rena made clear.

"Okay good," he sighed in relief. "So what's the problem again?"

"We've been kidnapped and escaped," Zachary explained once more. "Those bad people are still out there and our parents are probably here too because our alligators showed up. They're probably in danger too."

"Alright I'll call for help," he said going over to his phone. "You two just sit tight until the police arrive."

Knowing they finally found help, Zachary and Rena felt more at ease but still couldn't help worrying for their parents knowing their lives were in danger.

"I hope mom and dad are okay," Rena said worriedly.

"Don't worry Rena," Zachary said putting his arm around his sister. "There's nothing that mom and dad can't handle."

Back on the yacht below the deck within the secret compartment, Vincent tried tending to his arm. Not only was he massively bleeding, but the bottom of his humerus bone was also protruding directly out of his skin thanks to the damage Esma caused. Snatching his belt off from around his pants, he wrapped it around his arm to temporarily stabilize his now disabled limb. He held the end of the belt in his mouth while pulling the other end with his left hand. Aggressively biting his teeth down on the belt while groaning in pain, he successfully managed to insert his bone back immobilizing it. Afterwards, he wrapped the entire belt around his bleeding arm but it still couldn't subside the severe pain he was experiencing. In utter rage from the fact that Dylan and Katie always got the best of him, he saw nothing but red. He planned this idea for years only to have it go up in smoke. Someone of his status used to have it all until that unfortunate night he decided to drink behind the wheel. If he had enough common sense he would've taken full responsibility for his actions and left the whole situation alone. But not Vincent. His narcissistic nature only proved his arrogance to punishing individuals when he didn't get his way. And now from the current situation, he was boiling with absolute anger that couldn't be contained. His main goal used to be just focusing on making Dylan and Katie suffer but now in an instant, murder was on his mind. His new objective was to remove them from this earth.

"I've had it with these damn creatures!" he yelled going through the compartment room. "Why did it have to be their car I rammed into that night? Because of them, my life is spiraling down to shit. No more! I've had it. I'm getting rid of them once and for all."

Violently knocking over multiple boxes in his way, he came across just what he was looking for. It brought him back to those days after his reputation slowly plummeted down the drain. Losing his friendship with the mayor, including most of his colleagues from his law firm after Dylan and Katie won their case in court, he dragged himself to local bars to drown his sorrow in self-pity. He could still hear their voices taunting him in the back of his mind.

"How could you be so stupid Blake?"

"You just made yourself and this whole office look bad."

"Good luck finding clients who'll want you to represent them now."

"It's your ass that's going to burn for this asshole."

"You allowed your reputation to take a nose-dive over a stupid error."

"It doesn't matter that they were cartoon creatures, you still killed an innocent baby because of your arrogance."

"You might as well forget those glorious days of being the mayor's friend, cause he wants nothing to do with you anymore."

Before the tragedy, his drinking was minor until it spiraled out of control. It became a common routine where he was known as a regular generally making the bar his second home. He equally got into bar fights more often than not whenever someone dared comment on how he foolishly lost his case against two cartoon creatures. After he was banned from the bars from getting into far too many fights, he expressed his anger by obtaining weapons such as guns, artillery, and grenades. Getting lost in his own sick delusions believing he was a soldier in the war, he would sneak out to the farthest desolated woods whenever he could find the time and go on a killing spree hunting and slaughtering innocent animals. It became a sick hobby where killing the animals became a favorite pastime activity to calm his nerves. Sometimes he would shoot at nothing in particular just savoring the moment. Then one day, he came across a particular animal which reminded him of Dylan and Katie. That's when it hit him. Why take out his anger on these defenseless animals when he can go after the real thing. That's when his plans came into action and he vowed his vengeance on what he considered "the two freaks of nature". He played it calmly at first getting in touch with Amber after finding out about their history together and saw it as a perfect opportunity to manipulate the situation. However, it was a hard struggle trying to get Amber to play the part by getting her clean which wasn't an easy task. He never liked her to begin with but she was the perfect ploy in his evil scheme to get back at Dylan and Katie. Once the plan came into action, Amber was able to talk him into just running away with her kids, which he wasn't willing to go along with at first but figured it was a delicious act of revenge to really hurt the two parents. But now, right here at this moment, his hunting skills were resurfacing where all acts of rationality was just thrown out the window. Those were the times when he was exultant of being free to slaughter anyone in his path without any restriction. Now reliving that same moment once again, there was no way he was going back to being subtle. The compartment surrounding him distorted to the dark isolated woods he fondly remembered, desperately wanting to be that wild and free tyrant roaming the area as a madman without any restrictions.

Back on the surface, Katie continued trying to claw her way through the secret door Vincent disappeared into.

"Katie what about the kids?" Dylan desperately mentioned.

"You jump after them," she ordered. "Someone's got to obtain Vincent before he'll cause more trouble."

As soon as the words left her mouth, a random bullet blasted through the floorboard nearly hitting Katie across the shoulder. Falling backwards Katie immediately got out of the way as more bullets began shooting all over the place. The two anxious creatures quickly tried running from the attack barely making it out alive.

Even the bodyguards and Amber had to retreat. Vincent went crazy firing a machine gun at the ceiling above him hoping to hit somebody. Due to the rage he was feeling, he didn't even care if he hit Amber or any of his bodyguards. The flying bullets managed to hit the control panel causing the ship to halt and just sit in the middle of the water.

"That psychopath has flipped his lid!" Dylan cried out.

"Ya think!" Katie shouted back.

Unfortunately one of the bullets managed to strike Dylan through the tail causing him to fall over.

"Dylan!" Katie cried as she rushed to his aid and helped him away from any more attacks. They took cover heading near the second floor of the ship.

"Dylan are you alright?" she asked with great concern.

"Just got me in the tail," Dylan squirmed caressed it trying to stop the bleeding. "That's the second time my poor tail has been abused by our foes in one night."

"That does it! I've had it with this asshole!" Katie yelled leaving her husband's side.

"Katie stop!" Dylan shrieked, however, he was unable to stop his wife from her abrupt departure.

The aggressive female creature assertively rushed back around the area with the flying bullets. Since the floorboard was already weak due to the countless holes, Katie attempted to plummet her body like a torpedo straight through the deck, taking advantage of the bullets weakening the floorboard. First jumping high in the air, she amazingly crashed right through heading straight in the direction of Vincent knocking him over in the process. The dazed man tried to gather himself from the unexpected blow as Katie did the same from the violent impact. As he tried retrieving his gun,

Katie immediately pulled it away. Instead of getting upset Vincent just looked on in amusement.

"So—you think you've won," he said giving her a smug expression.

"Let this end now," Katie warned him.

"Oh it will," he said struggling to get up. "I'm not going to prison. The only way I'm getting out of here is by going out, but not without taking you guys with me."

Vincent then brought a grenade from behind his back raising it in the air.

"Oh you sick son of a bitch," Katie glared.

"I came prepared for this moment," he explained. "If I wasn't going to accomplish stealing the kids from you and Dylan, then I was going to take all of us out. It was my main mission as the ultimate triumph at defending you abominations."

"I care less about me, but my kids are another matter. Are you telling me if the kids still would've been on board then you would've killed them too?"

"I've got nothing else to lose."

Angrily gritting her teeth, Katie lost all self-control and launched herself towards Vincent before he could pull the pin. Dropping the grenade to the floor, Vincent fought with an enraged Katie on top of him scratching and punching him to death.

"You already took my first child away and now you're trying to take the ones I have now!" she screamed in a fit of hysteria. "If any of us deserve to be taken out, it's you!"

Vincent was in bad shape but wasn't going to allow himself to be defeated, so using all of his strength, he shoved Katie off of him. He then struggled to retrieve the grenade. Katie once more tried fighting with him before he could use it. They both tussled with the weapon chaotically. It tossed and flipped in the air bouncing off their hands and paws until it eventually sprung to the surface back on deck. Katie tried rushing up to it but was immediately dragged down by her tail from Vincent as he rushed right past her and made his way to the deck first. Katie quickly made her way back on deck, but by then Vincent had retrieved the grenade and looked on victorious as he once more raised it the air.

"I win!" he wickedly shouted.

Knowing there was no reasoning with someone like this, all Katie could do was look on in horror as she watched Vincent pull the pin from the grenade. The deranged man laughed on sadistically as he was prepared to accept his fate while taking everyone out with him. Knowing there wouldn't be enough time to escape, Katie sadly looked on not realizing it would end this way. She wished she had one last moment with her kids. Dylan was too far to reach Vincent in time also, so he equally looked on in despair just preparing for the worst. Time froze as the inevitable was beginning to happen while Vincent continued holding his weapon high in the air waiting for the destruction to take place, only to have it taken completely off guard by an unknown object. In a swift move of bravery, Jerry had leaped his whole body flying across the sailboat and managed to bite Vincent's hand clean off along with the grenade. As Vincent screamed in excruciating pain dropping to the floor, Katie and Dylan both watched Jerry as he dropped back into the water making a big splash. The minute his body hit the water, the grenade went off causing a great explosion that drastically shook the yacht amongst the waves. After observing this, Katie and Dylan frantically ran to the railing looking for Jerry.

"JERRY!" they both shouted in a fit of panic.

After a while, nothing surfaced from the water until the two witnessed a gruesome pool of blood much to their horror.

"Jerry!" they cried out once more.

After a couple of more terrifying minutes, Jerry finally surfaced.

"Jerry, you're hurt!" Katie cried.

"No I'm fine," he said faintly.

"Then what's all that blood," Dylan demanded.

"It's nothing but a flesh wound," he brushed off.

"Jerry I..."

"Listen you guys, try not to worry so much," he told them. "Look you're close to shore. Just operate the boat and park it there."

"That asshole broke the control panel. We can't operate it," Katie said.

"I'll help push the yacht so you guys can make it there."

"Jerry don't," Katie begged, but much to her dismay, their shark swam underneath the yacht popping up on the other side and helped shove the sailboat into the direction of land nearby.

Vincent was clearly out of willpower to fight anymore after losing his left hand and ultimately admitted defeat. Katie and Dylan cared less of dealing with him after fearing for their shark, who they knew was in critical condition despite what he told them. As the yacht slowly made its way to shore, help had finally arrived thanks to Zachary and Rena coming across the stranger who contacted them. They arrived sooner than the ones Katie told Shelley and Brandon to call because they were closer within the district. The coast guard, police vehicles, and even a helicopter came into the picture. Zachary and Rena looked on in suspense as they saw the sailboat coming their way. Spotting their mom and dad from the deck of the yacht, they frantically called out to them.

"Mommy! Daddy!"

"Kids!" Katie and Dylan madly called back.

Before the yacht was even close enough to shore, the two parents jumped from the sailboat and eagerly swam to their kids. After all this time of suspense and close scares, the four were finally reunited once again. They all wrapped themselves in a huge embrace hugging each other tightly while also sharing a few tears.

"My poor babies," Katie wept while also kissing them. "Are you kids alright?"

"Yes mommy, we're fine," Zachary assured her.

"We were so worried about you," Dylan cried. "Please forgive us."

"It's not your fault mommy, daddy," Rena softly wept. "All that matters is that we're together again."

"Yes, and I promise I'll never let anything happen to you guys again," Katie deeply expressed.

When the cops finally came to their aid, the family told them who was responsible for this mess. They swarmed the yacht taking in Vincent, Amber, Chloe, and all of his bodyguards in handcuffs one by one. While this was going on, the family immediately noticed Jerry come along the shoreline being pushed by Esma and Baxter who helped shove him the rest of the way. His body slowly turned to the side revealing a massive chest wound from where the grenade exploded from. The family frantically rushed to their pet shark trying to help him.

"Damn you Jerry," Katie cried trying to cover up his wound. "Why did you do it?"

"Hey, we're family," he breathed slowly. "You do anything for the people you love."

"Don't worry Jerry, we're going to get you some help," Dylan said trying to help his wife cover up the wound.

"It's too late for me at this point," Jerry spoke vaguely.

"Don't talk like that Jerry," Katie told him.

"Mommy, is Jerry going to be alright?" Rena said tearing up.

"What's Jerry saying mommy?" Zachary asked.

Katie was unable to answer her children as she realized how severe his injuries were. "I—I…" she nervously stuttered.

"Tell the kids for me that it was an honor having them as part of the family," Jerry said to Katie and Dylan.

"Jerry please just hang in there," Dylan cried emotionally. "You'll be alright."

"I'm finished," the shark confessed peacefully. "My life on this earth is finally done. It wasn't easy, but the life I had with you guys was one I've been blessed with. I appreciate all of you and thank you."

Emotions hit Dylan and Katie hard as they were unable to reply. Zachary and Rena couldn't hear Jerry speak, but witnessing their pet shark in this anguished state was enough to cause them to equally break down. Jerry slowly moved his head to get one good last look at his family. No doubt he had a hard life and some might say it was unethical and was better off living in the ocean the way all sharks are supposed to live, but living with creatures such as Dylan and Katie gave him more personality and an existence unlike any other. He was proud to be a part of their family and given a unique life from two loving creatures who always shared that same love to him in return.

"I love you guys," he softly sighed taking his one and final last breath.

Right before all of them, Jerry sadly passed away as his unresponsive body stood motionless. Dylan and Katie stood frozen unable to comprehend what just occurred as Zachary and Rena went up to Jerry trying to wake him up.

"Jerry, Jerry wake up," Zachary cried.

"Please don't go Jerry," Rena sniveled. "Come back. Please come back."

The motionless shark didn't and never would respond again. This unexpected tragedy of Jerry being absent from their lives was a loss they weren't prepared for. He was a big part of the family ever since Dylan bought him. In a way, Jerry helped heal the couples during their time of bereavement due to what they went through after losing their child. He was like an adopted child they've grown fond of over the years. He wasn't only a member of the family; he was a friend, a guardian, a protector, and a loyal companion. And he just gave his life to save Dylan and Katie, allowing them a chance to still be in their kid's lives.

This heartrending moment caused Zachary and Rena to weep with great despair. Katie held Rena close while Dylan held Zachary. The two parents tearfully cried as well, the same emotions of loss and grief from losing their child resurfaced, thanks to the careless acts of Vincent... yet again. The alligators even surrounded their shark companion, representing their loss by relaxing their scaly bodies up against Jerry's.

41

While the police escorted the disgraceful humans to their vehicles, Amber took a moment witnessing the situation that she solely caused. For once in her sad life, she felt remorse for her actions and now had an epiphany of how right everyone was about her all along. Amber knew this was her only chance to set things right for herself and asked the guard who was escorting her for a moment to talk with the grieving family. Still held in handcuffs, the cop brought her over to the family who was still crying. They slowly took notice of her once her presence was known to them.

"I—I—I don't deserve your forgiveness," she sadly murmured. "You guys were always right about me. I never thanked you for all the good you've done for me. My actions have only caused nothing but pain to those around me. I'm so sorry for everything." She looks towards Zachary and Rena saying, "I will never bother you guys again. I just hope someday in your hearts, you'll be able to forgive me." She then stares at Dylan and Katie in tears saying, "I'm really, really sorry."

No one said anything to her. What she caused was enough to make them loathe her and she didn't blame them in the slightest. After saying what she needed to, the cop escorted her back to the police car. While placing a gravely wounded Vincent on a gurney into an ambulance, he was still yelling in pain from massive blood loss. Chloe equally screamed in pain the moment they made her sit down. Either way, the villains knew the creatures would have their day of retribution for what has happened here.

Of course this story hit the news the minute the media found out what happened. It spread like wildfire all over social networks and television just like when Dylan and Katie first adopted Zachary and Rena. This time however, they had so much support from the tragedy they suffered after losing Jerry. Generous people had come forward and donated money to the family. Although they didn't ask for it, Dylan and Katie respectfully thanked those who were thoughtful enough to donate and put the money towards the cause. For one, they wisely saved half of it, and the other half was put towards a proper funeral they wanted to do in honor of Jerry. A week later after that horrible night, Dylan and Katie requested Jerry's body to be cremated. They placed his ashes in an urn and planned to scatter them out to sea. The urn itself was beautifully designed with a picture of the ocean and sharks swimming around it. Carved in the center of the urn were the words, "Jerry Lloyd, Beloved Shark Family Member."

On this specific morning, Dylan and Katie rented out a large boat for them to use. The whole family was present on it, including the alligators. The ocean was far and wide just like when Zachary and Rena first went on the cruise with Amber before it turned ugly. This event was depressing too since Jerry was no longer in their lives but they wanted to give him a proper farewell. Rena was the one who held onto Jerry's urn while Dylan was at the control panel and stopped the boat when they came out far enough. Sitting right in the middle of the ocean, the family stood together on the deck looking out at the sea on this bright delicate morning. Dylan walked beside his wife while their kids stood in front of them.

Taking a deep breath Dylan announced, "I'll go first." He deeply gazed out at the ocean remembering the fond moments he and the family shared with Jerry. "I remember the very day I first got Jerry. He was no smaller than a cat in a small fish tank. He was scared and knew of his inevitable doom that awaited him of being eaten. My heart immediately went out to him when I saw how terrified he was. When I realized the humans were going to eat him, I knew at that moment I had to save him. Saving his life was like a redeeming aspect for when I was unable to save our first baby. Once I brought him home and presented him to Katie, he was still timid but eventually warmed up to us. His favorite hobbies were sitting in the tub while watching shark videos on his laptop. Regardless, he was still always an enjoyable member of the family. I'm proud I was able to stroll through the market that day and come across him. Thank you Jerry for fulfilling our lives with happiness and helping heal us when we suffered our own loss."

Katie went next by saying, "I'm so sorry Jerry. I regret a lot of awful things I used to say to you whenever you broke something or ate our food. It wasn't your fault that you're a natural predator who probably deserved to be released in your own habitat. But you've told me time and time again that you'd rather live with us. It showed us how much you appreciated me and Dylan. I will also never forget how you protected us from intruders. You were always a loyal family member and I appreciate every moment we had you in our lives. Losing our child was still a devastating experience, but if it never happened, then we probably never would've had you. Thank you Jerry and I love you."

Zachary decided to speak next after clearing his throat a bit. "You were always my friend Jerry. It was because of you why I like swimming. I remember the first time I was scared, you helped encouraged me and my sister. If we slipped or fell, you were always there guiding us and protecting us from drowning. There will never be another one like you Jerry. I just wish we could've heard you talk like mom and dad but either way, I still loved you."

Last but not least Rena was to finally say her speech. "I really, really loved you Jerry. Thank you for always protecting us and being there for us when we needed you. I'm so sorry for what happened to you but thank you so much for saving mommy and daddy. I just wish we could've saved you, but I know you're in a better place now. And I just pray whenever our time comes, we'll get to see you again. You're the greatest shark that I know Jerry and I will never forget you. Good-bye, my friend."

The family couldn't help sniveling soft sobs of grief after they each reminisced on their fond memories of the great white shark. After Rena wiped away her tears, Katie kneeled beside her softly saying, "Go ahead honey."

Everyone watched Rena as she slowly opened the top of the urn then carefully dumped Jerry's ashes out into the sea. Once they were gone, the alligators left the boat jumping into the water. They swam in circles around the area the ashes were dumped as their way of showing Jerry their condolences to their old friend. The parents held onto their kids knowing this was a depressing moment for all of them but were satisfied to do this to honor their friend. He would always be remembered and somewhere deep into their hearts, they knew they'd see him again someday.

"Do you really think we'll see Jerry again mommy?" Rena questioned.

"As long as there's a God, then I truly believe we'll be reunited with our loved ones. Humans, animals, and creatures alike," she reflected.

During the same time the family was grieving over their loss, the villains had their day in court after facing several charges. This time Vincent didn't get off like he did the first time when he killed Dylan and Katie's baby. He was facing time in prison and if it weren't for Amber who ironically testified against him, he probably never would've had received such a rightful sentence. It was Amber's way of redeeming herself trying to recognize her mistakes and do something right for once in her life. Her sentence was reduced thanks to her testimony, but she was still going to do time for her part in it. As for Chloe, her career as a lawyer was finally over. All the information about her wrongdoing was finally revealed and came down like an avalanche. Previous victims and deceitful friends ultimately came forward when they heard Chloe was arrested and exposed to a multitude of fraudulent things she's done. She faced nearly the same sentence as Vincent which was equally justified. One thing for sure of what Chloe has learned from this was to never use sex as a mechanism to get her way again. Not that she would enjoy it anymore from the hemorrhoids she regretfully developed. Her painful rear was always a daily reminder of how she fully regrets ever hitting upon Dylan.

Once the criminals had their day in court, Dylan and Katie never came to trial. It was too much for them to bear after everything they've been through and there was no way in hell they were going to drag Zachary and Rena through another trial ever again. The damning piece of evidence against all of them was the confession from the cell phone that Dylan recorded which came in handy when the family refused to show up in court. Also, thanks to Amber's testimony and the preexisting hard evidence was enough to still put the three away. However, Vincent would never have a second chance in court. When he was already found guilty on so many charges, he took the coward's way out by hanging himself in prison.

He truly lived up to his word when he said he was never going to prison and couldn't live with himself to pay for his punishment. The moment Dylan and Katie heard about Vincent's death, it was almost as if a big weight had been lifted off their shoulders. Since the day he took away their baby and now Jerry, that weight has always stayed with them like a sickness. Now with him gone from this world, they could breathe a little better.

It was going to take a while for the family to recover after that horrible night but Dylan and Katie knew they've always been through a lot and as long as they continued showing that strength towards their kids, they'd make it out strong. Two weeks later after Dylan and Katie received the news of Vincent's death, the two parents laid up in bed that night while Zachary and Rena were already asleep in their bedroom.

"Who'd ever thought that idiot would take the coward's way out," Dylan commented with his arm wrapped around Katie.

"Good riddance to bad rubbish," she scoffed. "And to that no good Chloe also."

"Yeah her dirty schemes had finally caught up to her. I'm glad because I didn't want to face her in court after what she did to me."

"I think she's the one that would've been worried facing you after what you did to her. From what I heard, that tramp is now wearing diapers," Katie slightly chuckled.

"I guess that's the best punishment she deserves," he smiles, but then instantly changed to a solemn look. "You know, Amber really stepped up when she testified against Vincent and Chloe and then plead guilty herself. Do you think she deserves a second chance?"

"I don't know. It was already hard enough the first time but after what she put us through, I'm not ready to forgive her just yet," Katie said. "Rena was the one willing to give her a second chance and Amber destroyed that trust from her. That's something I can never look past. Unless the kids will someday forgive her, then maybe I will."

"I guess that's understandable but living with this resentment will only make us bitter and angry," he told her. "We're going to have to let go of all that hatred towards her. Despite what we've been through, we always want to set a good example towards the kids."

"I know Dylan," she sighed. "You're right. But these wounds are still fresh and it's going to take a while for all of us to heal from it."

"Yes, it is going to take a while and there's no rush. The kids are still grieving over Jerry's death. We all miss him just the same."

"Yes, it's still been heartbreaking," she said sadly. "Every time I step outside into the backyard, I'm expecting to see Jerry in the swimming pool or hearing him shout, 'Feed me!' As annoying as that was, I'm really going to miss hearing it from him. He was a great companion."

"Yes he was. I love the alligators too but I miss having a shark since he was our first pet."

"Me too," Katie says then looks at Dylan's tail which was bandaged up from the incident when a bullet went through it. "How's your tail been feeling," she said gently massaging it.

"It's a little better but it's still kind of sore," he admitted. "Too bad it'll be out of commission for a while before I'll start using it the way I love to."

"Please, you don't always have to use it for that purpose," she said rolling her eyes. "But back to seriousness. Brandon and Shelley will be coming over tomorrow. We still haven't paid them back for when they told the cops about the phone call you recorded."

"Yeah, we'll spend time with them while Zachary and Rena will spend time with Malachi. But I have to make a quick trip somewhere tomorrow."

"Where? You didn't tell me this until now."

"That's why I'm telling you, but I can't tell you where I'm going. It's nothing serious baby, just running a quick errand."

"Whatever. Just don't be gone all day. I don't want to have to cook all the meals by myself."

"Don't worry, it'll be worth it," he assured her.

42

The next morning was bright and cheery considering the harsh past few days the family had suffered. Around 9:15 am, Brandon and Shelley came over along with their son. Dylan had already left earlier around 7:02 am and hadn't come back yet. During this time Katie made a big meal in the kitchen with Brandon and Shelley happily assisting her the whole time. Zachary, Rena, and Malachi were in the living room with the alligators who were keeping them company. Since the death of Jerry, the children haven't been in the mood to play outside in the swimming pool anymore. It pretty much destroyed their spirits in that department, since their beloved shark would no longer be around to either assist or encourage them. Katie only hoped they'd find the strength to want to do it again someday.

"So Dylan didn't tell you where he ran off to?" Brandon questioned bringing over sauce for the ribs.

"Last night he just told me he had an errand to run," Katie explained while she mashed potatoes. "He'll be back soon. But we wanted to thank you guys for helping us that night we asked you to come over."

"It's no big deal Katie," Shelley said bringing out soda from the fridge and placed them on the counter. "I'm just sorry the minute we called the cops, they didn't come in time to you and Dylan."

"It's alright Shelley. They wouldn't have made it in time from the distance Amber had taken our kids the minute they boarded that cruise. Luckily our children ran into someone who called the police for them within the district they came across. Either way, it still worked out."

"I still can't believe what Amber planned on doing this whole time," Brandon said trying to wrap his brain around it. "I could only imagine the resentment you must feel towards her."

"Oh trust me, I feel a heavy resentment towards that woman, but for the sake of the kids we're trying to not let it fester within us," Katie said.

"I admire your guy's strength," Brandon acknowledged. "A lot of people would've broken down already."

"That's part of the process of being strong," she said finishing up the potatoes. "One good thing that came out of this though was that we will never have to worry about Vincent and Chloe ever again."

"Oh yeah, it's hard to believe your past nemesis was also part of this whole operation," Brandon said. "Who would've thought."

"It was a shock for us too, but those two had finally paid the price for their evil deeds."

"How are the kids holding up?" Shelley asked her.

Katie looks across from the kitchen to the living room where the kids are happily playing with the gators while watching TV at the same time. "It's going to take a while but they'll be okay. They've bounced back from the deplorable conditions they suffered by the hands of Amber when they were just babies. They can do it again."

"All thanks to you and Dylan," Shelley smiled. "Kids hardly make it without the love and strength of their parents."

"Thanks, Shelley."

After the grown-ups finished working together, they had a big meal cooked and ready to eat. "Kids," Katie called out, "Brunch is ready so stop playing those games for now."

The kids momentarily joined their parents in the dining room to sit down and eat with them.

"Mommy, where's daddy?" Rena curiously asked.

"I don't know sweetie but he said he was running a quick errand," she replied. "Don't worry, he'll be back soon."

"Mommy, can we go outside?" little Malachi gently asked.

"Oh honey," Shelley said with a look of disappointment. "We probably can but I'm afraid Zachary and Rena aren't feeling up for going out there, cause I know you want your friends to join you."

"No one is rushing you guys, but when are you going to start going back outside to start swimming again?" Katie asked her kids.

"I don't know mom," Zachary sadly replied poking at his food. "It just isn't the same without Jerry around."

"I know it isn't, but I don't want you two to resent swimming because Jerry is gone. It was devastating what happened to him but like all pets, they eventually pass away. It's a part of life and we're going to have to move on from it. I just don't want you guys to be against swimming or going out in the backyard again because of his absence. And I know Jerry wouldn't want that for you. He would want you to continue to be strong and thrive the way he inspired you. Understand?"

"Yes mommy," both Zachary and Rena said.

After everyone nearly finished their meal, Dylan had finally arrived back home.

"I'm back!" he called out.

"It's about time!" Katie shouted back. "Where the heck were you?"

Coming into the living room, everyone witnessed Dylan pushing in a hand platform trolley cart, and there sitting on the cart was a medium-sized fish tank. Inside the fish tank were two baby sharks swimming about. Both were about 4 ft long and each had their own characteristic marking. While they both had the same white underside complexion, one had a coloring of light blue while the other had a light brown tone to him with dark brown stripes resembling a leopard shark.

"Surprise," he softly announced.

The kids screamed with excitement gathering around the tank while the parents equally came into the living room to witness this surprise.

"Dylan, what is this?" Katie said astounded.

"No one will ever replace Jerry, but I remember what I told you last night when I said I miss having a shark. Besides, these two needed a home just like Jerry did. And the kids this time will have someone they can grow up with, just like the gators. This could also be a great motivation to help them start swimming again. I hope you're not too mad but I thought this would be a nice surprise," he said.

"Oh Dylan of course I'm not mad," Katie said hugging him. "This was a nice surprise and really sweet of you. I'm sure the kids will be grateful."

"Man Dylan, you got two sharks!" Brandon said flabbergasted. "You guys already had your hands full with Jerry alone. Are you sure you can handle having two?"

"After everything we've been through, there's nothing we can't handle," Dylan replied. "Besides, how many folks do you know can handle keeping a great white shark as a pet?"

"I got to stop doubting your guy's way of living," he said shaking his head while placing his hand on his friend's shoulder. "You creatures really are unique."

"Aww thank you daddy," Rena said looking below the tank at the two sharks. "Can we really keep them?"

"I already bought and paid for them so I don't see why not," Dylan smiled. "They're a male and a female by the way."

"Can we name them?" Zachary asked.

"Sure," Katie said. "I think it's only fair since Dylan and I had Jerry. Well, he told us his name already, so technically we didn't name him."

"I want to name the boy Jerry Jr.," Zachary proclaimed.

"That's so sweet Zachary," Katie acknowledged.

"I want to name the girl—Ruby, just like another name for Diamond," Rena said.

"That's silly," Zachary said. "Diamond may work for the alligator but Ruby for a shark doesn't make any sense."

"Zachary now, it's only fair she gets to come up with any name she wants since you named yours," Katie pointed out.

"Yes mom," he said.

"So there are our new additions to the family," Dylan smiled. "Jerry Jr. and Ruby."

"This is such a sweet moment," Shelley acknowledged. "No doubt it's going to make you guys more famous on social media when this hits."

"We still try to keep our private life subtle, but now these days it's nearly impossible," Katie said. "Still we thought it was generous of people to donate money to us when they heard what we went through after the death of Jerry."

"Now you guys can call this a new chapter in your lives," Shelley said.

"It's still only the beginning, but we have come a long way," Katie smiled holding onto her husband. "Thank you for always being there for us Dylan."

"Thank you for making my life worthwhile," he said kissing on her on the head. He then turns towards his friend and said, "Oh Brandon, last time you were here you asked about us playing our guitars. I admit I was reluctant at first, but now I'd like to show you and Shelley we still have the skills."

"Now that's what I was hoping to hear," Brandon happily said. "Bring out the music."

"How about it baby, are you up for playing for our friends?" Dylan asked her.

"I guess I feel like reliving my sophomore moments again," she smiled back.

A little bit later, Dylan returned to the living room and brought out his cherished guitar along with Katie's.

"I have a feeling I'm going to enjoy this," Brandon smiled sitting on the couch with his wife.

Zachary, Rena, and Malachi sat on the living room floor with the alligators as they all anxiously waited to hear the two creatures play. After Dylan hands Katie her guitar, he looked upon her as the female creature he first fell in love with since the moment he first laid eyes on her. They swore the moment they got married that they would always be there for each other for better and for worse. The couple had gone through great trials and tribulations, but it only strengthened their relationship more, enduring all the hardship they suffered through. It only proved how strong their bond and love was for one another. They might have faced ugliness, encountering the wrong people, and negative situations but throughout it all, they never would've had the loyalty of their best friends; Jerry, seven alligators, two trustworthy friends, and two wonderful human children. They were blessed and thankful for what they had and couldn't ask for anything better. Now with two new shark members to the family, they knew they had a new path ahead of them, but if they made it this far then they can make it the rest of the way.

Confidently raising his guitar, Dylan felt the same rhythm he always felt whenever he held his musical instrument close. It drew him to Katie as she held up her guitar and started to gradually play. Whenever they played, it always brought them back to that same moment they first met. Drawn on a level beyond people's comprehension, the two creatures blissfully played as the music equally drew their friends in. Brandon and Shelley happily cheered as Zachary and Rena joined in. As shy as Malachi was, he couldn't help but be drawn into the music as well. The flowing music helped soothed any anguish the family was probably still carrying after the death of Jerry. This was a pleasurable moment that the family truly appreciated. All past sorrow was temporarily forgotten for the time being as the family and friends happily enjoyed themselves amongst each other.

It was still going to be a long road from here, but one that the family was willing to undergo. Zachary and Rena always knew better that Dylan and Katie weren't their biological parents but regardless, they would always be their real parents because of the unconditional love they've always given them. On the outside, society may perceive this family as dysfunctional; with two cartoon creatures as parents, dangerous predators as pets, and a moral structure that most people would envy, but it was their family, Dylan and Katie's dysfunctional family.

Printed by Libri Plureos GmbH in Hamburg, Germany